A
HEALING
JUSTICE

KRISTIN VON KREISLER

KENSINGTON BOOKS
www.kensingtonbooks.com

KENSINGTON BOOKS are published by

Kensington Publishing Corp.
119 West 40th Street
New York, NY 10018

All Kensington titles, imprints, and distributed lines are available at special quantity discounts for bulk purchases for sales promotion, premiums, fundraising, educational, or institutional use.

Special book excerpts or customized printings can also be created to fit specific needs. For details, write or phone the office of the Kensington Sales Manager: Kensington Publishing Corp., 119 West 40th Street, New York, NY 10018. Attn. Sales Department. Phone: 1-800-221-2647.

Kensington and the K logo Reg. U.S. Pat. & TM Off.

eISBN-13: 978-1-4967-0046-9
eISBN-10: 1-4967-0046-5
First Kensington Electronic Edition: October 2018

ISBN-13: 978-1-4967-0045-2
ISBN-10: 1-4967-0045-7
First Kensington Trade Paperback Printing: October 2018

10 9 8 7 6 5 4 3 2 1

Printed in the United States of America

For Clell Bryant,
my dear friend, writing mentor,
and model for kindness and strength.
With love and thanks.

Praise for Kristin von Kreisler and Her Novels

Earnest

"Dog lovers will adore this beleaguered Lab, who only wants to preside over a united household in his favorite 'library lion' pose."
—*The Seattle Times*

"A sweet and appealing story of a pet's effort to bring his pack together again!"
—**Heroes & Heartbreakers**

"Delightful . . . Von Kreisler's strength in her earlier works—penetrating character developments and tantalizing story lines—are prominent on this emotional, bumpy ride. She is an incredible storyteller."
—**American Kennel Club**

"An insightful and uplifting story . . . a great read for those who know the power of pets."
—*Modern Dog* magazine

"A highly readable story of what devotion and love really mean. Once again, von Kreisler, one of the best authors of animal-related fiction and nonfiction out there, brings readers a dog and a book they will cherish."
—*Best Friends* magazine

"The best part of von Kreisler's novel is Earnest . . . a sweet, lovable canine."
—*RT Book Reviews*

"*Earnest* lives up to his name. He is a dog who earnestly desires only one thing, to keep his family intact. Kristin von Kreisler deftly spins a tale of human failings and canine devotion that will have the reader reaching for the tissues."
   —**Susan Wilson**, *New York Times* best-selling author
of *Two Good Dogs*

"Kristin von Kreisler captures the emotional intelligence of Earnest, a dog who provides much needed guidance to a human couple spiraling into catastrophe. When Anna and Jeff both feel the depth of betrayal, only the steady loyalty and unwavering love of Earnest can save them."
   —**Jacqueline Sheehan**, *New York Times* best-selling author
of *The Center of the World* and *The Tiger in the House*

"Be prepared to fall in love with Earnest, a yellow Labrador retriever adopted from a shelter who teaches his humans a thing or two about resilience, loyalty, and forgiveness. . . . A truly charming story sure to please dog lovers everywhere."
   —**Amy Hill Hearth**, *New York Times* best-selling author
of *Miss Dreamsville and the Lost Heiress of Collier County*

"If you've ever wondered whether animals were smarter than humans, Kristin von Kreisler's *Earnest* is the book for you. This charming tale (pun intended!) leads us through the kind of conflict real families face and shows us, through the wisdom of a dog, what matters most in life."
   —**Nancy Thayer**, *New York Times* best-selling
author of *The Island House*

"Kristin von Kreisler's deep understanding of both people and dogs shines through in her compelling new novel, *Earnest*. Animal lovers will fall for the yellow Lab who saves his favorite humans from heartbreak."

— **Jeffrey Moussaieff Masson**, *New York Times* best-selling author of *Dogs Never Lie About Love*

An Unexpected Grace

"A heartwarming and beautifully written tale about trust and compassion. Grace provides the story with a wonderful balance of humor as her heroine, Lila, poignantly brings the reader into her frame of mind. Dog lovers will be particularly enthralled with the novel."

— *RT Book Reviews,* 4 Stars

"The talented Bainbridge Island author, who has previously focused on nonfiction, makes a smooth transition here into fiction. Von Kreisler is at her best with colorful metaphors throughout this striking adventure that exudes a combustible feel around every corner."

— *Seattle Kennel Club*

"*An Unexpected Grace* is a poignant contemporary . . . Readers will appreciate Lila and Grace helping each other heal."

— *Midwest Book Reviews*

"*An Unexpected Grace* is beautifully written. Kristin clearly knows dogs. The novel is filled with compassion. All pet lovers will relate to the story."

— **Pet News & Views**

"Devoted dog parents will read *An Unexpected Grace* and relate to the deep bond and heartfelt connection that can develop

between the human and canine species. Von Kreisler's passion for dogs is the underlying theme throughout the book and easily relatable by dog lovers wanting a happy ending. For that reason you will enjoy the book."
— *Seattle P. I.*

"A terrific, uplifting novel . . . Von Kreisler deftly shows how the love between a dog and a person can prove transformative."
—*Modern Dog* **magazine**

"A heartstrings-tugging novel with many a heart-stopping incident, the story of a beautiful dog in search of a loving home. Basically, it's a love story. Read it, if you can, in the sunshine."
—*Hudson Valley News*

"In Kristin von Kreisler's heartfelt novel *An Unexpected Grace*, a woman and a dog rescue each other from violent pasts. This is a story that underlines the irrevocable bond between dog and man—or, in this case, between dog and woman."
—*WV Gazette*

"Kristin von Kreisler is an acute observer of dogs and a fine novelist. Her novel about the healing powers of dogs is enchanting. I was captivated from page one and I learned a great deal from this heartwarming, thrilling book."
—**Jeffrey Moussaieff Masson**

"Kristin von Kreisler weaves a modern tale that seems at first to be a relentless search to understand a workplace shooting. But wait; von Kreisler takes us deeper into the powerful connections between humans and animals who are wounded by the incomprehensible and bound together by love."
—**Jacqueline Sheehan**

"In *An Unexpected Grace,* Kristin von Kreisler deftly tackles the age-old question of how to make sense of tragedy. When Lila's world falls apart, she learns that hope can come from unexpected places. With vivid descriptions and true-to-life characters, von Kreisler proves it's possible to heal, trust again, and love deeper than before. A heartwarming story on the healing power of dogs."

—**Susy Flory**, *New York Times* best-selling author of *Thunder Dog*

"Kristin von Kreisler understands the unique bond between survivors of trauma in this captivating novel of a woman and a dog learning to trust each other in a threatening world. You have to root for them as the damaged heroines of *An Unexpected Grace*, woman and dog, find the healing power of trust and love in each other."

—**Susan Wilson**

"A sweet and charming story of the tender, patient, and forgiving nature of our canine friends, Kristin von Kreisler's *An Unexpected Grace* will warm the heart of anyone who has ever loved a dog."

—**Amy Hill Hearth**

A
HEALING
JUSTICE

Books by Kristin von Kreisler

FICTION

An Unexpected Grace
Earnest
A Healing Justice

NONFICTION

The Compassion of Animals
Beauty in the Beasts
For Bea

PROLOGUE

ANDREA

October 2014

Like most everything else in life, the firs around Andrea Brady's
house were both a plus and a minus. The trees gave her privacy,
but they constantly rained needles and cones. As Andie swept
her porch, she internally grumbled about her love-hate relationship with the firs—or the yard's perps, as she'd say on the force.
For seven years, Andie had been a cop on San Julian Island near
Seattle.

As she emptied her dustpan into a garbage bag, she got the
prickly feeling that she was being watched—an intuition
finely honed at work. She glanced down her driveway. A German shepherd she'd never seen before was emerging from the
autumn morning's mist. He slowly made his way toward her.

He was magnificent, if slightly thin and a little on the rumpled side. His black muzzle looked as if he'd dipped it in an
inkwell, and he had a black star on his forehead. A black saddle
marked his back and sides, but the rest of him was tan with
swaths of rust brown, which in the watery sunlight looked almost as red as Andie's hair. Though not quite a German shepherd Mr. Universe, he was powerful and muscular. He moved
with the assurance of an army general.

"Well, hello, you." Andie held out her hand to encourage him to come down her flagstone path and have a sniff.

He walked toward her with quiet dignity and accepted the invitation. As he explored her lavender hand lotion's smell, he breathed out little puffs of air that warmed her creamy skin, which the sun could burn in minutes. He pressed against her leg; though only five foot four and slim, Andie was plenty strong enough to support his weight.

"You're a handsome gentleman. You know that?"

The dog pricked his ears and cocked his head the way dogs do when they are listening. In a slightly formal manner—after all, they'd just met—he seemed to say, *Modesty prevents me from bragging about my appearance, but, indeed, I* have *been called elegant.*

His gorgeous brown eyes tugged at Andie. Some people might say they looked sad, but, to her, they revealed character and depth. She would bet that he was the kind of dog who gazed into the distance on warm summer afternoons and con-templated his strong opinions: *I do not tolerate cowards. A disloyal dog ranks lower than a flea's antenna.*

"Are you lost? Has someone abandoned you?" Certainly, the answer to both questions would be yes. Cruel people took the ferry over and dumped unwanted animals; Andie had found homes for many over the years. She parted the fur on the dog's neck and found no collar and tag. *It's happened again,* she thought.

Those people he'd loved and trusted had turned on him and left him to fend for himself in the cold. He'd never under-stand why they'd repaid his loyalty with cruelty. Perhaps he thought he'd done something wrong and was being punished. Perhaps dogs' feelings could be as hurt as people's.

"Wait here a minute. I'll get you some water and food."

Andie hurried into the house, a two-story shingled Crafts-man that, thank heaven, she'd been awarded in her divorce. Rushing toward the kitchen, she ran her hand along the back of her white denim sofa and over her wicker "gratitude basket," into which she tossed daily lists of three things she was thankful for. Today one would be meeting this beautiful dog. She filled a bowl with water, grabbed a package of sliced turkey, and went back outside.

The dog was waiting on the flagstones a few feet from the porch's steps, the easier to bolt if Andie turned out to be unworthy of friendship. "Here." She set down the water and noted a black heart-shaped spot on his tongue as he lapped. On her palm, she held out half a turkey slice. Though she expected a ferocious chomp of teeth, he took the turkey politely—but then gulped it down, no chewing, that was it.

She sat on the bottom step, wrapped an arm around her knees, and handed him a whole slice. "You know, I used to have a shepherd named Noble. He took care of me when my father died." It hardly seemed possible that nearly thirty years had passed since then. She'd been in third grade. "Noble was a clown, but you seem sober as a judge. Someone should name you Justice."

He seemed not to mind the name as his eyes emphatically informed her, *I would greatly appreciate more turkey.*

Andie set the rest of the package in front of him and watched his eager bites. It felt so natural sitting with this stranger dog. It was like he personally chose her this morning and the universe might be sending her a gift. She wanted to keep him.

But, then, she had no time for a dog right now. She told Justice, "I work full-time. My husband left me last year because he couldn't stand my long, unpredictable hours. It would be irresponsible to adopt you when my life is so complicated."

Andie was nothing if not responsible. By age eight, she'd had to become an adult.

But—and all arguments, even in her head, always had a "but"—*but* Justice was so beautiful. (*Stop thinking of him as Jus-*

tice! Don't get attached!) *But* she loved how he plopped down on the flagstones as if he were claiming her house as his own and he fixed his brown eyes on her green ones.

His furrowed forehead seemed to say it all: *I can tell you're on your own, and underneath your strong exterior, you're vulnerable.* He tilted his head as if to emphasize, *You need someone to cover your back—and maybe offer friendship.* He tossed his licorice-gumdrop nose in the air. He could provide those things. No problem.

As Andie well knew.

The nose toss did it. And his eyes. They said as clearly as any dog's eyes ever said anything, *I would like to be your dog, but I would never stoop to pressure you.*

Besides, clearly hidden in his confidence was a love muffin. When she patted his shoulder, he nuzzled her hand. As a police officer, Andie kept her heart under wraps to protect it while she did her job, but this was different. Justice cracked her heart wide open.

Okay, so if she was going to take a rash, unintended step like adopting a dog, she needed support. She pulled her phone from her down vest's pocket and speed-dialed Meghan, who, besides being her next-door neighbor also happened to be San Julian's Saint Francis of Assisi. Today she was setting up her new interior design office downtown, but she'd drop anything for a needy animal.

"Hey. Do you know anything about a lost German shepherd?" Andie asked.

"You found one?!" At the prospect of a rescue, the usual uptick of excitement sounded in Meghan's voice.

"He's here. Somebody dumped him in our woods."

"Any ID?"

"No. I want to adopt him. You have to see him. He's gorgeous."

"I'm sure he is, but you need to try and find his family first." Meghan sighed.

"I don't *want* to find them. Not if they've abandoned him."

"You don't know that for sure. You need to put up FOUND DOG signs and have Dr. Vargas check him for a microchip. Don't fall in love yet," Meghan warned.

Andie pictured her, knitting her brows and fingering the tiny silver Eiffel Tower she'd worn around her neck since her student days in Paris. Nothing made her worry more than an animal in trouble. Andie, too. But Meghan was right. If Justice had a family he loved, he should go back to them.

Still, Andie wanted to keep him. "Justice is sniffing the flagstones. Maybe he could be a drug sniffer. He could be my K-9 partner." Andie petted his fluffy fur.

"Oh, my. I hope nobody shows up to claim him," Meghan said. "Guard your heart."

CHAPTER 1

ANDREA

November 2016

Andrea turned her patrol car off the highway and started toward downtown. At last Halloween was over, and for a year she wouldn't have to contend with injured and malicious trick-or-treaters. Now she could concentrate on drug dealers, domestic abusers, and burglars. Not that there were many. Most people were law-abiding in her community of twelve thousand people. No one had intentionally killed anybody since 1965.

As Andie made her way down Main Street, she waved to a boy whose stolen computer she'd found abandoned at the ferry dock, and to Haluk, whose Oriental rugs were yanked off hooks outside his shop and thrown into the street last March. She headed toward the druggies' mecca: Mel's Groceries' parking lot. In the backseat Justice sensed a hunt for dealers might be on, and he panted with excitement. He was now her best friend and drug-sniffing K-9 partner.

When Andie drove into the parking lot, no dealers were hanging around and looking suspicious—not even the brazen one everybody called the Beast. She was about to check Waterfront Park when her cell rang: "Be Happy" with whistles and finger snaps.

Her friend Stephanie, the station's senior police clerk, said, "Sorry to tell you, but the Laser Lady just called."

Groan. Every few weeks Evelyn Bastrop insisted that her enemies had aimed lasers at her to annihilate her in a puff of smoke. "I'll get over there and tell her we've turned on the shields."

"That's not the problem this time. It's one of her cats. She's scared he's going to attack her."

"Great. Let the cop get mauled." Andie pictured claws hooked through her jacket sleeves and shredding her arms.

"We could always send over the SWAT team," Stephanie joked.

Andie opened a vent to keep Justice's breath from fogging the windows, drove six blocks, and stopped in front of the Laser Lady's house. When on a "knock and lock" to serve an arrest warrant, Andie parked down the street so the suspect wouldn't spot her car and escape through the back door. But the Laser Lady was as benign as the inflated Thanksgiving Pilgrims and turkeys in front of her white clapboard house. She'd hung a cornucopia of wheat shafts on her picket gate.

Andie turned around toward Justice, confined by metal bars to his half of the backseat. The other half was reserved for criminals, at whom he didn't hesitate to growl. He was sitting in his usual ready-willing-and-able position, his front legs propping up his torso, his isosceles triangle ears alert for trouble.

"Okay, Big Guy, you want to visit the Laser Lady and check out a rebellious cat?" Andie asked.

As always, when about to confront any perp, no matter the species, Justice's eyes shone. He loved the job as much as Andie did.

"You have to be on your best behavior. No kitty abuse." Andie got out of the car, opened Justice's door, and hooked a leash to his collar. When she stepped aside, he leapt to the street. All business, he heeled down the Laser Lady's sidewalk to her house.

She answered the door in a fuzzy pink housecoat that matched her cheeks. Her blue eyes made Andie think of worn-out denim. Her only sign of what cops called a reality challenge was wild gray hair. Each strand seemed to spew out of her scalp, confused in which direction it should grow.

Andie flashed her shield, though the Laser Lady had seen it many times. "What's up, Miss Bastrop? I hear something about an angry cat."

"It's Alistair. One of my ferals. He's got a perfectly good home in the shed out back, but this morning I found him in my kitchen cabinet."

"How'd he get in the house?"

"I must have left the back door open." The Laser Lady's hands fluttered like wrens that Alistair would love to catch. "I went to get some tea, and he hissed. Scared me half to death."

"He didn't jump out?"

"No. He acts like he intends to sit on my shelf forever."

"May we see him?"

At "we," the Laser Lady glanced suspiciously at Justice, as if she thought he might sink his teeth into Alistair's neck.

"Don't worry about him. He loves cats. His best friend is a tabby," Andie reassured her.

Though the Laser Lady looked at him as if he belonged on her paranoia list, she led him and Andie to the kitchen, where he politely stationed himself beside the stove.

When Andie opened the cabinet door wide enough for a peek at Alistair, the cat snarled. His glare informed her, as loud and clear as an ambulance siren, *Open that door another inch and you're doomed.* He hissed.

He was sumptuous, part Siamese. He had buck fangs. His face's dark markings made his nose look like it was veering left,

and the ragged tears in his ears testified to fights and van-
quished foes. But Andie refused to be intimidated. She'd faced
down worse than Alistair. If he took her to the mat, she'd win.

Justice also refused to be intimidated. When Andie opened
the cabinet all the way, he and Alistair locked eyes, and Alistair
snarled again. Justice might love cats, but, to him, trespassers
were intolerable. He assumed his most elegant Czar Nicholas
posture and gave Alistair an imperious look that let him know,
You are an impertinent little twit.

Andie rested her fists on her hips and stared down Alistair.
"Okay, buddy, you're guilty of criminal trespassing in the first
degree. That can get you ninety days in jail and a thousand-
dollar fine. Now out."

Alistair did not budge.

"If you don't get out of here I'll add loitering to your
crimes, and that will bring your fine up to thirteen hundred
dollars." Andie walked across the kitchen and opened the back
door to provide an escape. "You've got a good home out there.
Now beat it! Scram!" Andie clapped her hands to make sure he
got the idea.

Anyone would have expected him to make a run for it. But
Alistair's scowl and defiant eyes informed Andie, *You want me
out, you make me go. How would you like being ripped to confetti?*

"He's brave." The Laser Lady tugged nervously at a bath-
robe sleeve.

"Let's try Plan B."

Plan B called for a bowl of Meaty Treat, heated in the mi-
crowave for an irresistible smell and set outside the doorway—
and a line of Pounce leading to it like crumbs leading Hansel
and Gretel out of the forest. As Andie readied Plan B, Justice's
nostrils flared and let her know he'd love a snack, but, for a
Czar Nicholas dog like him, lunging at lures would be un-
seemly.

When they were in place, Andie urged, "Come on, kitty. We don't have all day. Give us a break."

So that Alistair would feel safe—not that a rabid boar could frighten that cat—Andie, Justice, and the Laser Lady went to the living room of chintz sofas, organdy curtains, and cat figurines. Andie asked the Laser Lady about her Thanksgiving plans. Andie brought up the weather. Justice looked back toward the kitchen and chuffed frustrated breaths that asked, *Why are you mollycoddling that ill-mannered peon?*

The Laser Lady was unaware of Justice's contempt toward Alistair. She was more concerned about her enemies. "Thank goodness no lasers are aimed at me today. Alistair is all the trouble I can handle." She swiped at her nose with a crumpled tissue. "Usually communists are behind the attacks. Or Republicans. Lately I've been wondering if the man down the street might be involved. He dropped a piece of green string on my sidewalk last summer."

"Green string, hmm?" Andie asked tactfully. "How about we check on Alistair?"

In the kitchen, Plan B had worked its magic. The Pounce had disappeared, and on the porch Alistair was smacking Meaty Treat. Andie closed the back door.

When she signed up to be a cop, she'd thought she'd be chasing criminals, not squatter cats. But, whatever the task, she'd been put on earth to do her work. Like father, like daughter. Andie took pride in wearing his shield.

Andie's headlights shone through heavy fog as she and Justice traveled down her driveway through the woods. The moon hid behind clouds and made the night feel gloomy. She was glad to get home after a long day of Alistair, a man whose chicken statue had been stolen from his yard, and a couple who'd come upon a vagrant hiding in their basement. Just as Andie had been about to leave for home, an Iraq vet's wheelchair batteries had gone dead in a crosswalk, and he and the dachshund who rode in his lap had kept her at work an extra hour.

Now at nine fifteen it was time to leave behind her work and hang up her Kevlar vest and duty belt, to which were attached twenty-seven pounds of equipment. She'd build a fire in her potbellied stove, fix Justice his kibble and canned Chicken Supreme, and reheat white bean soup for herself. After dinner, she'd whip up a batch of Bad Guy Macaroons for her colleagues, then cuddle up with Justice under her Courthouse Steps quilt. They'd watch *Wild Kingdom* on Animal Planet, his favorite channel, and he'd rest his head on her lap and get his bliss expression—his eyes half-closed, the corners of his mouth turned up in a smile.

As Andie anticipated this peaceful evening, her headlights shone on her birdfeeder, tossed out of the plum tree by marauding raccoons. She pulled up to the parking area in front of her house, and the motion-detection light did not turn on. Yesterday she'd forgotten to change the bulb. *Drat. Another chore for the morning.* She turned off the ignition, got out her flashlight, and climbed out of the car.

Eager for freedom, Justice whimpered as she opened his door. The instant his paws touched the ground, he changed from a responsible K-9 to a joyful puppy. He pranced around her legs, swished his tail, and whined. *Whoopee! No leash! We're home!* He dashed to the rhododendrons, where Rosemary, Meghan's cat and his best tabby friend, often sprang out at him like a jack-in-the-box.

Andie expected Justice to sniff around for Rosemary, and if she wasn't there he'd bound up the stairs to the porch. But he froze. He pricked his ears. Every muscle in his body tensed, alert. He stepped forward and, growling, peered toward the woods. Barking low-pitched rumbles from deep inside his chest, he shot into the darkness.

He could be after a coyote, or raccoons might be snooping around for more birdseed—plenty of wildlife roamed the island. Andie called, "Justice, come! Come back here!" For the first time since his K-9 graduation, he didn't come back. *What's going on?*

Wind swayed the firs as Andie shone her flashlight toward the woods and started after him. When she scanned the underbrush, the light's beam passed a man crouched in jeans and a black hoodie that concealed his face. Her breath caught in her throat. *Who is that?! What's he doing here?* When she aimed the light directly at him, he rose from the bushes. Justice closed in, snarling, then stopped, as if he recognized who was there.

The man raised his arm. Andie's flashlight glinted off something metal in his hand. *A gun? A flashlight? A cell phone?* Andie squinted into the shadows and strained to make out what it was. Her heart sped up as her training kicked in. "Police! Who are you? I see a knife!"

Her shouts seemed to startle the man. He dropped his hand to his side. Justice growled and barked again.

Andie yelled, "What are you doing here? Put down the knife!"

The man raised it above his head. He lunged at Justice and stabbed him. A shriek echoed through the woods—a sound Andie would never forget. Another stab and shriek. Whimpering, Justice sank to the ground.

No! NO! Not Justice! Fury heated Andie's face. Her pulse pounded at her temples. She screamed, "Stop! Drop the knife! Put up your hands! Do it *now!*"

The man came toward her. When the knife flashed, it looked like a machete, smeared in blood. Her vest stopped bullets, but not blades. He could slash her to pieces. Terror zigzagged like lightning through Andie. *Justice can't help me. I'm alone.*

She had no time to run behind the car for safety. It was too late to Tase or Mace the man. If those defenses didn't stop him, he'd stab her before she could get out her gun and shoot. *She had to stop him. Now. By herself. I don't want to die.*

Andie pushed the red emergency-call button on her radio and drew her GLOCK from its holster. Her hands trembling, she took aim. "Get on the ground, or I'll shoot. Do you hear me? Stop! Or I'll shoot."

He was deaf, or bullets didn't scare him. He raised the knife above his head and charged.

Shoot or don't shoot. I don't want to do it. Decide. He's going to kill me. I don't want to hurt him. Decide!

Andie gritted her teeth, steadied her aim. A running target. She fired. He kept coming. *This can't be happening!* She shot again. Not eight feet from her, the man fell to his knees, then toppled onto his chest.

Andie tried to control her voice's shaking as she spoke into her radio. "Eight-two-two." Her police ID number. She realized that she was panting. She could hardly swallow. "Shots fired. I need help at my house. One on the ground at gunpoint. Eight-one-five just stabbed." *Please, Justice, my beloved eight-one-five, don't die.*

She riveted her eyes on the man, sprawled on his face in front of her, his arms outstretched like he was crucified. She hated him for hurting her dog. *The man could be pretending to be shot. He could jump up and come at me again.* "Stay on the ground!" she yelled so hard her throat burned.

With slow, cautious steps, she approached him. She nudged his foot with hers. "Can you get up?" she demanded.

When he didn't respond, she stepped over to his knife and kicked it out of reach. She saw Justice dragging himself across the grass toward her. To his dying breath, he'd try to protect her, and everything in her wanted to run to him. But their safety required that she secure the man. She ordered him, "Put your hands behind you."

No movement. *He might be waiting for the right second to attack again.*

"Now. Hands behind you *now!*" she shouted. *Maybe he is hurt.*

She holstered her gun and cuffed his wrist, then yanked the other wrist behind his back and cuffed it too. When she rolled him on his side, she saw a pool of blood, then his ashen face. He moaned and fluttered his eyelids.

Andie gasped. *It can't be. It just can't.*

"Christopher, what are you *doing?!*" A kid from down the road. Years ago she'd bought a Cub Scout raffle ticket from him, and countless times she'd waved to him, pedaling along on his dirt bike, his knobby knees sticking out at odd angles, his baseball hat backward. That was her image of him, not this brute who was sprawled at her feet.

Andie checked his pulse. He was alive, but blood was seeping from his thigh. She ran to her car, got a towel, and wrapped it tightly above the wound. As she tied it for a tourniquet, she urged him, "Hold on. I'm with you. We'll get you to a hospital. You're going to be okay." Now was not the time to demand, *Why did you stab my dog and try to kill me?*

Justice had reached the parking area but could not marshal strength for the last few feet to Andie. He was whimpering, and his blood was oozing onto the ground. When he tried to raise his head, he couldn't.

Feeling sick to her soul, Andie ripped off her jacket, bent down, and pressed it against Justice's wounds. She stroked his ears. "Please, Sweet Boy. Stay with me. Help is coming. We'll take care of you." Pressing harder, she blinked back tears.

But then she reminded herself, *Cops don't cry. Cops build a wall between their feelings and the outside world.* But this was not the outside world. It was Justice, her family and partner.

In the distance, sirens were approaching from every direction on the island. Some were crossing the bridge from Nisqually County's mainland. The sounds were eerie in the darkness. Andie glanced at Christopher and noticed that she was covered in blood. She squeezed her eyes closed and begged, *Please, help us. Let Justice be okay. Let Christopher live.*

CHAPTER 2

ANDREA

Crouched beside Justice, Andie willed herself not to feel anything, though on a Richter scale her stress could have measured 10.0. Her bloody hands were trembling. Despite the cold, beads of sweat trickled down her spine as car after car barreled down her driveway, doors slammed, and police came toward her, their heavy boots thudding on the damp earth. The north side of Andie's yard and the parking area in front of her house would now become a crime scene.

Andie stood and wrapped her arms around herself to contain her emotion as her brain leapt from one thought to another. Christopher's contorted face flashed through her mind. Then Justice's struggle to breathe. She couldn't focus. Everything was jumpy, twitchy. Repeatedly, she cleared her throat as she explained what had happened.

With guns drawn, police tore into the woods to make sure all was clear before ambulances came. Other officers checked Christopher's pulse—weak, but he was alive. They rummaged through his pockets for a wallet and ID as Andie knelt beside Justice and tried again to stop his bleeding.

Though Christopher was unresponsive, an officer, following protocol, read him his Miranda rights, which seemed to wisp through the air and disappear into the fog.

"You have the right to remain silent." *As if he could remain anything but.*

"You have the right at this time to an attorney." *First, he needs a doctor.*

"Anything you say can and will be used against you in a court of law."

Andie's stomach lurched. It hit her like a whiplash that if Christopher died and she was found at fault, someone could be reading these rights to *her*. His death could change her identity from cop to criminal suspect in danger of a homicide conviction. Every cop's worst nightmare.

Hold it together. Do. Not. Feel. Anything.

To ward off distress, Andie concentrated on the here and now. A policeman's shout: "Scene is safe and secure!" Fire trucks and ambulances, their lights flashing red against Andie's house. The fire department's LED searchlights, bright enough to illuminate a football field. Gurney wheels unfolded by EMTs. A staccato conversation about blood loss and shock. The glow of the ambulance's taillights as it sped down the driveway.

A paramedic hurried to Justice as Andie cradled his head in her arms. "He's my partner. He's been stabbed."

The man squatted next to her and lifted her bloody jacket off Justice's side. "The poor dog," he muttered. Andie read worry around the paramedic's eyes.

"Please, please, get him to the vet," she said.

The paramedic waved to his colleague and shouted, "Bring the gurney over here!"

Helpless, Andie watched the men lift Justice and set him on the padding. As they covered him with a blanket and strapped him in, she stroked his neck to reassure him and lowered her face to his. "Be strong for me, Big Guy. I need you. I love you. I'll get to the vet the minute I can." She thought her heart might splinter into tiny pieces when he tried to lick her hand.

The men wheeled him to an ambulance and put him inside. She had to fight herself to keep from climbing in with him—but policy required her to stay where she was. When the paramedics closed the doors, she swallowed against the sharp stone in her throat. Never before had Andie begrudged the force's rules, but now her resentment chafed against her obligation. Then worry clouded them both.

CHAPTER 3

TOM

Tom Wolski walked out of Pedro's Grande Taqueria and climbed into his patrol car's welcome silence. His head ached. His mouth was dry. *Damn, what a night, and it isn't even ten o'clock.*

He'd just answered a backup call. The bartender had tried to get some drunks to leave, but they hadn't liked breaking up their party early. Thugs, all of them. Getting their attention had taken four police and Tom, a deputy sheriff—plus handcuffs to finish the job. Nothing like the click they made when closed around a bad guy's wrists. Very satisfying.

Eight years in the Nisqually County Sheriff's Department had led Tom to plenty of tussles like tonight's, but his square jaw had not met many fists. He was a solid six foot four and barrel-chested. His muscular build fell somewhere between that of a tackle, the position he'd played at Oregon State, and that of a double-door refrigerator. He had powerful hands, hazel eyes, thick brows, and sandy brown hair in a Marine cut, though not shaved down to skin on the sides. Tom had *been* a Marine. *Semper fi* was in his blood. But now he was also faithful to the Sheriff's Department, Sammy, his golden retriever, and Lisa, his nine-year-old daughter, who lived with him most weekends.

Grateful that he hadn't had to take the drunks to the

county jail and wait around while they got booked, Tom took a slug of his coffee, now cold, and stuck his key in the ignition. Usually, he worked in the homicide unit, but tonight he was on patrol to earn some overtime. With luck, for the rest of his shift he could cruise quiet county roads with owls for company at this time of night.

Fat chance. Dream on. There's always something. He started the motor, and the car spewed out a cloud of exhaust. As he was about to back out of the parking lot, his cell rang. *Here comes the next "something."*

"Wolski," he answered, though colleagues often called him Polack, as if that were his last name. After forty-three years of Polack jokes, Tom hardly listened anymore: A Polack thought his wife was trying to kill him when he found her "Polish Remover." Polish names end in "ski" because Poles can't spell "tobbagan." *Real thigh slappers, those jokes.*

"Hey." It was Tom's boss, Sergeant Alan Pederson, supervisor of the sheriff's Investigation Unit. "Just got a call from Rex Malone. You know him?"

"Yep." Tom had met San Julian P.D.'s chief many times.

"Big deal going on over there. A cop shot a neighbor kid in front of her house. She says he stabbed her K-9 and she was defending herself."

"Bad news," Tom said. "Who's the cop?"

"Andrea Brady."

Oh. For a blink, Tom paused. "I . . . um—"

"They need somebody from the outside for an OIS investigation," Pederson interrupted. "I want you to head it up."

Tom had never taken the lead in an Officer Involved Shooting. A chance to prove himself. "Fine."

"I'll put Murphy and Jackson on your shoot team and send them and some technicians over to Brady's house. It's at Six-Five-Seven Valley Road. Just off Highway Twenty-One."

Tom scribbled the address in his logbook.

"You far from there?" Pederson asked.

"Maybe fifteen minutes." Tom could take the two-lane bridge to the island.

"Good," Pederson said. "The kid's Christopher Vanderwaal. Parents are Franz and Jane. They live down Valley Road at Nine-Six-Six. You got that?"

"Yep." Tom's writing looked like a palsied chicken's scratching, but he could read it. "Is the kid on his way to the hospital?"

"Should be."

"His parents?"

"Don't know where they are. The chief sent two of his people to their house a few minutes ago. The cops will stay till you get Murphy or Jackson to secure the scene."

"Right."

"Get over there. Let me know how it's going. Call anytime."

Tom opened his mouth to tell Alan what he'd started to say about Andrea Brady. It was something he should probably explain: They had an awkward history. They'd almost gone out together.

When she'd been a rookie on San Julian's force, a friend had set them up for a blind date. But the day before they were supposed to go out to dinner together, she'd called Tom and said, "I can't go out with you. I just broke up with someone. I'm not ready to get involved with anybody again."

Yeah, right. Why didn't you bring that up when I called you last week? And how can you be so sure I'd want to get involved with you?

From a mile away Tom could smell the get-lost-buddy line. She must have done some investigating and decided she didn't want to go out with him. On the one hand, maybe he wasn't God's gift to every woman on the planet, but he was attractive enough, and most women liked him. *To hell with her.*

On the other hand, maybe she'd done him a favor. Freshly

divorced from Mia, Tom had no time for more grief from a woman. Still, Andrea Brady's brush-off had chipped his pride, especially after he finally met her in person at a Homeland Security meeting. Though she was pretty, he made it a policy to avoid her. When they ran into each other once in a while on the job, he got away ASAP.

Tom closed his mouth without revealing this humiliating situation to Pederson, but he wondered, was he wrong to keep quiet? If Pederson knew, he might take Tom off the case. The opportunity would slip through his fingers and be handed to someone else.

Tom wanted to head this investigation. It would be tough; but if everything worked out, it could mean another success for his file. Another step on his path to making sergeant. He planned to take the three-striper's exam next summer.

Besides, he told himself, this business with Andrea Brady had happened more than five years ago. Since then, she'd married and, he'd heard, divorced. Lots of water had flowed under her bridge. His too. Their broken date was not worth mentioning. It wouldn't be acting unethically to forget it ever happened.

Eager to get to Valley Road, Tom turned on his siren and flashing lights. An OIS investigation sure beat patrolling empty roads. He told himself that he could handle Andrea Brady. He'd ignore the past and focus on the job. He sped toward the island.

CHAPTER 4

ANDREA

By the time the ambulance had driven Justice away, all eight cops in Andie's department, except Chief Malone, had shown up, on duty or not. They set up the incident command post and defined the crime scene and the path to it with yellow tape, then stood around, talking and waiting for the sheriff's team. Andie also waited, out of the way on the stone path to her house. She took deep breaths to calm herself. They didn't work.

Mario Capoletti, the department's disheveled part-time psychologist, walked around the crime scene's perimeter and greeted Andie. "Terrible this has happened to you. I'm so sorry." His eyes were kind.

Ron Hausmann, the guild attorney, appeared in a coat and tie, odd for a Sunday night. Jingling coins in his pockets, he said, "I got here as fast as I could. We can meet tomorrow if you're up for it."

How could I be up for it? Andie was thinking when, finally, Chief Malone arrived out of uniform and out of breath. He'd been at a cousin's birthday party in Seattle, he told Andie, but on the ferry he'd contacted the Sheriff's Department. "They'll be here in a minute. Everything's on track." He took her arm and led her to the porch.

Malone was a galumphing Saint Bernard of a man—he didn't walk, he lumbered, and his life's purpose was to rescue people. He seemed friendly till someone crossed him, at which time he would raise his hackles and growl. Every time he got excited, bits of foam appeared in the corners of his mouth.

"Brady, I wish I didn't have to be the one to tell you," he started slowly.

"Tell me what?"

"Christopher Vanderwaal died as soon as he left here. He didn't make it to the end of your road. One of your bullets nicked his femoral artery, and he bled out."

Andie's stomach dropped as if she were in an airplane, losing altitude. The news knocked the breath out of her. The porch seemed to distort and spin, like she was looking into a carnival mirror and everything around her was wavy and awry. Shock numbed her brain and shut it down.

"I know it's upsetting. It's the last thing any cop wants to hear," Malone said.

Andie moved her lips to speak, but no words made their way through her constricted throat.

"Are you all right?"

An invisible puppeteer pulled a string and made her nod.

"You don't *seem* all right." Malone peered into her face.

Andie managed, "I'm okay." *A lie.* She wasn't okay by a long shot. The Chief had just shattered her world.

"Look, Brady, I'm going to put you on administrative leave. Take some time off. You need to recover from tonight. You'll still get paid."

Andie nodded again.

"Everything's got to be confusing to you now. Before you talk to anyone, you'll need twenty-four hours to settle down. You'll start to get a handle on what's happened."

"Um . . ." Whatever she was going to say drifted off, out of reach.

"On Tuesday morning the OIS team will need you to give a statement. And on Wednesday I want Capoletti to debrief you. I'll assign Stephanie to be your peer counselor. She'll help you through the process. That sound okay?"

"Yes," Andie whispered, though she hardly understood what she was agreeing to.

"Do you have family to see you through this?"

Andie's parents were dead, and no one could count on her brother, Ray, who lived in New York. "Justice is my family. Do you know if he's all right?"

"I haven't heard anything yet," Malone said.

"I want to see him."

"You have to go to the station first."

It isn't fair.

"Look, we're here for you twenty-four-seven." Beads of Saint Bernard foam were gathering on Malone's lips. "I know you know this, but I want to remind you—don't talk about the case unless it's with Capoletti or Hausmann or the sheriff's team."

Malone looked over Andie's shoulder and beckoned to someone. "Come on over here, Wolski." Malone said to Andie, "He's a good guy. He'll be heading the investigation."

She turned around and saw Tom. *No. Surely not. The Chief couldn't find anyone who thinks less of me.*

Tom ducked under the crime scene tape and took the porch steps two at a time. He and Malone shook beefy hands, but Tom did not extend his hand toward Andie. From his imposing height, he looked down at her and said formally, "Hello, Brady." His face seemed starched.

"I'll leave you two. People are waiting to see me." Malone patted Tom's back and left.

Tom watched him go down the steps, then said to Andie, "I want to talk with you about tonight."

"The Chief told me not to say anything till I have time to get my head together."

"Did you know Christopher Vanderwaal?" Tom asked anyway.

"Not really."

"What does that mean? You either knew him or you didn't."

I can't handle this. Andie felt cornered. Her face flushed as survival instincts unsheathed their claws and warned: *Be careful.*

She had every reason not to trust Tom. He didn't like her, and now he had the power to ruin her career or, worse, get her sent to prison. On the rare occasions when she'd seen him since she'd broken their date, she'd felt nothing from him but disapproval. And she felt it from him now.

"You can't interrogate me tonight. I can't think straight." Andie rubbed her forehead, as if that could get her mind to work.

Tom stared at her, perhaps trying to decide how hard to push. "Okay. I want the keys to your patrol car. You can't drive it on leave. And your house key. Christopher Vanderwaal may have broken in earlier. We need to check it out."

Andie reached into her pocket and pulled out her key ring, from which dangled a silver German shepherd. "Here." Docile, she worked off the keys and dropped them onto Tom's palm. *This must be how suspects feel when they're under investigation. Required to follow orders. No longer in control of their own lives.* A seasoned cop who'd chased down drug dealers and hauled perps to jail, Andie had been fearless. Now she was scared.

CHAPTER 5

TOM

Tom gathered his team around him. There was so much to do at once. It had to be done right.

"Okay, Murphy and Jackson, get over to the Vanderwaals' house. If they're there, persuade them to go to a hotel. If they refuse, keep an eye on them so they don't sneak out evidence. Look for drugs, journals, photos, anything suspicious. Get the kid's electronics. I'll be over later."

"We're on it." Ross Jackson's ruddy cheeks looked chapped.

"Dawson, go to the vet clinic and take photos of the dog's wounds, preferably before anybody sews them up. And, Sanchez, get pictures of the sole of every shoe that came through here tonight. Firemen. Paramedics. Cops. Andrea Brady. Christopher Vanderwaal."

"Done," Dawson said. He and Sanchez picked up their camera gear and headed out.

"Chan and Lindstrom, set up an outer perimeter of tape and keep everybody back. You can hear the press out there on Valley. Matter of minutes till they stampede down the driveway," Tom said. "The rest of you know what to do, so get to work."

Tom stepped over to the incident command post and kept watch on the crime scene. As minutes crawled by, his technicians flashed cameras on footprints, Andie's bullet casings, and Christopher's knife in place. Diagrams were drawn of where he'd waited in the bushes, where his head and feet had rested on the dirt, and where Andie's shells had landed. Distances between these locations were measured.

Those calculations would be crucial. *Everything has to add up if this case goes to court. Maybe not if—when.* Even if the evidence showed that Andrea Brady had been justified to shoot, no way would Christopher Vanderwaal's parents take his death lying down. Whether criminal or civil, a lawsuit was looming out there on the horizon.

Tonight Tom had to make sure that everyone went slowly, took meticulous care, made no mistakes. There was no room for slipshod evidence collection or muddled computations. He had to be ready to defend his team's conclusions against lawyers, reporters, and higher-ups. He'd be exposed, professionally on trial. He and his team would be pressed between glass slides and put under a microscope.

Though grateful for the chance to prove himself, Tom felt the challenge weigh him down. Since childhood, a streak of hesitation sometimes showed up in him, a trait few would guess a sturdy man like him could have. Again tonight the streak presented him with stumbling blocks of caution, but Tom hooked his thumbs in his pants' front pockets and mentally kicked them away. *No room for self-doubt here. Get on with it.*

He thought of his coach at Oregon State barking at the team. "I want to see you fight!" he told them, circled around him, their heads bowed before they ran onto the field for a game. As they left the locker room, he'd pat them on the back and shout, "Get out there and kick ass!"

That's what Tom would do for this OIS investigation.

CHAPTER 6

ANDREA

Gathering evidence, Tom and his team took over Andie's yard. They stomped through her chard and kale beds and snapped branches off her camellia bushes. The destruction didn't register on Andie because her house now felt like public property. And whatever knife and bullet shells the team might find wouldn't bring Christopher back to life or answer the most fundamental question: Why had he done what he did?

Andie was too numb to think about it. But shock was a gift that flipped a switch inside her to protect her against debilitating guilt. Until she could face it, shock stored it away in her mind's darkest corner. Shock also split her into two disconnected parts: the exterior Andie who did her duty even at a time like this; and the interior Andie who was immobilized, incapable of absorbing that she'd killed someone. The two parts allowed her to do what was asked, but she felt like someone besides her was going through the motions.

Her only lucid thoughts were about Justice. When Tom asked one of his deputies, Tina Morrison, to drive Andie to San Julian's police station for processing, she got into the patrol car itching with impatience to go to the veterinary hospital. More than she'd ever wanted anything, she wanted to get over there and see for herself if Justice was still alive. Not knowing was torture.

Tina, clearly in no hurry, drove at the maddening speed of a three-toed sloth. She looked like one too. Her eyes drooped, her hair was shaggy, and her long nails curled under like claws. She talked slowly, as if sedatives were her closest friends. She might have spent the afternoon languid in a eucalyptus tree, munching leaves and shoots.

Andie kept thinking, *Hurry!* As they inched through the intersection of Highway 21 and Puget Road—two blocks from the vet—she wrung her cold hands together and mentally begged her big guy to hang on.

The station was built of concrete bricks soon after World War II. Inside were speckled gray linoleum floors, pea-soup-green walls, and smells of dust and age. There were no halls, so the rooms were a jumble; the force referred to their station as the "rabbit warren." Tonight, to Andie, it felt more like the unfamiliar barracks of a foreign army. In her daze, she wasn't sure she could find her locker or the restroom.

Tina guided her past the station's two jail cells to the back, where drunks took Breathalyzer tests and perps were lined up against a wall for mug shots. "We need photos," Tina drawled.

Andie stood against the wall, and Tina flashed the camera—face forward, then profile, then Andie's full body, showing her uniform's splotches of blood and Justice's shed fur. The photos were supposed to record what she'd looked like when Christopher had run at her. No longer simply tired from a long workday, she was pale and bedraggled. Her blank expression informed the camera, *Inside my head, nobody's home.*

Investigator Stan Carson, who had a beanpole physique, took her gun for ballistics tests to discover whether its bullets matched those at the scene. He swabbed her hand for residue to document if she'd pulled the trigger. Finally, in the women's restroom, Andie changed into a sweat suit that Tina found in her locker, and Carson collected Andie's uniform to test whether the blood on it was Christopher's and Justice's.

"Did you see those storm clouds? Sure looks like rain," Tina said.

"Give me snow in the mountains. The last ski season was the pits," Carson said.

"What do you think, Brady?" Tina's sloth lids sagged over her eyes.

I think we should stop wasting time. I want to see Justice. "What do I think about what?"

"Earth to Brady." Carson's words sounded fuzzy, as if spoken underwater. "We're talking rain."

Andie looked as if she weren't sure what rain was. She said vaguely, "It's fine."

Clearly, Carson and Tina were trying to distract her and keep the conversation light. If they talked directly about the "case," as the worst night in her life had become, they would jeopardize the investigation and a possible legal trial.

After Carson left to take the evidence to the Sheriff's Department, Tina handed Andie a use-of-force report form and settled her at Stephanie's desk, which was behind an interior window just inside the station's front door. Then Tina leaned back in a metal folding chair against the wall, leisurely flipped through a *People* magazine, and gave Andie space to collect her thoughts.

Andie couldn't focus. The form's words seemed to sprout little fins and swim off the page. She needed all her concentration to understand the questions, much less to fill in the blanks with facts that shock had tucked away in her mental muddle. "Officer's name"? "Suspect's name"? "Weapon used"? "Location"? "Time of day"? "Lighting"? "Why was the weapon used?" "Briefly narrate the incident."

Andie made herself pick up the pen. As she started to answer, her handwriting looked like a stranger's scraped into the paper rather than her own loops and swirls. Her words might have been written in Coptic or Urdu for all anyone could tell. But always responsible, even in shock, Andie tried to fill out the form.

"Hey, girl!" Stephanie bustled into her office, bent down and hugged Andie, and engulfed her in a cloud of perfume called Glow. "The Chief assigned me to be your peer counselor. That's a new term for 'friend,' which I already was." She chortled. "So you've taken over my desk."

"Just for a little while," Andie said.

"I don't mind as long as you don't muck it up with a glue gun or something." Stephanie plucked a dead leaf off her desk's ivy plant, which she was forever forgetting to water. "By the way, you look great in that nasty sweat suit. Did the Laser Lady's cat drag you in?"

Stephanie's chipper talk didn't fool Andie. It was meant to distract her, like Carson's and Tina's. Still, the presence of her friend reassured Andie, and a tiny spark began to thaw her inner ice.

Stephanie should have been an actress. She wore only red, and she painted her nails scarlet, garnet, or rose. She also went through life like every moment ended in an exclamation point. On the stillest afternoon her hair looked wind tousled, and for now it was colored Beeline Honey, but who knew about next week? She set her red bucket bag on her desk and leaned back in a folding chair next to Tina.

"She doing okay?" Stephanie asked Tina, referring to Andie, as if Andie couldn't hear.

"Traumatized, but she's okay," Tina said. "After she finishes the form, she can leave."

"Want to go home or spend the night with me?" Stephanie asked Andie.

"I want to see Justice. I don't know how he is."

"I just called the clinic. He's in surgery," Stephanie said.

So he's alive! Alive!! Thank you! With relief, Andie closed her eyes and exhaled from somewhere so deep that her shoulders lowered a couple of inches. Then she remembered he might still die. "Did the vet say anything else? Will Justice be all right?"

"I don't know. Everyone in that place is sure aware of him. Cops and deputies must have poured in over there," Stephanie said.

"We have to hurry."

Andie scratched her pen faster. When she finally finished, she set down the pen and handed the form to Tina. "Let's go," Andie said.

As Stephanie drove toward the veterinary clinic in her red Toyota, Andie was quiet. Suddenly she heard herself ask, "What if Justice dies to punish me because I shot Christopher?"

"That's crazy. Life doesn't work that way," Stephanie said.

Andie wasn't so sure. Guilt was beginning to nibble at her barely thawing edges. It was waiting for the chance to chomp.

Chapter 7

Tom

At the end of Andie's driveway, neighbors and reporters gathered around Chief Malone. Blocked from the crime scene by a wall of firs, he stood on a makeshift platform and blinked against the TV cameras' lights. A forest of microphones had been placed on stands in front of his chest, below which his stomach was locked into an ongoing battle with his belt. Malone's slumped shoulders said, *I don't want to be here.*

I wouldn't want to be there, either, Tom thought as he stamped his feet in the cold, away from the crowd.

News had traveled fast. TV and newspaper reporters had scrambled to get to the island from Seattle and Bremerton and as far away as Olympia. By morning, national crews might show up to cover Andrea Brady's use of deadly force.

It was a sensational story, guaranteed to hook audiences. Dog lovers' hearts would melt at Justice, whom Tom had heard could be a poster dog for law enforcement. And half the U.S. population would hope to see what they'd call a trigger-happy cop get hers. All police in America were aware of the negative sentiment against them, and it had only been getting worse. Cops were a hot topic. The use of deadly force was forever debated. Controversy sold newspapers.

Tom felt sorry for Malone, facing down the wolf pack.

Tom had seen the press chew up and spit out plenty of sheriffs and chiefs. But this press conference would be different because it was about *his* case. *Pay attention. Lots to learn here.*

"I'm sorry to report that one of our officers has shot a suspect," Malone began. "The officer was not injured. The suspect is dead. The officer's K-9 is in critical condition at the veterinary hospital."

A reporter in a black down coat shouted, "Where did this happen?"

"At the officer's residence." Malone did not mention that it was located in the woods behind him, but a reporter with half a brain could figure that out.

A man with a dirty ponytail and a pen behind his ear asked, "Can you tell us about the victim?"

Victim. Already the word "suspect" had been shelved for a more sensational and biased term. Anyone could see where this was going. The train had left the station and was rumbling down the track toward a town called Gotcha. Inevitably, some of the media would twist the story against Andrea Brady.

Avoiding the trap about the "victim," Malone said, "The Nisqually County Sheriff's Department is taking over the investigation. You'll have to talk with them for more details."

"Why did the officer shoot?" asked a woman reporter wearing a blue knitted hat.

"As soon as more is known, the Sheriff's Department will give you information," Malone said.

"If the shooting took place at the officer's residence, the officer surely knew the victim," a reporter badgered.

"I don't want to impede the investigation by providing more details at this time," Malone said.

A woman at the crowd's front raised her hand. "Is this the officer's first use of deadly force? Or have there been others?"

Probing for the bad. Looking for chinks in the armor, Tom thought.

"Once the investigation is finished, the details will be available," Malone said.

"When?" she asked.

"Hard to say. Could be as soon as three weeks. We'll let you know."

Malone tugged at his collar as if it were too tight. The reporters kept pressing, and in a dozen different ways he repeated that he couldn't give more information now. When bits of foam piled up in the corners of his mouth, he mopped a white handkerchief over his lips and forehead.

Sitting in the hot seat can sure singe your pants, Tom thought.

He warned himself that he'd have to be on guard. He'd need to run the investigation exactly right so these buzzards couldn't pick his bones. They'd be circling for the chance to swoop down on mistakes. He damned well wouldn't let them.

In his time he'd faced down worse opponents than the media. Years ago as a Seattle rookie cop, he'd stood in a skirmish line, wearing a helmet, clenching a baton, and pitting his heft against an angry mob. They shoved and hit and yelled about the unjust Iraq War's Operation Phantom Thunder. Tom planted his feet on the ground and warded off blows.

"Bastards!" the cop next to him shouted. "My brother got killed in Baghdad last week. I have more reason to be pissed off than they do."

As Tom was being jostled and screamed at in the face, he managed only, "I'm sorry for your loss." He was also sorry for the damned state of the world, all the anger and violence. His job might not be as dangerous as a U.S. soldier's in Iraq, but every time Tom showed up for work some punk could hurt or kill him.

Now as he surveyed the reporters on Andrea Brady's street, he knew that coiled beneath their questions might be a mistrust of police, but journalists' words couldn't break Tom's bones. Reporters didn't throw bricks. They fired questions, not bullets. He'd seen far worse.

CHAPTER 8

ANDREA

So that the island's pets could always get medical attention, Drs. Vargas and Upton kept their clinic open twenty-four hours a day, seven days a week. Their message was clear: *We care about your animals.* You could sense it when you drove into the parking lot, where a row of imitation fire hydrants encouraged canine patients to attend to their biological needs.

Inside, the waiting room was a cozy houseplant jungle. Comfortable wingback chairs were placed around a diamond-patterned area rug, and café curtains hung on the multi-paned windows. Half walls enclosed most of a toy-strewn corner, over which hung a sign: TWO-LEGGED KID ZONE. Next to it were stations for coffee, tea, cookies, dog biscuits, cat treats, and the latest editions of *Modern Dog, Popular Mechanics, Sunset, Outside,* and the *San Julian Review.*

Andie had brought Justice here many times, but never after one a.m. or for a life-and-death emergency. So late, the waiting room, though comforting, was missing its usual barks and meows. It felt lonely and off-kilter, as if the walls might fall in around her and pin her to the ground.

"Want me to go see Justice with you?" Stephanie asked.

"Maybe it's better for him if I'm alone."

"Just let me know what you need."

Andie nodded but knew she had no idea what she needed, except for Justice to be okay.

A technician in a dog-and-cat patterned scrub suit led her to an exam room where Dr. Mark Vargas, Andie's friend and vet, was waiting for her, his arms crossed over his chest, each hand cupping an elbow. Covering his heart that way seemed like a self-protective posture. Maybe he had bad news he'd rather not deliver. Maybe veterinarians, like cops, had to protect their feelings from the outside world.

Mark peered down at Andie through John Lennon–style wire-frame glasses. His rice-bowl haircut and bangs flopping to his eyebrows looked like a youthful Beatle's too. Tonight, however, lines of fatigue surrounded his eyes and he seemed more formal than usual. His distance scared Andie.

"Is Justice all right?" she blurted out.

"Before you see him, I want to prepare you," Mark said. "He's sedated in an oxygen cage. His prognosis is guarded."

"You mean *doubtful?* You think he'll *die?*"

"I hope not, but he could. It's too early to say. You need to be ready in case we can't save him, Andrea. We won't know if he's out of the woods for a couple of days."

As if Andie hadn't trembled a lifetime's worth of trembles on this long night, her hands started shaking again.

Mark pulled a paper cup from a nearby dispenser and filled it with water. "You're white as a sheet. I don't want you to faint on me." He handed her the cup. "Want to sit down?"

She took a sip. "I want you to tell me about Justice."

"Well, he was stabbed twice. You don't have to worry much about the wound in his shoulder. It should heal okay. I'm more concerned about the one in his thoracic cavity. We're lucky the knife didn't go to his lung because that would have finished him off for sure."

Andie scrunched her eyes and fought back tears.

"I promise we're doing all we can. Justice lost a lot of blood,

so we gave him a transfusion. We closed both wounds and su-
tured in drains."

"For what?"

"To drain off fluids—and air if it builds up in his chest and
presses on his lungs so he can't breathe. We'll keep checking his
red blood cell count and oxygen saturation. My main concern
is infection. We're giving Justice IV antibiotics. Now we wait
to see how this shakes out."

"I wish you had a magic wand. . . ."

Mark put his arm around Andie's shoulders and led her
into his surgery, where he left her and Justice alone.

No amount of preparation could have readied Andie for
the sight of him lying in the Plexiglas cage. He was wearing a
small oxygen mask over his nose and mouth, but what grieved
her more were the huge shaved patches of his fur, the thick
white dressings on his wounds, and the tubes bristling from his
flesh like stems after a deer has munched off the flowers and
leaves. The catheter piercing Justice's front leg and bound with
pink tape was the least of what had been done to him, and yet
it was also painful to see.

Still, the very worst was the sedation. Justice looked like he
was dead. With no twitch of an ear or flicker of an eyelash, he
was miles away, completely out of Andie's reach. She was used
to him sleeping on her bed, snuggling behind her knees' crook,
hogging up the space. Throughout the night, he snored or
sighed or shuffled his paws while dreaming. Now he was immobilized. Silent. The sedation seemed like a prelude to death.

Andie reached through an opening in the Plexiglas cage
and petted his haunch. She wanted him to sense on some level
that she was there—and if he died in the night he'd go knowing she loved him.

Meghan often said that you had to imagine what you wanted,
that a detailed mental picture was the first step in coaxing your
wish to come true. So Andie visualized throwing Justice's green,

blue, and red Frisbees—and him dashing across her grass to snatch them from the air. A champion of Frisbee catching, he snapped one at a time between his teeth without dropping any he already held. When he had all three fanned out from his mouth like a hand of cards, he ran a victory lap around the yard until Andie tugged them away and threw them again and again. When he finally got tired, he ran up to the porch and dropped the Frisbees at the front door. *Kerplunk.*

Andie had lived this scene with him countless times. Now she pictured it so hard that it felt engraved on her brain. If the sincerity of her imagining counted for anything, by tomorrow Justice should be bounding around the clinic, eager to go home to his Frisbees. But that was hardly likely.

She rested her forehead on the Plexiglas above the cage's opening, as close as she could get to his ears. Usually, they were raised at attention, like triangle sails on a toy boat beating into the wind. Now his ears flopped down from drugs.

"I'm sorry Christopher stabbed you, Sweet Boy. If I'd had time, I'd have moved heaven and earth to stop him," Andie whispered. "Don't worry. Everybody's rooting for you. Everything will be all right."

Even sedated, however, Justice was too smart not to detect a white lie.

So Andie amended it: "Sweet Boy, we all *hope* everything will be all right." That's all she could do about the dismal mess that her and Justice's life had become. *Hope.*

CHAPTER 9

TOM

The hardest part of Tom's job was knocking on a door and informing parents that their child was dead. Tom remembered every single person he'd had to shock that way. It had ripped out their hearts—and it would have ripped out Tom's if he hadn't blocked Lisa from his mind. Sometimes he couldn't help but feel sorry for people—yet he couldn't stop himself from feeling grateful that the kid had been theirs, not his.

Relieved that Ross Jackson and Mike Murphy had been the bearers of the Vanderwaals' tragic news, Tom stepped inside their barn-red clapboard house, removed his khaki hat, and hung it by the front door on a coatrack's peg. He found Jackson poking around the living room. "The Vanderwaals here?"

"Murph drove Franz and their other son, Joey, to meet Jane at Wilson Hospital. She's an emergency room nurse. Night shift. Too upset to drive her car."

"Can't blame her."

"They're going to a hotel."

"Better to have them out of our hair," Tom said.

"What little I've got," Jackson joked as the chrome light fixture hanging from the ceiling shone on his bald head.

Tom glanced around at the empty walls and coffee table's top. The lampshades were covered with plastic wrap, like they'd just that minute arrived from Home Depot. The only sign that someone actually lived in this room was a bowling trophy on a side table. A small brass man swung his arm behind him, about to whomp his ball into nonexistent pins. Below was etched "Franz Vanderwaal, 2013."

"So what's Franz like?" Tom asked.

"A shrimp. Napoléon complex. Reactive. When I told him Christopher had died from a cop's gunshot wounds, the first words out of his mouth were, 'I'll sue the hell out of you.'"

"No concern for Christopher?"

"If there was, it whizzed right by me," Jackson said. "Franz never wondered why he hadn't shown up for dinner tonight. Father of the Year."

Tom tucked that fact away for future thought. "What about Joey?"

"He's thirteen. He stood here, didn't say a word. Didn't dare cry."

"Could be some father-son problem going on."

"That's my take. Intimidation or neglect." Jackson picked up the bowling trophy, frowned at it, and set it down. "Damned shame."

The palm Tom ran over the gas fireplace mantel got dusty. "Franz say anything else? Any thoughts about Christopher?"

"Claimed nothing unusual was going on with him. No mental health issues or recent problems at school. Everything perfect. Gold stars all around."

"Maybe Jane'll be more open." Tom hoped. Uncooperative parents could be doors slammed in your face.

He followed Jackson through the kitchen and noted the sink of dirty dishes that Jane might be displeased to find. She also might not like the newspapers piled on the breakfast table next to greasy plates and jars of mayo, mustard, and peanut butter, onto which no one had bothered to screw back the lids. Attached to the refrigerator by magnetized frogs were to-do lists so long that the Energizer Bunny would lose heart. Tom didn't much like the feeling here. Something seemed out of whack. Nobody seemed to care about the house.

Jackson led Tom down a dark hall to Christopher's bedroom, which was a tidy day to the kitchen's grubby night.

"Whoa! No normal kid is this neat." Tom looked around at books set in even rows on shelves, and shoes lined up, straight as soldiers in parade formation, under the bed. "This is weird. A monk could have lived in this room."

"He's emptied the wastebasket. I have to threaten my kid with no TV for a month to get him to do that," Jackson said.

Tom poked the wrinkle-free plaid bedspread. "You could bounce quarters off this. There's got to be something out of place here."

Jackson nodded toward a poster of a young David Bowie. "That's the only hint of rebellion." In a sports coat and loosened tie, he had slicked back his hair, and a cigarette dangled from his lips. His famed different-sized pupils drilled straight into Tom. Printed in red letters above Bowie's pretty head was the name of his hit "Under Pressure."

Tom tried to imagine what David Bowie's gaze had meant to Christopher and how it might have drawn him in. "You think Christopher was gay?"

"Could have been. Ask his parents," Jackson said.

"Maybe they didn't know."

"He might have been trying to work it out. That could upset a kid."

"Sure could," Tom said. "Something was bugging him if he stabbed a K-9 and attacked Brady." *That is if Brady told it like it really was. It's too early in the game to know what's what.*

Tom and Jackson started a search of Christopher's room to answer key questions: What was he like? Who were his friends? Did he take drugs? Leaning toward the theory that drugs could have been involved in Christopher's alleged attack, Tom wanted to search out a hypothetical stash or anything else of interest.

He rifled through pockets of Christopher's shirts, Dockers, and jeans. His clothes were conservative and Spartan. His only nod to most teens' slouchy outfits was a fleece vest and jacket collection.

Jackson checked the toes of Christopher's shoes, unrolled balls of his socks, and reached under drawer linings. Tom ripped off his bedspread and sheets and looked for mattress slits that might lead to secret compartments. Together, they unscrewed and prodded behind heater vents, light switches, and plugs. While Jackson peeled David Bowie from the wall to see if Christopher had flattened drugs in an envelope and taped them behind the poster, Tom went to the bathroom and opened Christopher's deodorant stick and shampoo bottle. "Squeaky clean choirboy," he muttered.

Next, Tom and Jackson pulled Christopher's many books from three wide shelves and hunted for hidden pockets carved out of pages. Tom noted titles—*The Hunger Games, The Way of the Shadows, Catching Fire, Frankenstein,* and *Slaughterhouse-Five.* He flipped through Christopher's field guides to everything from worms to stars. Clearly, he'd liked to read, and widely. Nature meant something to him. Maybe he'd been a Boy Scout.

When Jackson found Christopher's San Julian High School yearbook, Tom thought they might have struck gold. But the yearbook index listed only two photos of Christopher. "Not exactly Mr. Popular," Jackson said.

In his class picture, Christopher was wearing a neatly pressed button-down white shirt, a cousin of those in his closet. He had sandy brown hair, cut short and as tidy as his room. His eyes looked sad and older than his sixteen years, as if he might have seen and felt too much too early.

"Could have been lots of mileage on that kid," Jackson said.

"But he's clean cut. You'd never believe a kid like that could do what Brady claims." Tom flipped to the yearbook's second photo, in which Christopher looked lost in the back row of the Computer Club. "Maybe he was a nerd."

Jackson bent down for a closer look. "Interesting about the club when there's no computer in this room."

"Could Franz have sneaked it out of here?"

"He never got out of my sight," Jackson said.

"What about Joey?"

"Nobody had the chance to take anything."

Tom walked over to Christopher's IKEA birch desk. On top sat a computer printer; its cable, coiled on the wood, was connected to nothing. Tom shuffled through the drawers and found the usual school supplies—printer paper, pens, pencils, a stapler, some paper clips. Nothing revealing. No iPods or video games tucked anywhere.

Tom wondered if Christopher had purposely cleaned out everything, including a cell phone that would tell investigators who he was. Tom made a mental note. *High Priority: Locate the electronics.*

CHAPTER 10

ANDREA

"They moved my geraniums off the windowsills." Andie looked around her living room for other signs of Tom Wolski's invasion.

"His team checked that Christopher hadn't opened a window," Stephanie said.

"They should have put my plants back."

"Not to worry. Easily fixed."

Stephanie moved the pots from the coffee table to the sills as Andie walked around the house to see if valuables were missing. Her grandmother's silver pitcher still sat in the kitchen cabinet. Her TV, CD player, and computer were safely in her bedroom. No one had taken her collection of silver teaspoons, started on a family trip to Canada when she was five, or the Native American jewelry she'd inherited from her mother but rarely wore. Andie's checkbooks were still tucked into one of her rolltop desk's drawers.

All but the geraniums looked the same as yesterday, but something wasn't right. It was a vague feeling in the air. Andie sensed that Tom's team had left behind ragged traces of their energy as they'd snooped around and pawed her windows and heaven only knew what else. Her house didn't feel like *hers* anymore. Like the north side of her yard, it reminded her of

Christopher, and it didn't feel safe. But, then, after last night, no place did.

Andie found Stephanie in the kitchen and winced at Justice's water bowl on her linoleum floor. "Nothing's missing except my beloved dog," she said. When they'd seen him this morning, he'd been awake and she'd been hopeful—until he'd tried to get up and hadn't had the strength.

Andie was still wearing the same nasty sweat suit dredged from her station locker. Not wanting to send Stephanie back here last night for toiletries, she'd brushed her teeth with her index finger and Stephanie's Colgate. She'd forgotten to wash her face in the shower. Her hair, usually puffy as a red cloud, was flattened against her head, and her spirit had flattened too. She knew how a punctured tire felt. *You don't see your dog stabbed, then kill someone without major emotional damage.*

But for Stephanie's sake, Andie tried to act normal. "Tea?" she asked.

"If you've got time."

"I don't have anything *but* time."

As Stephanie set spoons and place mats on Andie's round oak kitchen table, she chattered about the vacation she'd been saving for—to the Great Barrier Reef. "I've found a great way to raise more money. On weekends I'm going to be an artist's model. I can earn up to forty-five dollars an hour, and all I have to do is hold a pose for a few minutes."

Andie narrowed her eyes. "What kind of pose?"

"I don't know. No contortions, as far as I've read. It sounds easy. I could listen to music."

"You haven't mentioned if you'd be naked."

"Oh, that." Stephanie got Andie's sugar bowl from a kitchen cabinet. "Don't rain on my parade."

"What if the Green River Killer gets you in his private studio? You'd be totally vulnerable." *He could come at you with a knife.*

"You're talking like a cop."

"I *am* a cop." *At least for now.* A whistle from Andie's kettle pierced the air.

Without asking what kind of tea Stephanie wanted—the answer was always English breakfast—Andie set two tea bags into white mugs and poured in boiling water. "By the way, I know what you're doing."

"I'm trying to earn money for my trip."

"I mean right now. You want to make me think about something besides last night. You're trying to keep me from being upset."

"It *was* working pretty well."

It wasn't, though Andie didn't want to point that out. Stephanie was trying so hard to help. Even if her effort hadn't worked, Andie loved her for it. "You've been wonderful, Steph. I can't thank you enough, but now I have to take care of myself."

After Stephanie left, Andie poured herself another mug of tea and brought her wooden recipe box to the kitchen table. She thought she might make cookies and take them, as usual, to the station—till it occurred to her that she could only go there on official business now. Still, sifting and stirring always made her feel better, so she thumbed through her recipes and pulled out the index card for Al Capone Biscotti. If she were banished from the station, she'd make them for the senior center.

Andie read the card, but she couldn't seem to get the ingredients straight. She saw "flour," then moved down to "sugar," but had forgotten both of them by the time she got to "eggs." The ingredients she'd mixed together countless times now seemed incomprehensible.

As she stared across the kitchen, the afternoon sun shone through a crystal prism hanging in her window and cast a blurry rainbow on the wall. Her house's silence seemed to echo, and she longed for Justice more than ever. Andie closed her eyes. A big mistake. The movie she'd watched till dawn on Stephanie's living-room ceiling started up again on the backs of her lids.

The movie was *The Stab and the Shot,* starring Christopher Vanderwaal and Andrea Brady. It opened with Justice's shrieks, then showed Christopher's knife blade shining in a flashlight's beam and his hood casting shadows on his face. The soundtrack boomed Andie's words, "Decide! Decide!" In the last scene, Christopher's pool of blood seeped into her driveway's dirt.

Unnerved, Andie opened her eyes. Across the kitchen, Christopher leaned against her refrigerator door, one foot crossed over the other, his eyes boring into her. She turned toward the window, but he was out there peering in, his hands cupped around his eyes against the sun's glare on the glass. Andie pressed her fingertips against her temples. Her stomach tightened to a fist. She couldn't get away from him.

How could you not have seen Christopher on your own property sooner? she asked herself. *Why didn't you pick up from Justice immediately that Christopher was there? Why didn't you have Justice under control so he'd have come when you called? . . .* She pummeled herself with "shoulds": She should have been more vigilant. She should have yelled at Christopher more forcefully. She should have gotten off her lazy bum and changed the lightbulb so she'd have seen him when she first drove up.

Andie could list dozens of things that she should have done differently so Justice wouldn't have gotten hurt and Christopher would have lived. But she'd done none of those things, and she was to blame for all that had happened. It was her fault that Christopher was dead.

Since last night, shock and fear had ruled Andie. But now the guilt she'd staved off came at her with a cyclone's force. It blew down her power lines, stripped her trees, shattered her windows, and blasted through her front door, leaving her defenseless and exposed. She was as vulnerable as Stephanie posing naked for a maniac, but Andie's nakedness was emotional and inescapable. No one could hide from something so internal as guilt.

She buried her face in her hands, and tears pooled in her palms.

When Andie stopped crying, her brain felt stuffed with soggy paper towels. The kitchen was dark, and moonlight was shining on the table. She got up, turned on the lights, and poured herself a glass of water from the tap. *I can't go on like this. I can't spend the rest of my life unhinged. I have to get hold of myself.*

The problem was that she had no idea how. She'd never been in a situation that even vaguely resembled what she was facing. None of her colleagues had ever killed anyone; she had nowhere to turn for advice.

As Andie sank back into her chair, she wished her father were still alive. In scrapes even as a small child, she'd gone to him for guidance; he'd never failed her. *What would he do if he'd just killed Christopher?* she wondered. The answer that dawned on her was that he'd do what he'd always done: He'd be a tough, brave cop.

As far as she knew, he'd never used deadly force on anyone. But if someone had attacked him, she had no doubt that he'd have used any means necessary to protect himself—and, afterward, he'd have been honorable and strong. In an investigation, he'd have called on iron discipline. He'd never have let himself fall apart. He'd have kept his feelings in check, and, with unwavering courage, he'd have taken whatever was thrown at him.

Which was exactly what Andie decided to do.

She told herself that as a cop she had to survive not just physically but also mentally. She had to keep from getting

killed, and she had to keep from losing her mind. That required
staying controlled, holding in her emotions, and keeping her
own counsel. Whatever she felt, no one could know.

She would not just keep the wall that most police constructed between their feelings and the outside world; she
would rebuild the wall with granite boulders and fortify it
with her steel. She would make the wall so thick that nothing
could break it down or find a way through cracks to reach her
heart. Air hammers could not rat-a-tat a tunnel; earthmovers
could not scrape the wall aside. It would get her through what
lay ahead.

As usual before going to bed, Andie got a pen and index
card, and at the kitchen table she began her list of the three
things she was grateful for.

1. Christopher's knife didn't go into Justice's lung, and he's
    better today than yesterday.
2. I'm alive behind my granite wall.

As Andie was thinking what the third thing might be, a
thud on the kitchen windowsill made her jump inside her
skin. This time Rosemary, not an imaginary Christopher, was
looking through the glass at her. Unaware that Justice was
gone, Rosemary announced that she would grace him with
her presence for a game of Bat the Ping-Pong Ball Around the
Living Room. The moonlight on her tabby stripes changed
her from an alley cat to a feline princess.

Andie opened the window, scooped up Rosemary, and
hugged her. "You dear kitty! Justice isn't here, but thank you so
much for stopping by." With Rosemary, Andie didn't have to
be a tough cop; she could be her guilty, needy self.

For once, Rosemary didn't wriggle out of her arms and
leap to the floor with a resounding thump. She purred, nuzzled

Andie's neck, and willingly bestowed fur therapy. When Andie told her that she'd die if Justice never came home, Rosemary acted like she understood.

Andie carried her to the table. With the kitty in her lap, she finished the list:

3. Rosemary comforted me just when I needed it.

Andie tossed the card into her wicker gratitude basket and thought, *Even in the blackest times, there's something to be thankful for.*

CHAPTER 11

TOM

The Vanderwaals' living room was as cheerless this morning as it had been last night. It felt damp and smelled vaguely of mold. Tom had thought that sunshine would brighten up the house, but little light filtered through the trees. As to be expected after a child's death, misery hung in the air, clung to the walls, and fogged the windows.

Jane and Franz occupied opposite ends of a living-room sofa, separated from each other by more than four feet. She was thin and pale, and her mouse-brown hair was twisted and pinned above her neck. She looked as if an eraser had come down from the sky and rubbed life off her face. The rims of her eyes were red from crying. Her nervous hands twisted a white handkerchief.

Though Franz was only five foot three, he had a General Patton swagger about him. He puffed out his small chest and man-spread his legs—perhaps he thought that taking up more space would make him appear larger than he was. His beady eyes were too close together to see through most binoculars; bird-watching would be hard for him.

Tom flipped open his notepad and clicked out the point of his ballpoint pen, ready to pin down some facts and get to know the Vanderwaals, who sat across the coffee table from him as though they were all about to play a game of Go Fish. "How much did the deputies tell you about last night?" he asked.

"Just that the cop down the street shot Christopher because he supposedly attacked her. That's ridiculous!" Franz scowled.

"The deputies weren't sure what had happened. We're just starting the investigation. It's going to take a while to figure things out," Tom said.

"Christopher had nothing to do with any of it. That cop murdered him in cold blood," Franz said.

Tom absently pinched a corner of his notepad. "Christopher may have stabbed Officer Brady's dog."

"He'd never hurt a dog. He loved dogs. He begged us to get one, but Franz is allergic," Jane said.

"If Christopher *did* stab that dog, it attacked him first, and he was defending himself," Franz insisted. "Typical German shepherd. Menacing. He should be patrolling a prison, not threatening our neighborhood."

"You were afraid of him?" Tom asked.

"Of course not," Franz said as if Jihadi John couldn't scare a bead of sweat from him.

Tom doubted the courage. Brandishing a hatpin might strike fear into a man as well versed in bluster as Franz was. "Like I told you, we're not sure yet what happened. We're just starting to get the facts. Officer Brady claims Christopher ran at her waving a knife. She thinks he intended to stab her. Do you know why he might have done that?"

"That's impossible. He is—" Jane flinched. "He *was* a good boy."

"That cop is delusional. Christopher wouldn't have hurt her," Franz said. "If she mistakenly thought he stabbed her dog, she shot him for revenge, pure and simple." Franz looked pleased that he'd wrapped up the case when the sheriff's morons had barely started it.

"We won't take revenge off the table." Tom scrawled on his

notepad: "Brady trigger-happy?" He paused to regather his focus. "Okay. Let's talk about Christopher. Anything unusual going on with him lately?"

Jane shook her head sadly and studied the loops in her carpet's pile. She seemed to retreat to a lonely, windswept land, as far off as Antarctica or Mongolia.

But Franz's face tensed. "Have you asked if anything unusual was going on with that *cop?* I'll bet money she's Looney Tunes. Or evil."

"We'll find out." Tom kept his voice calm. Ross Jackson had pegged Franz right: He was hot under the collar. A peacock. There was no point agitating him any more than necessary till knowing the facts put Tom on firmer ground. "So if nothing unusual was going on, could Christopher have been upset or worried about anything?"

"No," Franz said, flat as a tortilla.

"No problems at school? With grades?"

"No," Franz said.

"With . . . um . . . sexual orientation?"

Franz bristled. "You implying he was gay?"

"Just asking. It's routine. We're trying to get a picture."

"Christopher was fine." Franz glanced furtively at his cell.

What on that phone could be more important than Christopher's death? "You didn't notice any change in his behavior lately, Mrs. Vanderwaal? Any sign of upset or worry?"

"No," she said.

"Any recent traumatic situation? Anybody bullying him?"

"No," she said.

"Any major loss? A death of someone he loved?"

"No." The carpet's loops seemed to recapture her attention.

Tom mentally growled with frustration. The Vanderwaals would give Johnny One Note a run for his money; their one note was "no." He wondered what they were hiding, but he decided to save more forceful grilling for another visit when Jane might feel more inclined to talk. On a good day she'd be fragile; today she seemed like a frightened cockroach—one stomp of his foot, and she'd skitter under a baseboard.

"Any indication Christopher was into drugs?" Tom asked.

"Of course not." Franz shook his head at Tom as if a fruit fly could beat him on an IQ test. He slipped the phone back into his sports coat's pocket.

"What about Christopher's friends? Can you give me names?"

"I don't know them," Franz said.

"Mrs. Vanderwaal?" Tom called her back from the distant Land of Carpet Loops.

"I work nights and sleep during the day. Dinner is my time to keep up with the kids. Christopher never brought any friends around then."

"Work can get in the way of close relationships some-times," Tom said to inject a little empathy.

"I was saving up for Christopher's college fund." When Jane closed her eyes, she might have been trying to process the horrible fact that Christopher wasn't going to need the money now. "I promise you we had quality time. I put effort into that. Christopher knew I loved him."

Tom made a mental note: *Jane defensive.* Working mothers' guilt was a staple in juvenile offenders' homes. Jane looked so pained that Tom moved on to the less emotional topic of Christopher's computer. "Where is it?"

"We thought you'd found it on his desk and taken it. A laptop," Franz said.

"Nope. It wasn't there. No cell phone, either. You didn't take them away last night?" Tom asked.

"What are you suggesting?" Franz's eyes looked shifty.

"That they're missing. They're important to help us under-stand what was going on."

"Your men stormed in here and followed us around while we packed to go to the hotel. You treated us like criminals." Franz showed his teeth. "How were we supposed to take out Christopher's computer when we didn't have a minute to ourselves?"

"I'm sorry we intruded at such a bad time, but we had to do our job," Tom said.

"Go do it at that cop's house," Franz said. "That's where you're going to find the truth."

Right, buddy. Thanks for the advice. "Did you know Officer Brady?"

"No," Franz said.

"Mrs. Vanderwaal?"

"Mostly to wave to."

"Any impression of her?" Tom asked.

"Franz doesn't like her." Jane glanced over at him as he stared off into the distance at an imaginary vanishing point.

"I thought you didn't know her, Mr. Vanderwaal," Tom said.

"I don't." He shrugged.

"Why don't you like her?"

"Because she drives through the neighborhood in her big, bad cop car. She thinks she's hot stuff. I don't like cops. It's a disgrace to our family that one killed Jane's son."

"*Jane's* son?"

"We married when Christopher was eight and Joey was four. Franz adopted them," Jane said.

When a flicker of regret crossed Franz's face, Jane looked back at her carpet.

Well, at least one thing is established: no happy marriage here.

Christopher's brother, Joey, looked green around the gills. On a normal day, he might have been a normal kid. But on the day after his brother's death, he made Tom think of an inflated mattress whose air had leaked out in the night—his body looked shrunken, and his voice had gone flat.

Tom shook Joey's limp hand and gestured for him to sit next to him on the narrow step up to the front porch—away from Franz's hostile ears. Their shoulders touched, so Joey was spared making eye contact. He chewed his index fingernail.

"I'm really sorry about your brother. It's got to be hard for you," Tom said.

"Hmng . . ."

Tom waited for him to continue, but he gazed at his basketball hoop above the garage door. "You doing okay?"

A shoulder shrug.

"I can come back if this is a bad time."

"Doesn't matter," Joey mumbled.

Like mother, like son. Maybe their shared defense to get through life was to fade away. "Joey, so far all we know is that your brother allegedly stabbed the K-9 down the street and was coming after Officer Brady. Had anything been going on that would have made him do something like that?"

"No."

"Any problems? Upset? Something to stir him up?"

"No."

"A fight with your parents?"

"No."

"A conflict between him and your stepfather?"

"No."

Saying no must be a contagious disease in this house. "When you got home from your walk just now, did your father tell you not to reveal anything to me?" Tom had heard whispers in the kitchen.

Joey's gaze dropped to his scuffed hiking boot, a possible sign Tom had hit a nerve.

"You need to be honest, Joey. We're not playing games here. For Christopher's sake, we've got to figure out what was going on."

"Nothing was. Everything was fine."

Sorry, kid, but I don't believe you. "You must be pretty shocked by what's happened, huh?"

"Yeah." Joey dug his finger into the rip of his jeans' knee and jiggled his boot. In a few years he might grow into his huge feet.

Tom tried again. "I need your help. I really need to know where Christopher's laptop and cell are."

"I have no idea."

Tom turned to look at him for signs of lying on his face but couldn't pick up any. "You're sure?"

"Yeah." When a group of teens passed by on bikes, Joey's wave in their direction was as peaked as his handshake.

"Friends of yours?" Tom asked.

"I see them around."

"Friends of Christopher's?"

"Maybe. I don't know."

"I'd like to talk with some of his friends. Can you give me names?"

Joey shifted his body slightly away from Tom as if he wanted to bolt. "Christopher knew people, like everybody does. I don't know who."

"Nobody came around here to see him?"

"No."

"Because your parents didn't want them here?"

A shoulder shrug. A look of sadness. Tom felt sorry for him.

CHAPTER 12

ANDREA

"I've been waiting for you." Stephanie peered at Andie, whose black turtleneck accentuated the dark circles under her eyes. "I hate to be the bearer of bad news, but you don't look so good."

"Oh, I'm fine." Andie pasted a smile on her face, though her anxious heart was thumping all over her chest. She'd rather spend today milking python venom than meeting with Tom Wolski, but at least Stephanie would accompany her to lend support.

To meet him in the conference room, they had to pass through the roll-call room, where officers drank morning coffee around a large oval table. When Stephanie opened the door, the men were laughing, but the instant Andie stepped into the room, they stopped. Three sets of eyes gaped at her. Eyes of curiosity, which didn't surprise her: *What the hell happened when she shot that kid?* Eyes of relief, which alienated her: *Thank God it's not me.* Eyes of pity, which she hated: *Poor Brady. The job doesn't get any worse.*

Andie's colleagues were used to handling scams targeting little old ladies, pranks on high-school graduation night, and complaints about chainsaws on Saturday mornings. No San Julian officer in history had used deadly force. She might just as well have walked in with a black cowl and sickle. The men didn't seem to know what to say to her.

Determined not to let them see her anxiety, Andie threw back her shoulders and stiffened her spine. "Good morning," she said, drawing strength she did not feel from some resolute corner of herself.

"Hey, Brady." Doug Baker had gone through rookie years with Andie. A tattoo above his wrist said: "What doesn't kill me makes me stronger." He asked, "How's it going?"

"You know . . . same old, same old." *A preposterous lie.* If Andie were honest, she'd say that she was overwhelmed. She'd admit that she could hardly get out of bed this morning, that she was writhing at the awkwardness here.

Baker, bless him, joked, "No cookies for us today?"

Andie forced a smile. "No time to bake." *Who am I kidding?*

"Keep moving. We're late." Stephanie touched Andie's arm and ushered her toward the conference room—away from mere social discomfort into the gaping jaws of stress.

The conference room's only window was covered with a venetian blind, tilted so that little of the overcast day got through the slats. Tom Wolski and Ross Jackson sat on one side of the hard-edged Formica table, and Andie, Stephanie, and Ron Hausmann sat on the other. The arrangement told Andie everything she needed to know. The battle line was drawn, and the troops were at attention. It was Brady versus Wolski.

The opposing side had all the heft. Together, Wolski and Jackson must have weighed five hundred pounds, and their reflection in the Formica doubled them to a thousand. Every time Andie looked down to avoid Tom's and Jackson's penetrating stares, the two men were still staring at her from the shiny tabletop, their faces stern, like they'd been chewing five-penny nails.

In contrast, Ron Hausmann looked like an overgrown

Pillsbury Doughboy; he had round cheeks and a round stomach that, if poked, seemed like he'd giggle, *Tee-hee!* But his cheerful appearance masked seriousness that Andie now saw in his eyes and yesterday had witnessed on the phone when he'd warned her in a grave voice, "Tom's supposed to be an impartial fact finder, but be careful. Whatever you say might come back to bite you."

When Tom leaned forward and laced his fingers together, Andie noted that he'd be attractive if the overhead fluorescent lights weren't giving his honest-looking face a blue-green hue. As usual for taking an officer's statement, he, as lead investigator, would ask her questions. Jackson was there for another pair of ears and eyes.

For the recording, Tom gave the date and listed everyone present. As legally required, he read the Garrity Warning, which reminded Andie of her Fifth Amendment right to silence and her protection from disciplinary action if she refused to answer questions. He picked up his pen and held it in his fist like a small nightstick. "Okay, Officer Brady, let's start with you telling us about Christopher Vanderwaal. How did you know him?"

"I bought a raffle ticket from him once. Years ago. Cub Scouts."

Tom pressed, "Any other contact?"

"I saw him around the neighborhood once in a while."

"Did you talk with him?"

"I waved."

"That's it? Nothing more?"

Andie felt backed against the wall already. When she grabbed her chair's seat to steady herself, she realized that the interview was going to be even harder than she'd thought. "Nothing more."

Tom turned a page of his yellow legal pad. "Okay, let's cut to the night in question. After work, did you come straight home or stop somewhere?"

"I came straight home. I'd worked late, and I was tired."

"Was anything out of the ordinary when you pulled into the driveway or got out of your car?"

"No."

Tom set Andie's use-of-force report in front of her. "You say here that your motion-sensor light was out." He tapped his pen on Andie's wobbly scrawl. "Wasn't that unusual?"

"I'm sorry." *Don't apologize.* Flustered, Andie tucked her hair behind her ears. "I forgot. Yes, the light was out."

"If it had been working, would it have lit up your yard?"

"Yes. I should have changed the bulb the day before, but I never got around to it."

"Any reason for that?"

"I was busy," Andie said, defensive. She had a right to put off a chore in her own home. "What difference does it make why I didn't change the bulb?"

"I'm the one who's supposed to ask the questions here," Tom said.

The reprimand, though slight, felt like a slap to her wrist, and it emphasized that he was the boss and she, the underling. She noted that he was frowning—*she* was the one who had the right to frown in this scenario.

"So your yard was dark. Did you have a flashlight?" Tom asked.

"Yes. Every officer carries one." *As you well know.*

"When did you first know Christopher was there?"

"When he rose from the bushes and stabbed Justice."

"Did you actually *see* him do that?"

"Not up close. But I saw him raise his arm, and I saw the knife in his hand, and I heard Justice's horrible shrieks."

"So you *concluded* he'd stabbed Justice, but you weren't certain," Tom said.

"What else could I have thought? I heard the shrieks,"

Andie argued. *Stay calm!* For a break from his gaze, she looked down at the table, but Jackson's reflection was staring at her.

"When did you draw your gun?" Tom asked.

"When he started coming at me."

"How fast?"

"A quick walk at first. Then a run."

"Why didn't you use your Taser?"

"If it hadn't stopped him, I wouldn't have had time to shoot," Andie said, then added to make sure Tom knew, "I didn't *want* to hurt him." Under the table she wrung her hands so hard that her knuckles turned white.

Tom squinted at her slightly, as if he were deciding whether he believed her. He said, "Some people might wonder why Christopher was a threat to you. He was only five-five. Weighed a hundred and forty. You're what? Five-four? A hundred and twenty-five? You're strong. You've been trained to defend yourself. You couldn't manage a less lethal way to do it?"

"Not in the seconds I had. I'm sorry." *Don't apologize.*

"So you chose to shoot," Tom said, like that was an established fact.

"I chose to survive."

"You were *sure* he was going to attack you?"

"I thought so."

Tom exchanged a look with Jackson and took a slug of bottled water. "Let's stick with this idea of an attack for a minute. I want to go back to Justice. He must have known right away that Christopher was in your yard."

"Soon after Justice got out of the car, he barked and ran at him."

"Did that threaten him?"

"Officer Brady can't know what was in Christopher's mind," Hausmann said.

"Justice was just warning him. He stopped barking when he reached him," Andie said.

"Why was that?"

"Speculation. Officer Brady can't know what Justice thought, either," Hausmann said.

"Maybe Justice knew him," Andie offered.

"How did your dog know him if you say *you* didn't?" Tom asked.

Andie blinked, confused. How was she supposed to explain? "I don't know. Justice saw me wave at him now and again."

"But Justice did bark at him that night, correct?"

"Yes."

"Could Christopher have thought he was attacking him?"

"I've told you that Officer Brady can't read minds," Hausmann warned.

"The Vanderwaals claim Christopher loved dogs and would never have hurt Justice. They think he attacked Christopher—and if Christopher did stab him, it was in self-defense," Tom explained to Hausmann. "I want to know how Brady responds to that accusation."

"I'll tell you how I respond." Andie leaned forward, her elbows on the table, the closer to Tom the better to make sure he got the point. "The Vanderwaals are flat-out wrong. Justice didn't attack anybody. I was there. I saw what happened." Her tone contained a dash of cayenne pepper.

"Would you say Justice is reliable? Well behaved?"

"Absolutely." Justice's refusal to come that night when Andie had called him flashed through her mind. Still, she said with confidence, "He's impeccably behaved."

"Some people might disagree with that." Tom set another document in front of Andie. "Will you explain this complaint filed against him at the Nisqually County Humane Society? He got rough with your neighbor's dog."

Andie shrank back, cornered. "That dog came into my yard and attacked Justice. He was defending himself. You can't blame him for that." Red splotches of irritation appeared on her cheeks.

"But according to this report, Justice did grab the dog by the throat."

"Justice didn't hurt him!" Andie said, too loud. "The dog was fine. There wasn't a tooth mark on him. And there won't be one on Christopher!" Stephanie rested her hand on Andie's arm. To warn or reassure her? To calm her down? "You can go after me, but it's not fair to go after my dog!" Andie said.

"We're not here to decide what's fair, Brady. We're here to get the facts," Tom said. *Another swat to Andie's wrist.*

She closed her eyes to regain her aplomb, but it lay shredded around her feet. With an iron will, she sat up straighter and told herself that she would not let Tom Wolski see how much he upset her. She ducked behind her granite wall.

Three hours later, Stephanie hugged Andie good-bye and Ron Hausmann walked her to the station's parking lot. Rain was pouring, but she was too exhausted to drag her umbrella out of her tote bag. As they passed her requisitioned police car, an insult to her injury, her legs became rubber that at any minute might buckle under her. Psychologically, Andie felt as if she'd been trampled on by hooves.

"Good work in there." Hausmann jingled coins in his pocket.

"Wolski's tough" was all Andie could reply.

"Don't let him worry you. He knows the score. Your use of force was a reasonable response."

"I'm not sure anymore."

Hausmann opened her Honda's door, and she climbed behind the wheel. Rain spattered his glasses. "Wolski can't twist a perfectly rational action into an irrational one. I dare him to try."

It looks like he's trying. And you're shoring me up just because this investigation has miles to go. It stretched out before Andie like a road through a war zone, and her only weapon for self-defense was a dandelion puff.

As the wipers squawked across her windshield, Andie turned into her driveway. Before going to see Justice, she wanted to change out of her sweaty clothes and take a shower. Otherwise, he'd smell her anxiety, and it could distress him when he needed all his strength to recover.

For the last four years, she'd parked in front of her house. But today she pulled up to its south side, opposite the north part of her yard where Christopher had hidden. Now the house shielded her from that nightmare spot, the crime scene, which had once been a peaceful place with her vegetable garden, apple trees, and rhododendron bushes. She went inside and closed the curtains on windows looking out to it. Because it was too painful to see, she mentally cut it off and pretended it didn't exist. She'd never recover enough emotionally to park there again—one more change, thanks to Christopher.

CHAPTER 13

ANDREA

A plaid sofa and reclining leather chair furnished the family room in Dr. Vargas's clinic, but Andie chose to sit on the Berber carpet so she could visit Justice eye-to-eye. Though limping, he burst into the room and threw himself at her. As his wagging tail thwacked the sofa, he licked her face. But then he hobbled to the door leading to the waiting room and pressed his nose against the knob. *Get me out of here! I want to go home! In this pernicious clinic, they do heinous things to innocent dogs!*

"He's getting stronger." Dr. Vargas's technician, Wendy, her arms weighed down with woven friendship bracelets, guided Justice away from the door. "He has to be careful. If he gets too rowdy, he'll rip out his tubes and stitches."

"You hear that, Sweet Boy?" Andie asked.

Justice relented and sat on the carpet, but his dark look let her know in the starkest terms, *I have done nothing to deserve incarceration. I do not belong in this barbarous place.*

"I'm so sorry, Justice," Andie said. "But it's great that you're more alert today!"

"Dr. Vargas wants to watch him for infection a little longer, but he thinks Justice is going to be all right," Wendy said.

"All right" was a feast for Andie's hungry ears. She felt like she could take a deep breath for the first time since that night.

For two interminable days, she'd hoped for this good news. It took the edge off her morning with Tom Wolski, whom she would not mention to Justice for fear he'd sense how hard it had been.

Careful of his wounds, Andie hugged him. "You're going home soon. We'll have a party with Rosemary. In a few weeks, we can go for *w-a-l-k-s.*" Andie spelled the word so he wouldn't leap around again.

Justice's tail thumped against the carpet.

When Wendy left, Andie handed him his squeaky carrot, his second-favorite toy after Bandit, his teddy bear. Normally, Justice squeaked whole symphonies of joy, but now he managed only one paltry squeak before he dropped the carrot on the floor.

"It's your *carrot!* You love it," Andie reminded him. Determined to make him happy, she dug a packet of iceberg lettuce leaves out of her bag. She'd brought only the crunchiest ones from deep inside the head because he turned away from flaccid leaves as if they were too vile to consider. "Here." Expecting unbridled ecstasy and a snap of teeth, she handed him a crisp leaf.

He sniffed cautiously, bit into it, and dropped it. *P-tooey!*

Justice was too honorable to sulk about not going home, but he was not himself. Andie wondered if pain medication was dragging him down, or if he might be suffering from emotional as well as physical wounds. He was the kind of dog who'd run into a burning building to rescue strangers, but he was also sensitive. Perhaps he needed time to recover psychologically. Maybe he had to work out in his own mind what had happened to him.

Ignoring the spit-out lettuce, Justice lay on his good side, rested his head in Andie's lap, and moaned a deep, expressive moan. As she stroked his ears and listened to his quiet breaths, he slowly shut his eyes. His and Andie's bond was so close that sometimes she felt as if they lived inside the same skin. Just as she'd do anything for him, he'd do the same for her. They belonged together. They'd worked so hard to become a team.

After Meghan's unsuccessful search for Justice's people, Andie had claimed him for life and taken him to meet Chief Malone. "Look!" She held out a tug toy—a rope with a knot on one end and a rubber handle on the other—and Justice grabbed the knot with the conviction of a snapping turtle. No matter how hard she yanked or where she dragged him around the Chief's office, Justice held on. "See how focused he is? Nothing can distract him."

And when Andie told him, "Leave it," Justice dropped the knot. "He also knows obedience. He could be a champion drug sniffer," she said.

"Maybe." The hard-boiled Chief would take a while to agree that the Earth was round. "Take him for testing."

Justice had passed the entry tests at the State Patrol Academy's Narcotics Canine School. Confident of his olfactory prowess, Andie took him to the Academy's gym for two months—220 hours—and taught him what and how to sniff.

First, they completed what seemed like six thousand "fetches" of his treasured tennis ball. Then out of his sight, she tucked it and a small tin of cocaine into a canvas bag and set it with four empty bags onto the floor. She called Justice and said, "Search!"

Justice looked up at her, cocked his head, and relayed to her as forthrightly as he'd ever relayed anything, *I don't speak English.*

"Search!" She pointed to the bags. "Go find the ball! Get the ball!"

The sun rose on Justice's mental landscape. He dashed to the first bag and shoved his pointed nose into the canvas opening. He rushed to the second. At last in the third bag he sank his teeth into the ball and brought it back to Andie. She grabbed it and said, "Sit!" When he sat, she told him he was the smartest, most wonderful dog ever born and she threw the ball for him. He bounded after it, brought it back, and dropped it at her feet.

After doing this exercise what also seemed like six thousand times, Andie hid only the drug; when Justice found it and sat, she threw the ball. Being a brilliant and cooperative dog, he understood that his job was to locate drugs and sit, and he learned the smells of cocaine, heroin, and meth.

In the last couple of years, Justice had sniffed drugs in houses, cars, and the county jail's cells, where incarcerated dealers had unsuccessfully tried to fool his blue-ribbon nose by concealing their stash in hot chocolate mix or ground coffee. He'd found drugs wrapped as Christmas gifts, hidden behind a car door's interior panel, and mailed in suspicious packages at the post office. And he'd alerted Andie to dealers' secreted cash because the smell of drugs was on the bills.

Whenever Andie said "search," Justice searched with ebullience, never hesitating, never grousing, always eager. If he'd been a person, human resources officers across America would have fallen all over themselves to hire him. Because of that joy, Andie grieved to see him now, too badly injured to do the job he loved. She ran her hand over the fluffy fur on his neck and gently patted his unhurt shoulder. She whispered, "I'd have given anything for Christopher not to hurt you."

It had been so unexpected. That was the thing about life. Lightning bolts struck out of the blue and rattled your teeth. The first time had been when Andie's mother picked her up at school and broke the news of her father's death. The second, when she'd come home from work and found her husband Rich's note informing her: "I don't want to be married to a cop anymore." Now the third was Christopher's attack, which had emotionally razed Andie to the ground. It had also chipped away at her sense of safety so she felt vulnerable and small, an ant crushed under an elephant's foot.

Thank heavens for Justice. She stroked his chest. A rampant hedonist even in infirmity, he flopped out his unshaved front leg to give her better access. "You're honorable and good, Sweet Boy. You don't deserve your hurt."

Yet Andie wondered if she deserved *hers*. Sometimes she felt that she was being singled out for shocks and tumult. Or maybe she was being punished. *But for what? Inadvertent misbehavior? Bad karma from a former life?* How could that be so when she'd always tried to be a good person and do the right thing? If she believed in justice, she had to trust that decency's reward would not be pain.

"We can believe all is well. But it's never true," Andie whispered to Justice. "Everything can change in a finger snap. Life isn't fair."

She closed her eyes and let his soft fur and steady breathing slow her racing thoughts.

CHAPTER 14

TOM

Tom scooted his spine-torturing metal chair to the computer. The cubicle he called an office was barely large enough for him, and the only personal touch was a wood-framed photo of Lisa jumping on a neighbor's trampoline. Tom would never know why he kept that picture when one bad bounce and Lisa could have ended up at Wilson Hospital, where two years before that photo was taken he'd spent agonizing days with her. Remembering them still gave him the shivers.

He turned on his computer, the slowest on this side of the Cascades, and waited while, as usual, it would grind on before icons showed up on the screen. While Jackson and Murphy had been working their way down the Valley Road neighborhood interview list compiled from Google Earth, Tom had gone to San Julian High School, searched Christopher's locker, and found only dirty gym clothes and a few paperback books. No clues. No stash, laptop, or cell.

Tom had talked with Christopher's counselor, a plump woman in Birkenstocks, with hopes she might know about his drug use, which would be the easiest explanation for what he'd allegedly done. But she was barely aware of him. She said, defensively it seemed to Tom, "It's a big school. He didn't stand out." Once the press got through with Christopher, Tom bet he'd stand out in glowing Technicolor.

At last on Tom's computer screen, the e-mail icon appeared. He clicked on it. *Good.* There was a message from Nisqually County Central Communications, also known as CENCOM. Tom had requested a recording of Brady's radio call. Though probing it for answers could be a waste of time, it might shed some light. You never knew what someone's words or tone of voice could tell you.

As of now, Tom did not trust Andie. She'd answered his questions, but sometimes he'd gotten the feeling that she was evasive or manipulated facts, such as when she'd claimed the raffle ticket was her only contact with Christopher. Justice would have kept barking if Christopher had been a stranger, and Brady's suggestion that Justice knew him from waving on the road didn't cut it. Tom couldn't shake the suspicion that something had gone on between her and Christopher. It could have started the whole deal.

Andie had also gotten riled up about the complaint against Justice. Tom had watched those pretty cheeks turn red. He'd bet she'd gotten angry when Christopher stabbed her dog too. Tom could understand that; he'd be mad if anyone hurt Sammy, his golden retriever—though not mad enough to fire a shot. As every cop knew, anger could cloud your mind and goad you into using too much force. When you were emotional, you got sloppy. Andie could have done that.

Tom leaned back and clasped his hands behind his head. The Vanderwaals might have put their finger on it: Maybe Justice attacked Christopher and he stabbed the dog in self-defense. Maybe Andie overreacted and shot the kid. Tom would have to figure that out.

He clicked on CENCOM's file and listened to her give her police ID number. She said, "Shots fired. I need help at my house. One on the ground at gunpoint. Eight-one-five just stabbed."

He pressed his fingertips together and stared at the gray wall. By necessity, an emergency required Andie to be short and to the point. When so many snoopers scanned police calls nowadays, she couldn't give away much more than she had. And she had to be quick in case another cop needed the airwaves to call for help. Tom had to hand it to her: She'd kept her cool and followed protocol.

Tom played Andie's words again. Five times. He listened for her feelings. Beneath her control, he picked up heavy breaths, like gasps, and trembles in her voice. A cynic might say she was stressed about getting her story straight before backup arrived, or anxious because shooting a kid could derail her life, or angry that Christopher had attacked.

But a more empathetic person could understand that she was scared if she'd just seen Justice stabbed and come so close to getting killed herself. Her knees could have been knocking together; she could have struggled to be coherent and keep from breaking down. Any woman cop in Andie's situation would have felt that fear.

Any man cop too.

He picked up a pencil and rested its eraser on his desk, then flipped the pencil and rested the point. He rotated the eraser and tip again. And again. *Thump, tap. Thump, tap. Thump, tap.*

Once on a midnight shift in Seattle, he'd gotten scared and mad enough to understand every tremble in Brady's voice. He and his partner, Cliff, were checking out a possible intruder in a Queen Anne apartment. Nice neighborhood, but that didn't mean squat. Whether you were called to a penthouse or an outhouse, you never knew what you might be getting into. A lone sadistic killer could blast you from a window with his semiautomatic, or Charles Manson and his family could be waiting, hopped up on LSD, ready to bludgeon you to death. On any call, you had to deal with that underbelly of courage: fear of the unknown.

Cliff had parked the car a block downhill from the apartment building. He rushed into the main entrance and climbed the interior stairs to the fourth floor. Tom circled around to the back and started up the fire escape in case anybody tried to flee. On the third-floor landing he looked up. Under the building's exterior light, a handgun barrel protruded through a crack as someone slowly opened the fourth floor's emergency door.

At six foot four and 240 pounds, Tom was no pygmy, but the bruiser who burst through the door shocked him. Tom could have been Jack of "Jack and the Beanstalk" facing down the giant who'd grind his bones for bread. It was the first time in Tom's life that he felt small.

As he pushed his radio's emergency call button and whipped out his GLOCK, the thug clumped across the landing, and the fire escape shook under his weight. *Sweet Jesus. Where the hell is Cliff?*

"Stop! Police! Drop the gun. Kneel down. Right there!" Tom shouted.

The man stomped down the stairs as if he intended to flick Tom onto the concrete parking lot below. His eyes looked crazed.

"Drop the gun! Do it now. NOW." Tom's heart pounded like a tiger was fighting to get out of his chest. "Drop the gun, or I'll shoot!"

The man kept coming. Tom fixed his eyes on the gun barrel, looming just ten stairs above him. He could taste fear, like sour milk. Sweat poured down his face. Between him and the perp was nothing but metal rails and stair slats, which could ricochet bullets and wound Tom in ways he didn't want to think about. *No way in hell will I let that bastard kill me. Lisa needs a dad.* As anger pulsed through Tom, he yelled, "Drop the $#@*! gun NOW!"

"Make me, pig." The man aimed his gun and fired.

A bullet whizzed by Tom's ear. He ducked. *Okay, you asked for it, bastard. Bombs away.* He shot. Twice. The perp doubled over on the bannister and slid to the third-floor landing. Tom cuffed him as Cliff staggered onto the fire escape, blood dripping down his face. Ambulances arrived, and the perp was now in prison.

Tom thought he'd fired two bullets, but the shoot team found seven casings from his gun. The difference testified to how adrenaline blocked unnecessary thought, like counting, so he could focus on survival—and how anger and fear could hype you up.

Tom could understand Andie's trembling voice when she'd called for help. If Christopher *had* come at her to kill her, Tom couldn't blame her for being mad and scared—and he could easily relate to whipping out a gun to protect yourself. But just because they'd both faced terror and chosen to shoot, he couldn't lose perspective. He could not let empathy for Brady get in the way of finding truth.

CHAPTER 15

ANDREA

"What's it been since we had a professional chat? Seven years?" When Andie had applied to join the force, Dr. Capoletti, the San Julian Police Department's part-time psychologist, had given her psychological tests and interviewed her several times. Today he was supposed to help her through what was called critical incident stress.

"Seven years sounds about right," Andie said.

"You've liked the job?"

"I loved it till three nights ago."

"I'm not surprised to hear you say that," Dr. Capoletti said. "Killing someone can be tough."

Andie looked around the conference room where yesterday Tom Wolski had raked her over coals of disdain. She'd agreed to meet Dr. Capoletti here to save herself a ferry trip to his Seattle office. If Justice were at her feet, she'd feel safer. Since he wasn't, the granite wall she'd built between herself and the outside world would have to protect her. Dr. Capoletti would not be allowed behind it.

He knitted his brows into a bushy, sympathetic line. "You must be upset."

"A little." *My upset is the size of Texas.*

"It would be understandable if you said 'a lot.'" Dr. Capoletti's warm smile complemented his kind eyes. The rest of him was rumpled. His blue shirt may never have seen an iron, and his curly salt-and-pepper hair needed to be trimmed. His razor also needed to be changed before it met his dimpled cheeks again.

"I've read your incident report," he said. "You're probably tired of repeating the facts, but would you mind going through them one more time? I'd like to know what you saw and what you did . . . if you're okay talking about it."

Andie grimaced, looked down at the table, and met Dr. Capoletti's reflection just as she had Wolski's and Jackson's. For the next hour, she dipped her toe into the dark waters of deadly force and then waded in waist deep—but only with facts. She sifted through "this happened" and "then that happened," her version of events sanitized of terror and guilt. Dr. Capoletti rested his elbows on the conference table and listened so intently that his whole body might have been covered with ears. When she paused, he nodded to encourage her to continue. Once in a while, he interrupted, "What was your reaction when that happened?" She answered only with what she'd thought.

Finally, she described the moment when she saw that her attacker was Christopher. Dr. Capoletti held up his hand for her to pause and brought up the bearded, iridescent polka-dotted elephant in the room: "What about your emotions? How did you *feel* when you realized it was Christopher?"

Andie paused to consider what to say. "I was surprised." *Totally shocked, if you want to know the truth.* "I felt a little guilt." *Enough to fill a moving van.* "Even though Christopher lived on my street, I'd never gone out of my way to know him. I feel bad that I didn't help him before he went out of control."

"You can't rescue everybody, Andrea."

"I wish I could rescue his parents. I want to apologize to them for killing their son."

"It's hard not to do what you feel is right, but legally you can't talk with them now. Ron Hausmann would tell you that." When Dr. Capoletti took a swallow from his Coke can, his Adam's apple bobbed. "You know if you take a life, even justifiably, guilt is perfectly normal. I'd be surprised if someone as sensitive as you *didn't* feel it. But we don't want it to debilitate you."

"Don't worry. It won't." *A shameless lie.* Guilt had already sucked so much of Andie's blood that she was emotionally anemic. "A friend showed me Christopher's obituary this morning. He sounded like a saint. He was supposedly brilliant, generous, beloved. There wasn't a word about him stabbing Justice and intending to stab *me*. It's not fair. I thought my dog and I were going to die."

"Andrea, I'm sensing some resentment underneath your guilt."

"Maybe." Andie had revealed too much. She huddled behind her wall.

"When people go through trauma, they can't help being mad. It's perfectly okay for anger to flare up sometimes. You can also expect sadness, depression, anxiety, irritability, emotional numbing. You could get paranoid."

Andie could check each box in that list. No problem.

"Officers in your situation inevitably go through a notable disruption, and some have long-term problems. We want to head those off." Dr. Capoletti took a pipe from his coat pocket, and in this no-smoking room he held the unlit bowl. "Any headaches or stomach issues?"

"No."

"Trembling, sweating?"

Too many times to count. "Not really."

"Are you going over and over what happened?"

Constantly. "Once in a while."

"What about flashbacks? When you relive what you went through. Same sounds. Same smells."

"No."

"Nightmares? Panic attacks? They can be common after trauma."

"I'm really fine." *Liar, liar, pants on fire.*

Dr. Capoletti clamped his teeth down on the pipe's lip; perhaps he wished Andie would provide responses he could sink his professional teeth into. "Andrea, I'm getting the sense that you've closed down."

"How do you mean?"

"Shutting off your feelings. Being numb."

"Maybe a little," Andie admitted.

"You don't have to be ashamed of being vulnerable."

"I'm not vulnerable." If Andie were Pinocchio, her nose would have grown through the window and across the parking lot.

Dr. Capoletti raised his eyebrows. As he paid inordinate attention to his pipe, silence filled the room. At first it pressured Andie to blurt out something, anything to fill the void, but then she thought she had a right not to spill her guts. For long, awkward minutes, she watched her hands, folded on the tabletop, until they ended up a sweaty pretzel in her lap. She heard two men in the roll-call room arguing about a Seahawks game. Finally, she asked, "What do you want me to say?"

"What do *you* want to say?"

That I'm going through a classic case of what you called a "notable disruption." That I feel horrible, and I'm not sure I'm going to get out of this mess in one mental piece. "I don't want to say anything."

"Why is that?"

Andie shrugged. "Because there's nothing to say."

Dr. Capoletti's frown may have had as many wrinkles as his shirt. She bit her lip and waited for him to start on denial, yet another common symptom after trauma. Silent again, he looked like he was trying to determine how hard to push but only said, "Okay. Do you have any questions?"

"One. Well, two, actually."

"I'm listening." He leaned back in his chair.

"Of all the people on the planet, why was I the one who got caught in a terrible thing like this?"

"What do *you* think?"

"I have no idea. I did nothing to bring it on. I barely knew Christopher."

"What's your other question?" Dr. Capoletti asked.

"When I shot him, did I do the right thing?"

"What's your answer to that?"

Andie's cheeks flushed, her involuntary signal of chagrin. "I don't *have* an answer. That's why I asked."

"I can see you're annoyed," Dr. Capoletti said. "I asked for your answer because I believe what matters most is what *you* think about whether you did the right thing. Once you know in your heart that you did, what anyone says or thinks won't matter, because you can face whatever comes."

Andie glanced at the ceiling's white acoustical tiles, which were riddled with holes. "I still don't know if I did right."

"I'd like to help you find an answer. How about if we meet regularly for a while? I'd say you have a lot to work through."

"There's nothing I can't take care of on my own."

When Dr. Capoletti leaned forward, she could see broken capillaries in his nose. "All right. If you want to do this on your own, then at least take time right now to be good to yourself. Get stable. You need to sleep and eat well while you process what happened. If your feelings become too intense or you start having flashbacks or panic attacks, get yourself over to see me. Do you understand?"

"Yes."

"You know, between fifty to seventy-five percent of officers who kill someone leave law enforcement within five years. Second-guessing their actions and feeling moral pain get to them. I don't want that to happen to you."

"It won't. I'm really okay," Andie assured him one more time. Her replay button was stuck. She hunched down behind her wall, but the granite felt cold and lonely.

CHAPTER 16

ANDREA

As soon as Justice realized he was about to taste freedom, he charged through Dr. Vargas's waiting room as if he intended to yank off Andie's arm. He was so happy to escape that he seemed to forget the white plastic cone secured around his head to keep him from biting his incisions. At the front door he yipped like a puppy. Outside in the rain he tugged Andie to the parking lot.

But then he stopped and peered across the gravel at Wendy in her green scrub suit and Meghan in a yellow slicker. They were standing on each side of a suspicious rubber-surfaced plank that led into the back of a strange car. Justice twisted the cone around and looked up at Andie. What was that board? Where was her Honda? What was Rosemary's person doing there?

"Meghan is driving you home in her Jeep Cherokee so you'll have lots of room," Andie said. "We've borrowed a ramp because you can't jump in."

Justice eyed it with scorn. Once he figured out that the women intended for him to walk up it, he stiffened his legs and dug intransigent paws into the gravel.

"Come on, Justice." To urge him closer, Meghan patted her thighs and kissed the air.

Andie pulled him, like it or not, to the ramp, and six determined hands guided him up to a blanket nest. Justice's disparaging glances at his oppressors let them know, *I do not appreciate coercion.* He plopped down with a groan.

As Meghan was about to close the door, he bonked his plastic cone against a window. His dark expression made irrefutably clear, *This is the Cone of Doom.*

"You'll only have to wear it for a week or so," Andie said. *Huff.*

At home, Justice limped down the ramp and burst inside the house like a Cavalry Scout. He padded stiffly through each room and checked that it was still in order and in his absence nothing untoward had taken place—no furniture moved, nothing carried off by thieves, no bucket accidentally left on the kitchen floor. He may have sniffed vestiges of Tom Wolski and his team, but their invasion seemed no cause for alarm. Determining an all clear, he joined Andie and Meghan in the kitchen just as Rosemary landed with her usual thump outside on the windowsill.

Andie let her in and removed Justice's cone—for now she could keep an eye on him and stop him from chewing his stitches. From his gold corduroy bed, which Andie called his throne, he grabbed his rubber carrot and paraded, squeaking, around the room—until Rosemary leapt out from behind the kitchen table's pedestal and ambushed him.

Their evening wrestling match began. Round one: Rosemary lay on her back and flailed her legs, her claws politely sheathed. Justice whimpered and prodded her with his nose. Round two: He took her head into his mouth, and she resisted with halfhearted bats at his muzzle. Round three: He picked her up and carried her around the ring until she squirmed loose; in an amazing comeback, she pounced on him again.

The contenders repeated the rounds, dog versus cat, no champion declared, until they got tired.

Usually, they cuddled up and napped together on Justice's throne. But tonight Andie was browning hamburger to celebrate his homecoming, and, lured by the sizzle of beef, Justice and Rosemary stationed themselves at her feet. The desperation on their faces was as if they were only a whisker away from starvation and if she didn't provide a heaping serving they would collapse, unrevivable, and slip away.

Meghan watched, her elbows on the breakfast table, her graceful hands folded under her chin. To keep her auburn hair from frizzing in the rain she'd pulled it back into a ballerina's knot. Her features were delicate and even. "Imagine we thought Justice might never come home. Look at him now," she said. "What do you think he's thinking about getting *s-t-a-b-b-e-d?*"

"I'm not sure, but I doubt he'll be happy to see another *k-n-i-f-e.*"

"Has he been upset?"

"At first he was depressed, but he seems better now." With a spatula, Andie rearranged the hamburger for an even brown.

Justice's and Rosemary's nostrils quivered. Justice moaned as if to underscore that certain death from malnutrition awaited him.

"You should see the photo my client from hell brought in today," Meghan said. "It shows some deranged Scotsman's den, and everything was Royal Stewart tartan plaid. I mean *everything*—the walls, lampshades, rug, tablecloth, upholstery. It looked like some bagpiper had gone mad in there. She wanted me to decorate her family room like that."

"What are you going to do?"

"I tried to reason with her. I gave her a quick lecture on excess."

"Did she understand?" Andie asked.

"I don't know. Put me in a room like that and I'd start

screaming in two seconds. I'm counting the days till this project's done and she's out of my hair."

Justice and Rosemary were counting the seconds till Andie stopped cooking and they could sink their teeth into beef. Before they keeled over from anticipation, Andie turned off the burner and dropped three ice cubes into the meat to cool it quickly. She could relate to Justice's, Rosemary's, and Meghan's impatience. Sometimes you got so anxious waiting for something to end, like Andie was waiting for Tom Wolski to finish his investigation—yet it had barely started. Hours of her days would go to combing through alternative outcomes for her future and wondering how she'd cope. And she had no control over any of it. She was trapped in a car without a steering wheel, and it was careening downhill, picking up speed as it went.

After Meghan and Rosemary had left and Justice had inhaled two more of Andie's Welcome Home Pupcakes, she made her nightly gratitude list: 1) Justice is home! 2) He's getting stronger! 3) Meghan is my dear, kind friend.

Andie dropped the list into her basket and hauled Justice's throne upstairs to her bedroom. Usually he slept plastered against her legs, but now his wounds prevented him from jumping onto the bed. Accepting exile from his regular spot, he curled up on the gold corduroy the best he could while wearing the Cone of Doom. Andie tucked his white fleece teddy, Bandit, next to his chest for the night.

She climbed between her sheets with dread because she knew what was guaranteed to happen. As soon as she was alone with her thoughts, they'd zero in on Christopher as surely as a compass needle pointed north. And so they did. She lay there wondering, what had Christopher been thinking when he ran at her with his knife? She'd told him if he didn't drop it she'd shoot. She'd given him fair warning *twice*.

Had he not heard? Or had he not believed she'd shoot? Or had he been determined to run at her, the devil be damned? What had he thought when she fired her gun? Did he have regrets? Was he angry that Andie followed through on her threat? Was he scared? The more she thought about it, she became sure that fear had ruled his mind as he faded away.

Andie remembered a night patrolling with a high-school tennis player who'd signed up for a Career Day program that allowed him to shadow a cop. As she drove along San Julian roads, her headlights fuzzy in the fog, he'd asked, "What's the hardest part of your job?"

"That's easy," Andie had said. "Nothing upsets me as much as someone being scared and I can't fix it. I hate letting frightened people down."

Now imagining Christopher's fear as he died tormented her not just because she'd been unable to fix it but also because she was responsible for it. And for his death. Causing harm went against Andie's every impulse as a cop and human being. It was contrary to why she'd joined the force and why she got out of bed in the morning. Because she'd killed Christopher, she was tied to him with an intimacy she'd never had with anyone. Death's unbreakable bond linked them. Forever.

To calm herself, Andie breathed in sync with Justice until, finally, at dawn she fell asleep. But into the Land of Nod she dragged her agitation, which was a lead albatross around her neck.

She dreamed that she was having coffee at Brewed Awakening and a man, whose face she did not recognize, peered at her through a window from the street. There was nothing unusual about him except that he looked menacing. He had a black aura of evil around him and could have been a universal, one-size-fits-all threat.

As he pressed his nose against the glass and stared at her, Andie had no idea what he wanted. Unsettled, she took a sip of coffee and was relieved when he walked away. But then he stomped through the door carrying a hatchet, and the skin on the back of Andie's neck prickled with fear. He swung the hatchet above his head and started toward her. Sure that he intended to kill her, she stood up and drew her gun.

She shot. *Click.* Again. *CLICK.*

He came so close that she could smell garlic on his breath. *Click, click, click, click, click* . . . The gun would not fire.

Andie screamed. When she woke, Justice was standing by her bed, his body pressed to the mattress as close to her as he could get. He was whimpering and straining against the cone to lick her face.

CHAPTER 17

TOM

After questioning people who lived around Brady, Ross Jackson had pointed out a dissonance between the local natural beauty and the dislike everyone had for one another. "I'd hate to go to a neighborhood potluck on Valley Road," he'd said. That observation came to Tom's mind as he was wrapping up his interviews. He knocked on the door of Eduard Kraus, who lived in one of seven houses between Brady and the Vanderwaals.

Kraus looked like an aged SS officer, tracked down somewhere in the jungles of Brazil. His white hair fell to his shoulders, there was steel in his blue eyes, and he stood as erect as rebar. The lines in his forehead suggested a chronic misanthropic scowl that would scare off those of lesser stuff than Tom.

Mr. Kraus was unaware that there had been a shooting. "On that night I drink schnapps. I listen to *Die Meistersinger.* I have no interest in these people." He swept his hand through the air to indicate those on Valley Road.

"Do you know the Vanderwaals?"

"They are Dutch." He spit out "Dutch" as if poison tulips were sprouting from the word. "Good-for-nothings."

"Why do you say that?"

"Garbage cans turn over. Nobody cleans. American slum."

Then why was Christopher so orderly? "Did you know the older son?"

Mr. Kraus grimaced. "Typical American teenager. Country goes to hell. Good-for-nothing lazy bums. All on drugs."

His interest piqued at "drugs," Tom asked, "Did you ever see Christopher high on anything?"

"No," said Herr Kraus. "When I was boy, we were honest. Now everything is crazy. Terrorists. Politics. Criminals. The world falls apart."

Tom could almost see his reflection in Kate Patterson's lip gloss. Her clothes may have been left over from a party the night before. She wore spike heels, a way-too-scoop-necked top, and a skirt as tight as a sausage skin. Her false eyelashes looked like the wings of a desperate butterfly.

The wings fluttered as she devoured Tom with a quick, full-body glance. "Well, hello there. What can I do for *you?*"

Tom flipped open his notepad to convey that all he wanted from her was information. "You know anything about the shooting two houses down from here?"

"Yes," she said. "Why don't you come in? I'll give you a cup of coffee."

Served up with what? "Thanks, but I've got lots of ground to cover today."

The butterfly wings drooped.

"That night, did you hear anything?" Tom asked.

"Gunshots. I thought they were firecrackers till all the ambulances and police cars showed up. It's the most excitement we ever had around here."

"Excitement's one way to look at it, I guess," Tom said. "You hear anything else? Any shouting?"

"No, but I wish I had so I could help you." Another flutter of wings.

"You see anything?"

"Just all the lights flashing through the trees. I thought of walking out onto the street to find out what was going on, but I didn't want to be a rubbernecker." Ms. Patterson picked her thumbnail's platinum polish.

"Did you know Christopher Vanderwaal?"

"I don't socialize around here. I'm divorced. I live alone," she said.

"Right," Tom said.

"I did see him outside once in a while. Dressed pretty well. Not like boys in those baggy pants falling down so you see their . . . buns." She smiled.

"No evidence of Christopher drunk or on drugs?"

"No." She shrugged.

"What about Officer Brady? You know her?"

"Not very well. We've met at the end of her driveway a few times. She's not very friendly."

Wanting privacy, cops often stay to themselves. "So you don't have knowledge of a friendship she might have had with Christopher Vanderwaal?"

A lusty chuckle. "What are you implying?"

"Nothing. I'm trying to find out how well she knew him."

"No idea. You think anything . . . *interesting* . . . was going on between them?"

"We're looking for a motive." Tom closed his notebook. "Thanks for your time."

"You're sure you don't want some coffee?"

Miss Mildred Hawthorne lived next door to the Vanderwaals and, in contrast to their supposed slovenliness, not a leaf or blade of grass was out of place around her ranch-style house. When she answered the door, a net was pressing down her hair and her cheeks were caved in because she'd neglected to put in her false teeth. "I wasn't expecting company," she said.

"I'm not company." Tom flashed his badge. "I'm here to find out if you saw or heard anything the night your next-door neighbor was shot."

Miss Hawthorne gummed imaginary food. "I heard about that awful woman murdering the child."

She's more biased than the press. "It's too soon to use a word like 'murder,' Miss Hawthorne. We're trying to figure out what happened."

"I was watching *Keeping Up with the Kardashians* that night."

"You hear any shouting?" Tom asked.

"The Kardashian girls shout sometimes when they get mad."

Oh, man. "I mean shouting at Officer Brady's home."

"I guess I had the TV on too loud. Didn't hear a thing outside."

So there goes that. "Do you know the Vanderwaals?"

"A little." Miss Hawthorne sniffed.

"Any impressions of Christopher, their older son?"

"Hmpf." Miss Hawthorne's lips looked like she'd spent the morning sucking lemons. "I'll tell you, I'm not nosy. I mind my own business, and I don't judge people. Live and let live, I always say, but if you ask me, that family is a bunch of losers."

"How do you mean?"

"The father works for some company nobody's heard of, and the mother works as a nurse all night. I'd hate to count on her for a proper dose of medicine when she drags around exhausted all the time. If I were her patient, I'd be up a creek without a pickle."

I can't have heard that right. "Are they good parents?"

"They let those kids run wild. I always felt sorry for Christopher." Miss Hawthorne leaned through the doorway closer to Tom and whispered, "Two weeks ago he and his dad had an awful fight. I went out on my back porch so I could listen. Franz called that boy a sissy and said he'd never amount to anything. Terrible to do that to a child. That man's a bully. I thought of calling the police."

"You're sure he was shouting at Christopher, not Joey?"

"Joey had already left. He goes somewhere on his bike every Saturday morning at nine, like clockwork. Sometimes when his parents aren't there, he brings home a girl. Who knows what those children are up to. I can't see into Joey's window."

"What about Christopher? Ever see him with a girl?"

"No."

"How about drunk or high on drugs? Any sign of that?"

"Not that I ever saw. He might have been scared of what his father would do if he caught him. Someone should take that man out and shoot him."

"Miss Hawthorne, did you ever have reason to think that Christopher could be violent?"

"No, but I'll bet his father could. I hope he's sorry his son is gone. That man buttered his bread, and now he has to lie in it."

As long as Tom was close to Andie's house, he walked over to take care of a clerical problem. The phone number she'd listed on her incident report didn't match the one on her department roster. Tom rang the doorbell, took off his hat, and was smoothing back his hair when he heard barking fierce enough to freeze his blood. Justice sounded like he was about to rip through the door and grab Tom by the throat. When he stopped barking long enough to take a breath, the dead bolt clicked.

Justice's curled lip told Tom, *One false move and you're going to meet your maker.*

At the sight of Tom, Andie stepped back, clearly surprised. She looked like she hadn't slept in a couple of months. Tom almost felt sorry for her.

"Hello." He held out his hand for Justice to sniff, though it was awkward with the cone.

"Um . . . hello," Andie said.

"Poor guy. Those cones are miserable," Tom said. "Justice seems to be doing well, though."

"He's getting his old self back," Andie said as her puzzled expression asked him, *Why are you here?*

"He smells my Sammy. She's a golden." It was pleasant to have almost a normal conversation after their encounter at the station. Tom reminded himself, *Back to business.* "I have a question."

Andie narrowed her eyes. "You shouldn't be here without Ron Hausmann. We're always supposed to have a lawyer present."

"You won't need him to discuss your phone number. In your incident report, you said this was yours." Tom opened his notepad and pointed to a string of digits, written with a black felt-tip pen.

When Andie leaned over to read it, the smell of her shampoo wafted to his nostrils. It was nicer than he'd have expected from a cop.

"That's my mother's old number. I guess I was too upset that night to think straight."

"So this is your number?" Tom pointed to the one below her mother's and got another pleasant whiff.

"Yes, that's it."

"Good to know. We might have to get ahold of you."

"Not without Hausmann."

Okay, lady, I get it. We play by the rules. Tom straightened up and looked into those green eyes. They looked right back. "As you know, we need the right contact information. We'll be in touch," he said.

CHAPTER 18

ANDREA

At last, a week after being stabbed, Justice was permanently free from the Cone of Doom. He polished off his celebratory dinner of cottage cheese and a broiled chicken breast, after which he pranced around the kitchen with Bandit in his mouth. He let the world know, *This is my own personal teddy, and nobody else can have him.*

Justice sat on his golden throne in the posture of a maharaja—his bottom firmly on the pillow and his front legs, straight as scepters, propping up the rest of him. His gaze steady, he surveyed the kitchen, his dominion, with Bandit, his loyal colonel, at his side.

Andie was finishing her own dinner, chicken-and-dumplings, which Doug Baker's wife had left on the front doorstep with a note: "We're with you, Brady. Don't let the jerks get you down." So far there had been just a single jerk, Tom Wolski, whose grilling had been bad enough, but why couldn't he have gotten her phone number from Stephanie at the station? Why did he have to turn up and harass Andie in her own home?

Unlike Wolski, Andie's colleagues on the force had shown nothing but support. Every day on her porch she'd found surprises—cards, flowers, pies, casseroles, loaves of homemade bread, and even bubble bath from Stephanie with a card urging

Andie to relax in the tub. On several nights, she'd needed to triple her gratitude list in order to mention all the kindness. Her kitchen counter was covered with empty dishes to be returned. Though her colleagues couldn't talk about the case, they'd let her know they cared.

Fortified by their reassurance, she speared a dumpling with her fork and asked Justice, "What do you think, Sweet Boy? Do we dare watch the news?"

He cocked his head, his triangle ears alert. She could always count on him to pay attention.

"You think a week has been long enough for the press to lose interest? I don't want to see myself dragged through the mud," she told him.

If Justice could talk, he'd have advised Andie to wait a few more days. A cautious and protective dog, he picked up even her mildest distress in a flash. Besides, he had his own TV viewing preferences. On the Animal Planet channel, he enjoyed reruns of the Puppy Bowl and *Glory Hounds*, and on the Hallmark Channel, he went wild over dramas in which someone rang a doorbell.

Justice loved doorbells—one bong and he jumped to his feet and barked, ready to take on the world. Yet as much as he cared for doorbells, he disdained those who sometimes came to the porch, especially petition-signature seekers and door-to-door salesmen. After Tom Wolski had stressed Andie over her phone number, he clearly wasn't a favorite of Justice's, either. In his brain, he'd stored the conviction that Wolski needed surveillance.

"How about if we look at the news and then your shows, Sweet Boy?" Andie asked. Sure he'd agree—Justice agreed to most anything as long as she was safe—she aimed the remote control at her TV and pressed the power button on. The TV was set to Channel Four.

The notorious Sid King was perched on a sofa, his toupee

slicked back in a European style. His shiny sports coat's arms were too short. He wore owlish horn-rimmed glasses to make himself look smart, not that his viewers had witnessed much of a brain. He rested his elbows on his knees and leaned forward like he was about to whisper sweet nothings into somebody's ear.

But Sid King was not known for sweet nothings. He was known for his barracuda tactics. He whipped his forked tail, exposed his razor-sharp fangs, and fixed his eyes on someone across from him. He asked, "So tell me, if you could say anything to her, what would it be?"

Who is "her"?

The camera answered Andie's question. Across the coffee table from Sid, Jane and Franz Vanderwaal were pressed together, side by side, as if they needed each other's body heat to get through their blizzard of grief. Jane balled a handkerchief in her hand; Franz's hands rested on his lap in fists. Christopher's framed school photo sat on a table four strategic inches from Jane's elbow so that the big brown eyes on his young face could melt viewers' hearts.

"I'd tell Officer Brady I hope she rots in hell," Franz said.

If Andie had squeezed the remote control any harder, she'd have cracked its case. Her wiser self demanded, *Turn it off! Turn it off!* But the devil, who happily resides in everyone, poked her with his pitchfork and chortled, *Oh, go ahead. You know you want to watch. Think how juicy all that hate is going to be.*

Except the hate would be directed at Andie, and it was exactly what she'd wanted to avoid. Still, her curiosity made her helpless.

"And what would *you* like to say to Officer Brady, Mrs. Vanderwaal?" Sid asked.

Jane looked like her limited strength had drained out on the floor. Her face was hard. She peered into the camera as if she were peering into Andie's soul. "I'd ask her: Why did you have to confront our defenseless boy? If you were scared, you could have called nine-one-one. Better police than you are could have protected him from you."

Protected him from me?! What about protecting me from him?!

"In all fairness, we've learned that your son allegedly had a knife, Mrs. Vanderwaal," Sid pointed out.

Yes, a knife! And the Supreme Court ruled that if cops are threatened, they can use force one increment up from the force they face. I had a right to use my gun.

"I'm glad you said 'allegedly,'" Franz responded for Jane. "We don't believe Christopher *had* a knife. That woman planted it."

Are you kidding me?!

Franz continued, "If we're wrong and Christopher *did* have a knife, he stabbed the dog in self-defense. That woman sicced him on our son."

Andie could have sworn Sid smirked.

"About the dog," he said. "This afternoon I talked with one of the first responders to the scene. He said when he arrived, Officer Brady was administering first aid to the dog, not your son. He was a few feet away . . . bleeding to his death, as it so sadly turned out." The sorrow in Sid's eyes expressed a mortician's practiced concern. "Do you think Officer Brady cared more about her dog than your son?"

"Absolutely!" Franz snapped. "She's guilty of far more than negligence. Attending to her dog like that was criminal."

"You may be pleased that others share your opinion," Sid said. "Are you aware of the highly influential San Julian group Islanders for Collaborative Policing? They've called for Officer Brady's arrest and criminal prosecution."

Surely not. It can't be. The kitchen floor seemed to shake; the walls trembled. Andie felt her world tumble down. She grabbed the remote and aimed it like a gun at the TV screen. She pressed "off" so hard that the button imprinted a small white oval on her thumb.

Well aware that Andie needed bolstering, Justice came to her and presented himself for her to cling to. His steady presence let her know, *Don't worry. I'm here.* As she draped her arm across his back, he leaned against her leg.

"It feels like everybody's after me," Andie told him. She'd expected media coverage of the shooting to distress her, but Sid King was more brutal than she'd imagined. It hurt that the Islanders for Collaborative Policing, whom she'd willingly have risked her life to serve, now wanted her behind bars.

She'd had a mere second to deliberate before aiming her gun at Christopher. Shoot and she'd be called a murderer; don't shoot and she'd have a knife stabbed in her heart. Yet for weeks—maybe months—everyone, including the vulture press, would leisurely pick over the carcass of her decision to use deadly force. They'd not bother to give her the benefit of the doubt.

What nobody seemed to understand was how badly she'd wanted *not* to shoot Christopher. No police officer wanted to shoot anybody. No sane person wanted to take a life. Nobody would believe that in Andie's own way she was as grief stricken as the Vanderwaals.

"I'm out there now, public property," Andie told Justice. "I can't let the press see I'm upset, or they'll win. They'll own me." *Don't let the jerks get you down.*

They already had.

Justice rested his head in Andie's lap.

CHAPTER 19

The Nisqually County morgue cornered the market on "grisly." The rooms were cold and sterile, and, were it not for the formaldehyde smell, you might think you'd walked into a hospital. But a sensitive person might wince at the blood and tissue samples tucked inside the specimen refrigerator, or at the saws, mallets, shears, and goggles hanging on the Autopsy Suite's walls. Or at the cooler's drawers, half at forty degrees and half below thirty-two, to accommodate the varying lengths of time that bodies would be stored—bodies of every age, gender, and stage of decomposition.

Tom had been here for the start of Christopher's autopsy, and now he'd returned to pick up the coroner's formal report. Eager to get home to study for his sergeant's exam, he parked at the back of the building and walked through the ambulance's unloading area, the Decomposition Suite, its fans humming, and the Autopsy Suite, its concrete floor slanted to a drain below the autopsy table. He finally entered the office of Lowell Burden, the Nisqually County coroner.

Burden was dressed in desert boots, black slacks, and a shirt that seemed too crisp and white for his profession. He pried his heft off his swivel chair and gripped Tom's hand for a shake that might have brought a weight-lifting champion to his knees.

He pulled a folder from a pile on his desk. "Here." He handed the report to Tom.

"The kid had no heart or brain disease. His last meal was a hamburger," Burden said. "One bullet shattered his humerus. The other hit his quadriceps fermoris. If that bullet had gone half an inch lower, the kid would be at school today. Cause of death was bleeding from the femoral artery."

"Tox screen have any surprises?" Tom asked.

"One." Burden half-sat on his desk's edge, one desert boot dangling and the other planted on the floor. "You said you didn't find drugs in the kid's bedroom, but you suspected they might be involved."

"Yes."

"You were wrong."

Tom's eyebrows arched at this news. "Nothing? Not a trace of *any*thing?"

"Zip. No drugs or alcohol in his system at the T.O.D. He was clean."

Tom exhaled, slow and ragged. So Christopher hadn't wigged out on something and gone after Brady. Tom's hope for that simple explanation was dashed. "There went that theory."

"Sorry to make it harder for you," Burden said.

"We're back to square one."

Burden, about fifteen years older than Tom, gave him an encouraging football-coach pat on the back. "Remember, he was a teenager. Hormones hopping. Peer pressure through the roof. Major life changes. Those have caused plenty of kids to do crazy things."

In high school Tom and his friends had toilet papered their share of trees, unhinged a few restroom doors, and had pizzas delivered to dorks. Those pranks had been wrong, of course, but nowhere near the league of stabbing a K-9 and attacking an armed police officer. "If Brady's story is true, I have no idea what was going through that kid's head."

Burden nodded. "Motive can be the hardest part of a case. You know better than I do how much can ride on it."

"Unfortunately."

At home, Tom's computer made the bonging tones for his nightly Skype call from Lisa, the best part of his day. When he talked with her, he had the pleasure of looking into her funny little face: big brown eyes, teeth that were about to cost him a fortune to straighten, a ponytail that had been known to thwack his cheek when she turned her head. She had toothpick legs and a pipestem neck, from which her shoulders extended like bunny slopes. Her giggles made him think of champagne bubbles.

He loved that kid so much it scared him sometimes.

"Dad, it's forty-one degrees Fahrenheit. It's supposed to get down to thirty-four tonight. Precipitation zero."

"Very good, kid." Tom grinned at his junior weather fanatic. He planned to give her a barometer for Christmas. When she grew up, she wanted to be a Channel Five forecaster.

"The wind velocity is fifteen miles an hour out of the north-northwest," she said. "Did you see the clouds this afternoon?"

"Can't say I did. I was busy at work. Forgot to look at the sky."

"Da-ad." Two syllables always registered dismay. "You should have looked. They were stratocumulus."

In clouds, some kids saw a sheep, or a shark about to chomp a fish, but Lisa saw the scientific types. How cool was that? "I'll check out the clouds tomorrow," Tom promised.

"Where's Sammy?" Lisa asked.

"Right here. She wants to talk with you." Tom herded his golden to the computer and lifted her up high enough for Lisa to see her face. Sammy sniffed the screen.

"Hi, Sammy!" A champagne bubble or two.

Tom stooped to waving Sammy's paw at Lisa. *Ridiculous, but anything for my kid.*

"Can I keep her next week? I want to take her to school. We're having a pet show," Lisa said.

Whoa. "Sammy lives here."

"She could stay with Mom and me for a couple of days."

Not when I don't trust your mother as far as I can throw her. Sometimes that lack of trust kept Tom up at night, blinking in the dark. How he'd ever married Mia he'd never know, except that he'd been young and she'd had long blond hair and a knockout body. Hopping hormones, as Lowell Burden said.

But when God handed out maternal instincts, spoiled Mia had been at the end of the line. Tom worried that she wouldn't bother getting up to feed Lisa breakfast or lock the dead bolt to keep her safe at night. Mia might forget to put down Sammy's food and water. If Sammy got stabbed like Justice, Mia would leave her to die. Even for Lisa, Tom couldn't let Sammy stay with his ex-wife.

"Honey, we'll work it out," Tom told Lisa. "Maybe I'll bring Sammy to meet you at school before the show. While I'm there, I could talk to your class about being a sheriff's deputy." *Kids love learning about law enforcement.* "Let's discuss Sammy when you're here this weekend. We'll make a plan, okay?"

"Okay, Daddy." When Lisa looked up at someone standing behind the computer screen out of Tom's sight, he knew that Mia was hovering around. "I have to go, Dad. It's time for *Orange Is the New Black.*"

Mia can't let her watch that! Resentment crept through Tom, followed by mind-clogging guilt. Maybe having a weekend dad wasn't enough for Lisa and he should never have divorced. Maybe when Mia ran home to her parents seven years ago, he should have gone after her and tried to work things out.

The day before she left, she'd called Tom at his new Sheriff's Department job. "You've got to come home. There's this awful thing. I can't stand it. It's on the deck."

Nothing could persuade her to lock the doors and stay in the house till Tom got home from work. So in the middle of a busy day, he drove twenty-four miles to investigate. The "awful thing" was an errant slug, minding his own business; maybe he was a little slimy, but no big threat. Tom scooped him off the deck floor with a garden trowel and dropped him into the bushes.

"Look, we live in the woods. So do slugs. They're a fact of life," Tom told Mia.

"I don't care. I don't want slugs on my deck. I don't like it here," she said.

Tom had quit the Marines because Mia hadn't liked being a military wife, and he'd left Seattle because she hadn't liked the traffic and his police job's long hours. There had been no pleasing her. About much of anything. Tom knew he had tried.

CHAPTER 20

ANDREA

Back in the station's conference room, the flickering fluorescent light made Andie jittery. Her stomach was churning. Tom Wolski had called her in to discuss new "issues," and she had no idea what they were. She'd be flying blind in unfamiliar territory.

Ross Jackson, for whatever reason, was absent. In order to attend today, Stephanie had offered to cancel her interview with a mattress company for a night job as a professional sleeper, but Andie had said that she already had enough support. The reassuring sleeve of Ron Hausmann's herringbone sports coat brushed her arm. And stretched out in his library lion position, Justice was blocking the room's only exit and keeping a careful watch on Tom.

She and Tom faced down each other across the conference table's no-man's-land again. He read her the Garrity Warning, folded his hands on the table, and said, "A new witness saw TV coverage of the shooting and came forward. She was walking her Chihuahua down your road and heard you yelling. She thought you were arguing with someone."

"I wasn't arguing. I was trying to get Christopher to put down his knife," Andie said.

"She said you sounded angry."

"You'd be upset if someone hurt your dog, wouldn't you?"

"We're not talking about me here," Tom said. "And there's a difference between upset and anger."

"Okay, then I was angry. I couldn't help it. I love Justice. It broke my heart to hear him shriek in pain."

At the sound of his name, Justice pricked his ears. His bristled eyebrows told Tom as plain as day, *Back off. Don't pressure her.*

"Did your anger make you lose perspective? Make you too quick to shoot?" Tom asked.

"No!" *Um, maybe. Could that be true?* Doubt took a flying leap at Andie's churning stomach.

"Officer Brady, would you say you have an anger problem? Are you hotheaded? Short fused?"

"No." *Well, once in a while.*

"What about this complaint filed against you last year?" Tom tossed a piece of paper on the table and pointed to the name of Mrs. Emily Zidd. "Her son was skateboarding down Ranier Street, and you confronted him in what she claims was an unprofessional manner. She says you were furious. You lost it."

Andie's exhale was heated with scorn. When her cheeks warmed, she knew they were flushed, and she wished she could hide her telltale sign of annoyance. "There was traffic. Anybody with a pea brain would know skateboarding on that street was dangerous," she said, prickly as holly.

Tom stared at her, clearly taking note of her red cheeks. "So you're huffy about a complaint about your anger? Looks to me like a short fuse working overtime."

Andie clamped her teeth together as her annoyance ratcheted up to resentment. She'd played right into his hands and let him goad her into anger—he'd weaseled behind her wall. *Get a grip. You cannot let him manipulate you.* "Mrs. Zidd's complaint irritated me at the time, and it still does." Andie spoke slowly, as if she were talking with someone who was learning English.

"She should have been grateful to me. Her son could have been killed."

"You couldn't have asked him to get off the street? You had to yell at him, and apparently for some time?"

"I *did* ask him to get off the street, but he ignored me and skated away. I had to stop him. I was justified to yell."

"I'm seeing a pattern, Brady."

"We're not here for psychoanalyzing," Hausmann warned.

"Addressing Brady's anger is important. She admits she got angry when Justice was stabbed. I want to know if she flew off the handle," Tom told Hausmann.

"I was protecting myself." Andie's response sounded as if she'd bitten it off a hacksaw blade.

Surely picking up the emotions flying around the room, Justice got up, flashed Tom a withering look, and wriggled under the table. He rested his chin on Andie's toes and announced unmistakably, *I am here to protect you from that vile buzzard. Don't be afraid.* His velvety ear against her ankle soothed her.

"All right, let's leave anger for now." Tom set another piece of paper between him and Andie. "I've got to say this report surprised me. On September thirteenth, 2012, you arrested Franz Vanderwaal for DUI. Anything to say about that?"

Hausmann coughed. He backed his chair away from the table and gestured for Andie to follow. His hand cupped around her ear, he whispered, "You didn't think to tell Wolski—or *me*—about that arrest?!"

"It wasn't important. I just wanted it to go away," Andie whispered back.

"It's not going *anywhere.*" Hausmann's usual calm seemed to have hitchhiked down the street to the corner of Shock and Pique. "If there was some problem about the arrest, tell me now."

"No problem. It was fine."

Hausmann's exhale was long and weary. "Okay, answer his questions."

Andie scooched her chair back to the table. "I arrested Mr. Vanderwaal after his car jumped a curb and hit a fire hydrant downtown. He claimed he'd dropped his cell phone and was reaching for it at his feet. You know, a typical lie."

"You're sure he was lying?"

"I was sure when I shone my flashlight into his red, watery eyes and the alcohol on his breath almost knocked me over. He claimed he'd only had two beers—you know that one." Andie scoffed. "He couldn't stand on one leg, and he sucked in breath instead of exhaling into the Breathalyzer. After I called him on that stunt, he inhaled like he planned to blow up an air mattress with a single breath, then exhaled just a tiny puff. Who did he think he was kidding?"

"I read that his blood alcohol level was .05 over the limit and he was cooperative, so the D.A. knocked the charge down to reckless driving," Tom said.

"Right, and I didn't have to appear in court."

Tom leaned back and crossed his arms over his chest. "I have one main question about this whole deal. Why didn't you think to mention something so important as arresting the father of a teen you've killed?"

"I didn't think it had any bearing on Christopher's attack."

Wolski scowled. "Surely you're not serious."

Andie scowled back. "The DUI was four years ago. I arrested Mr. Vanderwaal. I didn't have to testify in court. End of story."

"No, the story hasn't ended. How do you think the arrest might have affected Christopher?"

"She can't know that," Hausmann said.

"I'll turn the question around, then. Brady, has it never occurred to you that Christopher could have hated you for what you did to his father? He could have been trying to get back at you?"

"It took him four *years* to get around to it?"

"I don't intend to argue with you." Tom pressed his pen's point on the file that had contained the arrest report. "But the witness said you sounded angry shouting at Christopher. There was obviously a conflict. It could have been connected to the DUI or something else."

"It was only connected to getting him to drop his knife!" Andie snapped.

"Just so you know, yesterday I talked with the Vanderwaals. They're adamant that something more was going on than meets the eye. They're sure you had an inappropriate relationship with Christopher. If that's true, I'm going to figure it out eventually, so you may as well save us a lot of trouble and tell me the whole story now."

Andie reared back like she'd been slapped. "Here's what I'll tell you now. You're supposed to be impartial, but you're biased—you've made up your mind that I'm a criminal, and you're out to prove it. You're coming at me like Christopher did. It's an attack."

Hausmann's hand landed on Andie's arm and squeezed. She shut her mouth to stop herself from saying more.

A muscle tightened in Tom's jaw. "That comment doesn't deserve a response," he told Andie calmly.

As she crawled behind her wall, she heard a muffled conversation in the roll-call room and made out just two words: "hour" and "trap." She wanted to ask Tom Wolski, *Do* you *have an anger problem? Are you mad I broke our date a gazillion years ago? Is it payback time for that?* But he'd deny it, and now wasn't the time to get personal. She felt like a sinking ship.

CHAPTER 21

ANDREA

Andie's father used to say that work was the best antidote for worry. You had to stay active till your world could right itself. Since Tom Wolski's inquisition—Andie had quit thinking of it as an investigation—she might have put a bee to shame with all she'd done to keep busy . . . and to chase Tom's suggestion of an "inappropriate relationship" out of her mind. She'd done nothing to deserve the accusation. It sullied and infuriated her.

To divert her anxious and resentful thoughts, in the last three days Andie had reorganized drawers, cleaned out closets, dusted books, defrosted the freezer, cleaned the oven, and waged war on the shower grout's mold. She'd made Liver-Cheese Humdinger treats for Justice and Sardine Surprises for Rosemary. She'd baked and frosted legions of turkey-shaped Thanksgiving sugar cookies for San Julian's senior center and soup kitchen.

However, none of these tasks had managed to take her attention from the snarl that her life had become. Her administrative leave had boiled down to one word: "limbo." She was stuck in it as surely as if tar had grabbed her feet. And a corollary of limbo was irresolution. She didn't know if she'd be sent back to work, fired, or sentenced to prison.

To her, all three possibilities led to a dead end. She wasn't sure she wanted to return to a job that might require her to shoot someone again or risk her life for such ungrateful citizens as the Islanders for Collaborative Policing. If fired, she could never look for work on another force because wrongdoing would hang over her head. And prison was too terrible to consider. Having no trust in her future, Andie could only wait till Tom Wolski's findings determined which dead-end fork she'd take in her road.

Determined not to brood, she decided to clean her house. Who cared if she'd cleaned it two days before? *If my life is a shambles, at least my house can be tidy,* she thought.

As she plugged in the vacuum cleaner, Justice, who'd been lounging with Bandit in front of the potbellied stove, rose to his feet. The vacuum cleaner, his archfoe, was on par with the Cone of Doom. The high-pitched whine assaulted his sensitive ears, to say nothing of the beater bar ruthlessly nipping his paws when Andie got to cleaning full-force. Justice's look at the vacuum let her know emphatically, *If I had my way, I'd banish that machine from the house.*

A keen reader of Andie's housecleaning signals, he also knew that bleach would soon make an appearance—and he was not fond of the odor. Nor did he approve of her callous washing of his bed, which took him weeks of sprawling on to return to his olfactory satisfaction. To avoid her cleaning frenzy, he hobbled up the stairs to the bathroom and squeezed between the vanity and shower, his favorite place to ride out thunderstorms.

As Andie vacuumed the living-room rug, she got on her hands and knees to reach under the sofa, wingback chairs, and oak end tables. Then she went after dust around her gratitude basket and in the bookcase and shutters. While straightening a pile of *Bake Away* magazines on her coffee table, she thought of her ex-husband, Rich. He would approve of her efforts. He lived by the rule "everything orderly and on schedule," which had once seemed like balm of stability after the instability of her childhood.

Rich was an accountant—he liked keeping track down to pennies—though his innate precision would also have made him an excellent Amtrak engineer or computer-chip assembler. By eight every Saturday morning, Andie woke to the *scratch-scratch-scratch* of his brush cleaning the toilet bowl. By two every Saturday afternoon, he pursued his favorite hobby: picking up litter on the section of Highway 21 that he'd "adopted" in a Nisqually County cleanup program.

For Andie's birthday, Rich had given her a heart-shaped crystal vase, which her feather duster now accidentally hit, almost toppling it over. It was supposed to hold roses he would bring home to her on special occasions—except he discovered he didn't like petals falling on the table, or cloudy water that had to be changed.

At the beginning of their marriage, Rich had danced Andie around the living room and sung "My Wild Irish Rose," his name of endearment for her. It had all been a pleasure until a year or so later—Andie couldn't put her finger on the exact timing—when they seemed to dwell less on an Irish rose's blossoms and more on its thorns.

Not major thorns. Just thorns of this and that. "The porch needs sweeping," he'd complain, to which she'd respond, "You could do it. You live in this house too." Or she'd leave for the grocery store, and he'd want to know where else she might stop and at exactly what time he should expect her back. Sometimes she felt like she was heeling on his leash more than living as his wife. A vague mutual peevishness became their norm, but they glossed over it and kept going.

Until a night three years ago when Andie learned that sometimes a confluence of minor irritations could create a Noah's-ark flood.

She was supposed to have gotten home from work at six,

in time for dinner with Rich. At six thirty, aware of his need for routine, she texted him: "Car rolled over on Highway 113. Home within an hour." How was she to know that she'd get an emergency domestic violence call? And that she would pull up to a house in flames and she and Doug Baker would have to chase the arsonist perp through the woods? While Baker took him to jail, Andie rode to the hospital in an ambulance with the perp's pregnant wife. Finally, pale and exhausted, fir cones tangled in her hair, Andie walked through her front door at 11:10.

"Where have you been?" Icicles hung from Rich's greeting. He did not get up from the sofa.

Andie rallied from fatigue enough to describe her evening. "It was a high-wire act. I never had a chance to send another text."

"I made you dinner. I finally ate at nine," he said. "Now I know you can be anything from ten minutes to"—he checked his watch—"five hours and twelve minutes late."

"I'm sorry," Andie said to bring the conflict to an end.

Rich didn't take the bait. "You're always sorry. Tonight you set a record."

"Before we married, you knew my hours."

"I didn't know how unpredictable they'd be," Rich said. "As soon as I get used to your shift, it changes. I can't make plans. When I want to go out, you want to sleep. While you're off saving the world, I'm the lout who has to hold down the fort."

"Oh, Rich." Andie would not use her last drop of energy to stand there and be railed against. She took off her utility belt and its twenty-seven pounds of equipment and sank into a wingback chair across from him. She thought, *No one but another cop could understand the pressures of my work.* "You knew my job was stressful before we married."

"I wouldn't have gone through with it if I'd understood how bad it would be."

A new low. The sharpest thorn ever.

After a fourteen-hour day—and no lunch—Andie stormed into the kitchen and left him to sulk. Her stomach's growls now close to roars, she slammed the makings for a turkey sandwich onto the counter and slapped mayonnaise on wheat bread. As she was slicing a tomato, someone pounded on the front door and startled her. Rich held firm on the sofa to force her to answer.

Their neighbor Kate Patterson was wearing jeans tight enough to cut off circulation. Her pink angora sweater plunged dangerously into cleavage territory. "Sorry it's so late. I saw your lights on." Clearly having run over, she was panting. "I think I need help."

You think? "What's wrong?"

"A naked man was walking around my backyard just now."

"Do you know him?"

"Not by name. I may have . . . er . . . seen him at the Tipsy Cow."

"How does he know where you live?"

"Well . . . I'm not sure." Kate studied her suede boots' pointed toes. "I wouldn't have minded him out there if he hadn't rattled my back-door knob. He was trying to get in."

"Is he still there?"

"He disappeared. That's when I ran down here." Shivering, Kate hugged herself to stave off cold. "Please, can you come and look around? For all I know, he's hiding in my garage."

Every muscle in Andie's body ached, but as she'd told the high-school tennis player that night on patrol, nothing bothered her more than seeing someone frightened and not being able to help. As a cop, Andie was public property, to whom, 24-7, people felt they had a right. No matter how tired she was, duty called. She picked up her utility belt with its twenty-seven miserable pounds and told Rich, "Back in a little while."

Rich didn't bother to look up.

Andie searched Kate's yard and garage and found no naked man. When she dragged home, Rich was gone. He had not returned when she left for work the next morning. That evening she found an envelope, propped against the empty heart-shaped vase on the kitchen counter. In tiny but perfect block letters on his most formal business stationery, Rich had printed what looked like a PowerPoint presentation, including meticulous indentations and bullets.

With surgical precision, he outlined his grievances against Andie, most of which rehashed the night before. He saved his one new point for last: "I no longer want to be married to a cop." That was it. *Finito.*

Since by some estimates eighty percent of cops divorce, Rich's departure should not have bowled over Andie. Still, years after reading that letter, shock and hurt rippled through her all over again. She set down her feather duster, fell back into the sofa, and rested her palms against her eyes.

Maybe sometimes you have so much on your mind that cleaning your house can't distract you, she thought. Her worries, disappointments, and hurts added up, and their sum was steamrolling her.

CHAPTER 22

TOM

Alan Pederson's office was palatial compared to Tom's measly cubicle. And Pederson had windows. He could look out at the clouds that Lisa was always talking about—stratocumulus, cirrus, nimbostratus—and all day long mallards and Canada geese cruised around on a pond that glittered right under his nose. Tom, in contrast, stared at fuzzy gray walls, and sometimes in his small, dark space he felt like a besieged mole. If he made sergeant, he'd climb a ladder rung to a bigger office with a window or two. That prospect was a carrot that kept him galloping toward solving Brady's case.

Tom handed his boss a folder of interview notes and recent reports, including the coroner's. "No news yet on ballistics for the knife, but I'll be getting it this afternoon."

Pederson leaned back in his swivel chair and laced his hands behind his head. Perspiration rings darkened his khaki shirt's armpits, surprising on a cool November day. "So what have you learned?"

"There's evidence proving Brady shot the kid. If the knife's ballistics check out, we'll know he stabbed the K-9 and probably went after her. We haven't unearthed any sign of trouble for him, unless you can count having pieces of work for parents. His room was compulsively neat, but that didn't tell us much."

"Yeah, no crime in that," Pederson said.

"Brady arrested his father for DUI four years ago, but they both deny any hard feelings. She has a temper. I'm not sure yet how that played out. She claims she barely knew the kid."

"You think that's true?" Pederson sat up straight again.

"His parents are convinced more was going on, but we've found no evidence of it. And nothing else to suggest any other reason for what happened."

"You need to dig it up if you want to finish the case right. It doesn't sound like you've gotten very deep," Pederson said.

"We're digging as deep as we can."

"Dig harder. And faster. Funding for this investigation can't go on forever. It's the end of the year. The budget is running on fumes."

"Yes, sir. I understand." A flock of Canada geese flew over the pond in a honking V.

"Wolski, I gave you this case because I thought you could handle it . . ." Pederson said.

Tom braced himself for a "but" that he wasn't handling it as well as Pederson hoped. When no "but" followed, Tom breathed a little easier. "I appreciate the opportunity."

"That's good, but we need to wrap up this case. Soon."

"Yes, sir." When Tom left the office, his armpits were as damp as Pederson's.

On Tom's third visit to the Vanderwaals, he held out the knife found at the scene—an eight-inch kitchen carving knife with steel rivets, a wooden handle, and a steel blade that re-flected the ceiling fixture's light. The blade had an edge sharp enough to shave with and a point fine enough to pin a dust mote to the floor. Brandish it in front of anyone and that per-son would know fear.

Just back from the lab, the knife was secured in a clear plastic bag. Tom had intended for Jane to examine it, but she re-coiled at the sight of it and pressed her back into the sofa's pillow.

"Mr. Vanderwaal? Do you recognize this knife?" Tom handed it to him across the coffee table.

Arching an eyebrow with obvious distaste, Franz pinched a corner of the bag and held it at a distance like he was holding the tail of a dead mouse. He set it on the coffee table. "Never saw it before."

"Mrs. Vanderwaal? Is it from your kitchen?"

Jane shuddered. "That knife isn't ours."

"Why are you subjecting us to this?" Franz demanded.

"Because we just got a forensic report. Christopher's fin-gerprints and touch DNA were on that knife, and it's the same one that wounded the K-9. Since we know Cristopher had it in his hand, we can conclude he stabbed the dog. It looks like that part of Officer Brady's story checks out."

"Didn't you hear us? It's not our knife. Don't you under-stand plain English?" Franz insisted.

Because non-ownership trumps forensic results? "Christopher must have bought it. We'll talk to people at DIY Hardware and Village Vittles Kitchen Store."

"That knife belongs to Officer Brady. I told you she planted it," Franz said. "She squeezed Christopher's hand around it for the DNA and prints."

"Her own would be on it if she'd done that," Tom said.

"Not if she was wearing rubber gloves." Franz puffed out his chest as if again he'd outfoxed the pros.

"We'll see what else comes up. The investigation isn't over yet." Tom slipped the knife into its padded envelope as a cour-tesy to Jane, whose eyes were darting all over the room to avoid a direct look.

Franz must have felt he was on a roll to victory over Tom. He demanded, "What about that vicious dog? Have you put him down?"

"He's an outstanding K-9, Mr. Vanderwaal. An asset to the force." Before Franz could argue, Tom leaned forward, rested his forearms on his thighs, and said, "This afternoon I had a long talk with Christopher's homeroom teacher, Mrs. Rachlin. Have either of you met her at a back-to-school night?"

Jane shook her head no.

"Mrs. Rachlin said Christopher was very introverted. No friends that she knew of. Does that sound right?" Tom asked her.

"We told you we didn't *know* his friends." Franz pushed his way back to center stage. "I'm sure he had some."

"Mrs. Rachlin thought he might have been troubled."

"Not that we ever saw," Franz insisted. "We told you that too. How many times do you plan on asking us the same questions?"

"As many times as it takes to get answers." *You loser.* "And I'll ask you again, can you explain why Christopher went to Officer Brady's yard and stabbed her dog?"

"We said we don't think he did!" Franz bolted off the sofa as if he'd had enough of Tom; he leaned against the mantel. "Just so you know, Jane and I still think more was going on. That cop seduced Christopher—have you looked into that, yet? It's the only explanation that makes sense to us, isn't it, Jane?"

When she nodded, a pin from her French twist fell onto her shoulder.

"Look at high-school teachers and their students today. They hook up all the time. You see it in the paper," Franz said. "Why not Officer Brady?"

"I guess anything's possible," Tom said.

"You're damned right. She doesn't have a husband, so she was preying on Jane's son."

In the silence that followed, Tom noticed the refrigerator

hum. An ice cube fell into the receiving drawer. A branch scraped against a gutter. He took a breath.

He told Franz, "We're looking into all that." And he would. But as he spoke, he was also thinking that Brady wasn't the type to get involved in something so stupid. Or was she? Still, Tom's intuition was starting to suggest that Brady might be telling the truth.

CHAPTER 23

ANDREA

Andie worked a spatula under a Cherry-Top cookie and set it on her wire rack to cool. The kitchen smelled of cinnamon and nutmeg, and it was warm from the oven's 375 degrees. Justice, whose thick winter coat could stave off Arctic cold, sprawled on his golden throne as far from the oven as he could get.

All afternoon he'd napped on his back with his legs flopped out; if he'd been a person, Andie would have arrested him for flashing. And he'd sat at the back door and looked through the glass panes into the yard, guarding the house against his enemies, raccoons and squirrels. Now he was lying on his stomach in his sphinx position, staring at her. His intense concentration let her know that he was contemplating something, and Andie guessed it was his routine. In the last few weeks, it had drastically changed, as had hers. His world had shrunk to the confines of the house and yard, and he was as bored as she was.

A dog can only loll around so long, and I am not a wastrel. I am a disciplined German shepherd, and I have a job to do, his bristled eyebrows informed Andie. *Let's go nail the Beast. You know he's out there dealing drugs. Why are we hanging around here like flakes?*

Andie set another Cherry-Top cookie onto the rack. "We'll go out in a few minutes." She would take him to the yard for a bathroom break.

He groaned. *I am not a fluffy lapdog. I am opposed to rhinestone collars and high-pitched yips. I work!* He rolled over to his side and stared at the wall.

"Here, Justice. How about a little Animal Planet?" Andie wiped her hands on her red-and-white-checked apron and pressed the power button on her TV's remote control. Who should appear on the screen but Sid King? Andie grimaced. When would she learn not to turn on the TV when his program was on? Again, she could not help herself; she had to watch.

Sid King was interviewing a woman who looked vaguely familiar. She wore an eggplant fleece jacket whose color overpowered her pale skin, and she had plucked her eyebrows to near nonexistence. Above her narrow upper lip were the wrinkles of a perpetual lip purser.

"So you admit you blocked an intersection?" Sid asked.

"Yes, but it wasn't my fault. I was in terrible traffic for the Rotary Auction, and I sat through three light cycles before I could finally go. Then some jerk cut in front of me! I couldn't get out of the intersection. I was stuck!" *Purse, purse* went her lips.

"Couldn't you explain that to Officer Brady?" The red glass in Sid's high-school class ring looked like an albino gerbil's eye.

"I *did* explain. She said she hadn't seen the jerk ahead of me. All she saw was me in the intersection so she had to give me a ticket. *I* didn't break the law. *He* did."

"So you thought Officer Brady was unsympathetic? Callous?"

"I certainly didn't deserve the hundred-and-fifteen-dollar fine." *Purse, purse.* "Why wasn't she directing traffic? Why did she have to give a ticket to a decent person who was just trying to follow the law?"

Rancor heated Andie's face more than the oven had. She

quickly switched to Animal Planet. A lion was running after a sumptuous Cape buffalo. Each time his massive paws thumped on the savannah's grass, his muscles rippled and his mane shook. His teeth at the ready, he leapt in the air to pounce.

When Andie turned off the TV, she wished she could pounce like that on Sid King. *Can't he find someone else to torment? Does he have to hunt me every day of the week?*

Just yesterday he'd called and asked when he could interview her. "You could tell your side of the story. No one's feeling much sympathy for you right now. I'm giving you a chance to turn that around."

Yeah, right. You'd unfurl your scorpion stinger. Andie had wanted to work her fist through the receiver and along the telephone lines to bop him in the nose. Posthaste, she'd turned him down.

She raked another cookie off the metal sheet onto the wire rack and was still fretting when Meghan called. Before she could ask Andie how she was, she blurted out, "I am so sick and tired of Sid King."

"He *is* an awful man," Meghan agreed.

"He found some woman I gave a ticket to years ago. A hundred percent of people like that aren't happy about it, but I had no choice. I saw her break the law."

"Take a breath, Andie."

Andie could hear Rosemary meowing to Meghan for dinner—she was probably extra-hungry after her and Justice's rigorous game of Chase the Cat Around the House that afternoon. Andie pressed her fingertips against her temple, as if trying to dislodge her distress, but that didn't get Sid King out of her brain. "I'm sorry to dump on you," she said.

"I don't mind," Meghan said. "But promise you'll turn off the TV."

"I just did." For almost three weeks Andie had also avoided the *San Julian Review* and the Internet in general, where biased posts had grieved her. She was relieved she wasn't on social media. After a slew of hateful e-mails, she'd stopped checking her Gmail account too.

"You need to think about something besides that man," Meghan said.

"I'm baking cookies."

"That's not enough," Meghan insisted. "You can't stay home and brood till the investigation's over. You need to get out into the world."

"If I leave, someone might recognize me. Or I'll run into Jane or Franz."

"Don't worry about that. You can handle it," Meghan said. "Why don't you take Justice for a walk?"

"No matter who Sid King digs up to disparage me, I won't let him hold me captive in my own home. I will be tough," Andie muttered to Justice as they followed her flashlight's beam to the end of the driveway and onto Valley Road. "And you need to walk and get back your strength."

Since tonight would be Justice's first exercise since being stabbed, she would take him only past ten houses and turn around; then every evening she'd add another house or two till he got back his strength. If she met Jane or Franz on the road, she'd deal with it. As Meghan had urged, Andie would *not* sit at home and brood. Not anymore. No, sir.

Though limping, Justice was thrilled to be on the road. He skimmed his nose along the asphalt with the scrutiny of an anteater looking for dinner and searched for messages left by raccoons, squirrels, and neighborhood pets. He stopped and sniffed a sword fern's frond to discern who might last have brushed against it. His nostrils flared around Kate Patterson's mailbox post and Eduard Kraus's garbage can.

Though Andie was determined to be tough, the closer she got to the Vanderwaals' barn-red clapboard house, the shallower she breathed. She knew she should turn around and walk away, but just as curious drivers stare at a freeway wreck, she stopped in the shadows across the street and peered at the house.

Upstairs, a light shone from the window of one room and a TV flickered on the dark ceiling of another. Weeds grew between the stepping-stones to the front door, where a bare bulb was screwed into a porcelain socket that cried out for a light fixture. Attached to the garage's front was a basketball hoop, its mesh limp and gray and worn.

The house looked sad. Like Sleeping Beauty's castle, it seemed as if someone had cast a spell over it, but no handsome prince had come along and kissed anyone. Bushes grew over half the downstairs windows. Gloom seemed tucked into the roof's black shingles and the wilting azaleas by the front door.

I'm the one who cast the spell, Andie thought. She was to blame for the sorrow that permeated the house. "I wish I could snap my fingers and change everything," Andie whispered to Justice, who was pressed against her in his ready-willing-and-able position, his triangle ears at attention.

Andie thought, *If only Christopher and Joey could be playing* Gone Home *on their computers, and Franz could be upstairs, chuckling over a* Seinfeld *rerun. If only Jane could be chatting with hospital colleagues about an upcoming family ski trip. If only . . .*

Andie reminded herself, *You can't rewrite history. Some stories don't have a happy ending.*

When someone turned on the Vanderwaals' floodlights, Andie drew back into the darkness with a start. An electric charge shot down her arms into her hands. If Franz caught her there, it would be one more frame in the movie of her nightmare. She tugged Justice across the street to Miss Hawthorne's hedge.

Perhaps on a study break, Joey bounded out the front door. He dribbled a basketball along the driveway and tossed it into the garage's hoop. It hit the backboard, bounced around the

rim, and fell through the net. Joey caught the ball and dribbled
it back and forth around the driveway, dodging imaginary
guards.

He seemed like a smaller Christopher with the same chis-
eled features and clean-cut look. He also moved with Christopher's teenage gawkiness, so his uncoordinated limbs seemed
out of sync. Andie stared at him till her eyes stung. *He could* be
Christopher, she thought.

When Joey barged past an invisible opponent and dribbled
the ball toward her, it felt like Christopher was coming at
her—with the knife. She could almost see it glint in the floodlights and hear his shoes slap the wet grass. Each dribble of the
ball sounded like a gunshot.

Andie's ears rang. Her heart raced with the urge to run.
She reached for Justice and wrapped her arms around his neck.
He held her up.

*Maybe this is a flashback like Dr. Capoletti mentioned. Maybe I
have PTSD.*

But then Andie caught herself. *No! This is not a flashback. It's
just a bad memory. Nothing serious. I am fine.*

With discipline like Justice's, in the shadows she started
home.

CHAPTER 24

TOM

Stacks of reports, photos, diagrams, transcripts, statements, and notes covered the Sheriff's Department conference table, which could seat fourteen husky deputies. It was the only space large enough for Tom to spread out all he'd gathered in the last three weeks for Brady's case. As lead investigator, he had to organize the facts and present them in his own report, along with all documents and findings that might be needed at a trial. As if that weren't pressure enough, Tom wanted to write it all up in a manner professional enough to impress the many eyes that would see it.

The first eyes would be Alan Pederson's. If he approved the report, Tom would send it to the County Prosecutor, who'd determine whether Brady should be charged with a crime and, if so, what it should be. The Prosecutor's review would go to Chief Malone for his own judgment and sign-off. Were the shots good or bad? Was the homicide justifiable or criminal? It had to be one or the other.

Today Tom's job was to present facts that would speak for themselves. The time had come to fish or cut bait; but since he'd never been a lead investigator before, he felt like his fishing boat was adrift. Pederson could disapprove of Tom's results, the County Prosecutor could send back the case for more investigation, or Malone could upset the whole applecart. Plenty of hurdles needed jumping before Tom could breathe easy. Any trip-up could humiliate him, thwart his ambitions, and wrestle his pride to the ground.

He exhaled a long, slow breath and told himself to man up. He hadn't gotten into this business to doubt himself. *Over and out, Wolski. Get on with it.* His high-school English teacher, Mrs. Casey, who'd drilled grammar and punctuation into him, would be watching over his shoulder. She'd keep him on the straight and narrow.

Tom settled down with a cup of coffee. All morning he studied photographs and diagrams. He read every view anyone had officially offered on the case and again went through the coroner's and crime lab's reports. Finally, he picked up his pen and yellow legal pad. To organize his thoughts, he wrote basic facts and listed the supporting evidence:

1. *Christopher hid in the bushes on the north side of Brady's property, and he was the only perp.* Photos showed the soles of Christopher's shoes and his footprints in the dirt around the bushes.

2. *Christopher moved four feet and stabbed Justice with the knife found on the scene.*

   Photos showed Christopher's footprints. New interview notes from Jackson revealed that a teen matching Christopher's description had bought the knife at DIY Hardware with cash the day before he attacked Justice and Brady. Forensic reports concluded that Christopher's fingerprints and touch DNA were on the knife, whose steel blade matched Justice's wounds. Photos of them and of Justice's blood on the ground showed where he'd been standing when attacked. His blood matched blood found on Christopher's jeans and hoodie and on Brady's uniform.

3. *Christopher ran toward Brady, who was standing near the northeast corner of her house.* Photos showed his footprints in the wet grass and hers in the parking area's moist dirt. A diagram revealed the distance between her and Christopher when he'd started toward her: twenty feet and seven inches.

4. *Brady fired the gun found at the scene.* A ballistics report had just come in showing that the residue on Brady's hand and the bullets in Christopher's arm and thigh were from her gun, and shell casings found at the scene matched up. Diagrams and photos of the casings on the ground were added proof of where Brady had been standing because, as was typical, they'd fallen to the right and just behind her feet.

5. *Brady shot Christopher at close range; the first bullet didn't stop him, and he kept coming.* Photos of his blood showed where he'd fallen in Brady's parking area. DNA of the blood on Brady's uniform matched Christopher's. Diagrams indicated the location of his head and feet and the distance between his body and the shell casings from Brady's gun: seven feet.

Tom tossed his pen on the yellow pad and rubbed his eyes. He'd worked hard and lived through aggravation, but the findings made a verdict clear, as far as he could see. Brady's shoot was good. She was defending herself. If she'd gotten mad before she pulled the trigger, so be it. No law against anger.

Tom was still pondering when Jackson walked in with a two-foot hero sandwich, which filled the room with onion and salami smells.

"So how's it going?" Jackson pulled up a chair and sat across the table from him.

Colleagues had joked that Jackson should try intravenous feeding because he was such a sloppy eater. "Don't get mustard on these papers," Tom warned.

Jackson chuckled and pushed himself back a safe distance from the tabletop.

"Those sandwiches can fill you up for a day or two. You might ruin your Thanksgiving dinner," Tom said.

"A side of beef couldn't ruin my Thanksgiving dinner." Looking gleeful, Jackson took a hearty chomp. "You reached any conclusions?" he asked, his mouth full.

Tom nodded. "The evidence supports her story. The kid stabbed her dog and came at her. He meant business, and she shot to stop the threat. When he kept coming, she shot again. The force was necessary to save her life."

Jackson's cheek bulged with another hefty bite as he looked warily at Tom. "Aren't you forgetting her Taser? A blinding dose of Mace?"

"She said she didn't have time, and I agree with her. Look." Tom tossed a diagram of the crime scene toward him.

Jackson wiped his fingers on the paper towel he was using for a napkin and picked up the diagram. "What do you want me to see?"

"Christopher started over there." Tom leaned over and tapped his pen at the spot where Christopher had stabbed Justice. "She's over here." He pointed to where Brady was standing in her parking area. "Twenty feet, seven inches. The Twenty-One-Foot Rule applies." He didn't need to explain to Jackson that if you were less than twenty-one feet from a perp armed with a knife, he could run up and stab you before you could draw your gun, aim, and fire.

"The kid was an immediate threat. All Brady had time to do before he could kill her was shoot," Tom said. "It was *Graham versus Connor* pure and simple—her use of force was reasonable at the moment that kid came at her. If we'd been in her position, we'd have shot him too."

"So you're saying it's justifiable homicide," Jackson said.

"That's where the evidence points."

"It goes against my hunch."

"I don't know any other way to look at it. You've got to listen to the facts," Tom said.

"Except we're still not sure what was behind the whole damn thing."

"Yeah . . . well. We don't need the backstory to exonerate her."

Tom had wanted badly to get every duck in a row before winding up this case and handing over his report to anyone. But no one knew why Christopher had been violent, and his family surely hadn't shown any inclination to solve that mystery. Tom still didn't have Christopher's computer or cell phone, and he hadn't managed to get inside the kid's head. As much as Tom longed to congratulate himself for a job well done, he couldn't. *What happened to beginner's luck?*

"So you believe Brady didn't know Christopher and she had no idea why he attacked?" Jackson asked.

"I'm starting to believe her. She told the truth about everything else."

"She could have lied about their relationship."

"Maybe. But I'm thinking she didn't. We all know crazy things can come out of left field, and no cop with any sense would get mixed up with a San Julian High School kid."

When Jackson took another bite, in the silent room Tom could hear him chew. Mayonnaise had found its way to his earlobe, and a bit of sausage rested on his eyebrow.

Tom's eyes skimmed over the papers on the table. He'd done all he could to gather the facts; he couldn't feel bad about his work. Still, though the criminal part of the case might be over, there was plenty more that needed investigation. Unfortunately, Pederson would say there was no budget for it and he'd tell Tom to step down from the case.

But Tom wished he could keep digging for a motive. Hell, he'd crawl over broken glass to look for it even on his own time just as a matter of curiosity and honor—though working on his own was not allowed. Still, walking away from an unfinished job did not sit well with him. It was like getting a call about arson and leaving before the fire was out.

CHAPTER 25

ANDREA

Justice had his own internal Global Positioning System, and he could read Andie's mind. After she turned a few corners and stopped at familiar lights, he could figure out their destination when it was significant to him. If they were going to Mark Vargas's veterinary clinic, Justice got his most dispirited expression, flattened back his ears, and visibly drooped. If the destination was the Barkery, which sold gourmet dog biscuits, such as Beef Delights and Peanut Butter Wonders, he panted and marched his front paws in place on the car seat, hardly able to contain his excitement.

Today he'd clearly concluded that they were headed for the police station, his place of employment—his job! The corners of his mouth turned up in a German shepherd smile, and he pressed his nose against the windshield to get a better view of the road. At a high and fevered pitch, he whimpered, *Eeem! Eeef!* His other comments fell somewhere between a gargle and growl: *Grrrrrm! Mrrr!* Justice was letting the world know, *Wahoo! Hurrah! Hurry! Hurry! We're going back to work!*

Andie did not have the heart to point out to him that they might not be going back to work at all. Chief Malone had asked to meet with her, and he might fire or arrest her.

If she went to prison, she had no idea what would become of her beloved dog. Meghan would be the best choice for his family because he was fond of her and Rosemary. But he would want to continue as a K-9, and that would require teaming with an officer. Andie combed through a mental list of colleagues and weighed their pluses and minuses till her tortured thoughts became too much to bear. How could she ever entrust Justice to someone? She would be lost without him. He would never understand why she was giving him away, and he'd think she was casting him aside. He'd feel abandoned again. It would be unspeakably unfair.

Andie told herself, *Don't you dare cry.* She coughed and blinked so Justice wouldn't sense her sad thoughts. She gripped the steering wheel and drove on.

"Hey, Justice!" Bobbing in a swivel chair, Chief Malone patted him on the head as if he were dribbling Joey's basketball. Each time his hand whomped down, Justice's head bounced and involuntarily his upper teeth clicked against his lower.

Justice liked being gently petted on his star, but being bonked on the head was out of the question. *Never!* Too polite to snarl at his boss, however, he cast Andie a look of dismay. *This is intolerable.*

"Justice dragged me in here. He's really glad to be back," Andie told the Chief.

"Good, good. You had us worried, boy." When Malone reached out to dribble another round, Justice backed away and plopped down next to Andie, in a folding chair safely on the other side of the desk.

The Chief's messy office might have passed for another burrow in the rabbit-warren station. The tilted blinds subdued the light so you felt like you were a few feet underground. Overflowing the wastebasket were papers, which an industrious rabbit might have ripped up for a bed. An asparagus fern that could pass for a giant carrot top was shedding needle-y fronds on the linoleum floor.

"What about you, Brady? Holding up okay?" Malone asked.

"I'm fine!" She tried to make her facial expression match her words. "I miss everybody, but other than that, everything's good."

The Chief got up, crossed the room, and opened his metal file cabinet's top drawer. "I've got something of interest to you."

He pulled out what might have been a report, bound like a book with a plastic cover, and he handed it to Andie on the way back to his swivel chair, which squeaked under his weight. "Here's what Wolski came up with. His boss, the County Prosecutor, and I signed off on it. That's your copy. Take it home. Read it if you want."

In Andie's hands it felt as heavy as a barbell. She felt like she was holding her future, and she was scared to find out what it was. "Thanks," she said, barely audible. So close to a reckoning, it was hard to be tough.

"You'll be glad to know we all agree you acted within state and federal law and our department policy. It's a tragedy that Christopher Vanderwaal died, but you were right to shoot and protect yourself. It's a justifiable homicide."

The barbell in Andie's hands became a feather. For the first time in over a month, the stiffness in her shoulders eased, and she breathed a deep, relaxed breath. She felt more than relief; she felt like the Chief had issued her a ticket to a country called Freedom, and vindication was delicious. Sid King, his prejudiced colleagues, and the Islanders for Collaborative Policing could put "justifiable homicide" in their pipe and smoke it.

"Thank you, sir." Using facial muscles that had lain dormant for weeks, Andie smiled. A real smile.

She reached for Justice, who would now be her dog forever. No prison sentence would separate them! He got to his feet and looked at her, his head cocked as if he were checking that the palpable rush of emotion from her was positive and she didn't need assistance. She put her arms around his neck and hugged him. He licked her ear.

"I'm glad I could deliver good news," the Chief said. "Wolski did a bang-up job. His investigation was as steady and measured as he is. No one could have asked for more."

"I'll thank him." Next time Andie ran into him, she'd apologize too. She was sorry she'd gotten mad and called him biased. He'd only been doing his job.

"We need to talk about some things," the Chief continued. "This business isn't over. The press isn't going away anytime soon."

"Shouldn't Sid King back off once he hears I'm off the hook?"

"He won't. The Vanderwaals have hired a lawyer."

"A lawyer?" Andie should not have been surprised—these things happened when police used force, but, still, she reeled back in her chair. Malone had just stamped "void" on her ticket to Freedom. "Why?"

"The Vanderwaals think you and Christopher were . . . involved," Malone said.

"I didn't know him! How many times do I have to say it?" Andie lashed out, though the Vanderwaals, not the Chief, were her target.

Malone raised his hands, palms toward her to indicate, *Peace.* "I believe you didn't know him, Brady, but they don't. They claim their son would never hurt a fly, and the lawyer's pressuring us to find out what was going on. You can understand that they'd want an explanation."

"They should understand *I* want this nightmare to end. I did nothing to start it," Andie said, louder than was acceptable in a professional discussion. "And I don't have an explanation.

It's not like I haven't spent a gazillion hours trying to figure one out."

"I know. Nothing about this is easy." Andie's outburst must have caused the new foam in the corners of Malone's mouth. "I talked with Alan Pederson and Wolski this morning. We've worked out an arrangement so Wolski can earn overtime and keep investigating the case. He's glad about it. He wants to know what was going on with Christopher as much as you do."

That's hardly consoling. Who knows what Wolski might try to pin on me next?

"Wolski's bothered that he hasn't come across the kid's laptop and phone. He thinks that's where he'll find a motive," Malone said. "Just sit tight. Let this play out. I believe you didn't have anything to do with it. Wolski's inclined to agree."

"'Inclined' doesn't indicate a strong opinion," Andie said.

"He's on your side. I am too. We're just trying to avoid a lawsuit."

Andie shook her head, unnerved. A lawsuit meant she'd be under attack all over again. Discovery, depositions, and court appearances could drag on for years, and she could end up with a terrifying judgment against her.

But for now a lawsuit was too much to consider. She told herself, *Forget it! Don't borrow trouble. Pretend it doesn't exist!* With the same steel that fortified her wall, Andie shoved the possibility of a lawsuit out of her mind and shrugged back into her role as a tough, confident cop.

"You can come back to work as long as Capoletti agrees you're okay," Malone said. "Make another appointment with him."

"Yes, sir." *No fun there.* "If he clears me, could Justice ride with me right away? I know he can't run yet, but he's doing much better."

"That's fine."

The Chief got up and came toward Justice, who could read

his mind as well as Andie's. Justice knew perfectly well he was about to get bonked on the head again.

Pat, pat, pat. Bounce, bounce, bounce.

1. Justice is getting stronger and more limber. He'll be able to ride with me as soon as we go back to work. (And I *will* go back to work!)
2. Tom Wolski is "inclined" to believe there was nothing going on between me and Christopher. Maybe he'll stop confronting me.
3. I'm not going to prison! I won't be fired! Everybody agrees that I was right to shoot! It's justifiable homicide!

Andie put down her pen and stared at "justifiable," a verdict she'd longed for with such fervor, yet actually seeing the word was almost a shock. Her actions were deemed reasonable, defensible, legitimate. Everyone had agreed.

But then another word caught her eye: "right." Being justified to shoot and being *right* to shoot were vastly different. Her action may have been reasonable, but maybe it wasn't moral.

Though she'd expected exoneration to absolve her of wrong, again she asked herself, *Did I do the right thing?* The question sank its teeth into her and wouldn't let go.

Chapter 26

Tom

"Here, Sammy! Come on, girl!" Tom's whistle pierced the crisp December afternoon.

Her ears flopping, her feathery tail waving, his golden retriever galloped across the dog park toward him. As he'd worked for months to teach her, she sat in front of his toes.

Biscuit! Biscuit! I came when you called. Oh, please! begged her beautiful eyes.

No biscuit was forthcoming because Sammy had been looking pudgy lately and today Tom and Lisa were encouraging her to exercise. From across the park, Lisa called Sammy in a small, high-pitched voice and waved her red mittens. Sammy ran to her, then turned around and ran back when Tom shouted her name.

As she was halfway to him, a German shepherd darted across the meadow, ambushed Sammy, and leapt around her. He was hobbling slightly, but that didn't seem to dampen his excitement. *Come on! Let's play!* said his yips and bows.

"He wants to make friends. Do you mind?" A woman's voice behind Tom sounded familiar.

Puzzled, he turned around. He should have recognized the voice *and* the dog. Andrea Brady hurried toward him, her red hair flying. She was bundled up in a pink down coat, and her cheeks were pink from chasing Justice. Man, she was pretty.

"I'm sorry, Wolski. You don't have on your uniform, and I didn't recognize you from behind," she said.

I hardly recognize you head-on. She'd obviously gotten the good news from Chief Malone. What a difference it had made to wipe the resentment off her face. "I should have known it was Justice. I can't believe he's so much better. He's running almost like a normal dog, and it's not even been six weeks."

Two parallel vertical lines appeared between Andie's eyebrows. "It feels like a century."

Sorry about that. It took me a while to do my job. "Have you met Lisa?" In her red parka and ski hat, she was running around Justice and Sammy as they fake-growled at each other. Tom called Lisa over and told Andie, "She's my daughter. She's a little shy sometimes."

"I didn't know you had a daughter," Andie said.

"Best thing that ever happened to me. She lives with me on weekends."

"Oh."

Brady got the look that had crossed some women's faces when they'd added two plus two for the four of Tom's marital status. Usually, their eyes would sneak a glance at the fourth finger of his left hand, but Brady's eyes stayed on his face. She wasn't interested, not that it mattered.

Lisa arrived out of breath, her hat's pompom bouncing. "Dad, that dog likes Sammy."

"His name is Justice," Tom said. "This is his person. Andrea Brady. She's a San Julian cop."

"You don't look like a cop," Lisa said.

"I'm not wearing my uniform." Andie smiled.

Amazing. A first. And her smile didn't kill her.

"What's the weather going to be tomorrow, Lisa?" Tom asked.

"I already told you this morning," Lisa said.

"Tell Officer Brady. Show her what a good weather forecaster you're going to be."

Lisa sighed like her father was the king of dorks. She cleared her throat. "Okay, a storm is coming from the south-southwest. Temperature will be a low of thirty-eight, high of forty-three. Rain by midnight. The barometric pressure is falling. You can tell from all those birds over there." She pointed to crows roosting on a power line. "They're not flying around because the falling pressure hurts their ears."

"I didn't know that," Andie said.

"She surprises me all the time with what she knows," Tom said. "What kind of clouds, Lisa?"

"Da-ad, you said you'd learn the names."

"I've been busy lately." *Brady could vouch for that.*

"They're cumulonimbus." Lisa pronounced each syllable carefully, like she was talking around pebbles in her mouth. "They mean bad weather's coming."

"I'm impressed. Where'd you learn all this?" Andie asked.

"Some at school. I look online a lot."

"I have something you might like." Andie unzipped her black shoulder bag and rummaged around the way women did when Tom asked to see their driver's license. From the bottom of her purse, she pulled out a ring that looked like a plastic wedding band.

"Have you ever seen a mood ring? Here, take it. It's yours," Andie said.

Lisa shook off her mittens and tried the ring on her scrawny fingers, then slid it onto her thumb.

"The ring's a barometer of your feelings. When it changes color, it predicts your emotional weather," Andie said. "If it's black, you're stormy and scared. If it's pink, your sun is out, and you're happy."

Lisa beamed at Andie as if the sun rose compliments of her

each morning. *Good for Brady. Very kind,* Tom thought. He watched the ring slowly lighten to the blue-green of the Pacific on his and Mia's Hawaiian honeymoon, which he didn't particularly like to remember.

"Great color. Blue-green means you're in a good mood. You're pleased, upbeat," Andie told Lisa. "Watch out if it turns yellow because that means you're anxious. Or orange—you're angry or nervous. If you Google 'mood ring chart,' you can find out how to read every color."

"I'm going to hear her mood now along with her daily cloud report," Tom said. "What do you say, Lisa?"

"You don't have to tell me, Dad. I was getting ready to thank her."

"Sorry, kid."

Lisa hugged Andie, a shock to Tom. He'd never seen his shy daughter do anything like that to someone she'd just met.

"Thank you." Waving her hand—and her mood ring—she danced off toward Sammy and Justice, who were taking a sniffing break along the gravel path around the park. They were surely friends by now. If they were people, Justice would be asking Sammy for her phone number.

"Lisa's thrilled," Tom said. "I've never seen her warm up so fast to anyone before."

"I'm honored."

"Where'd you get the ring?"

Before Andie could respond, a woman with a long face stormed up to them. She was carrying a fox terrier whose woven leather collar sagged on her scraggly neck. "Is that your German shepherd?" she asked.

"Yes," Andie said.

"Off *leash* like that?!"

"This is a dog park. That's why there's a chain-link fence. The leash law doesn't apply here," Andie said.

"You shouldn't let a vicious dog like that run free around

that child. What are you *thinking?*" The woman shook an ink-stained finger at Andie. "Your dog could tear that girl to pieces, and he'd kill my Trixie with one bite. Thanks to you, I have to leave the park."

"You don't have to worry," Tom said. "That dog happens to be a K-9 in the San Julian Police Department. He's perfectly trained."

"I don't trust him. I've seen those dogs snarling in Nazi movies. They're unpredictable. I can't stand the sight of them." The woman hustled Trixie off to the dog park's gate.

Tom looked down at Andie. He'd seen that flush on her cheeks when her annoyance had been aimed at him. "I wonder what color her mood ring would turn."

"Neon orange. She's furious."

"It's her loss." As Tom glanced across the grass to check on Lisa, he pulled his muffler tight with his hands as if he were about to buff the back of his neck, like a shoe. "It must be hard to have a dog some people are so prejudiced against. I'm sorry you had to go through that."

When Andie didn't respond, Tom looked down at her again. Her face looked like she'd walked into her house and an unexpected crowd had shouted, *Happy birthday!* He asked, "Why the surprise?"

"No reason," Andie said.

"Because I have a heart?"

His honesty seemed to ruffle her. "Well, if you really want to know . . . I didn't realize you could be sympathetic. Toward me anyway."

"Because I was cruel and heartless during the investigation?" Tom's smile crinkled his face.

"You're harassing me." Andie's second smile for the afternoon told him she didn't mind.

"I know you thought I was after you, but I wasn't. I went into that case stone cold. I had to do my job," Tom said.

"You did a good one," Andie admitted. "I read every word of your report. I'm grateful you were careful and fair. Thank you. I'm sorry I got mad and called you biased."

"I've been called worse," Tom said.

Andie looked sincere. Her eyes were like deep green lakes when not a whisper of wind skims the surface. Tom never thought she'd have it in her to apologize. He'd misjudged plenty of people in his life, but he'd bet his next paycheck that Andrea Brady was honest. He felt sure she hadn't known Christopher Vanderwaal.

"Since it's legal for us to talk about the case now, do you have any idea why that kid came after you and Justice?" Tom asked.

"Not a clue. I swear. If I knew, I'd tell you."

"I'm still looking for a motive."

"So the Chief said." Andie pushed a strand of hair away from her face. "I'm happy to help you any way I can. We've got to figure it out."

She said "we." We! Brady, welcome aboard.

CHAPTER 27

ANDREA

On the ferry to Seattle, Justice stuck his head out of Andie's Honda window and, in ecstasy, sniffed the fishy smells. He pricked his ears at squawks of gulls circling the boat and watched suspicious passengers who might be sneaking in dope from Canada. Because he was so fond of the ferry, he looked downcast when the ride came to an end. Andie drove to a similarly downcast redbrick building on Capitol Hill and persuaded him to step onto an old squeaky elevator, which took them to Dr. Capoletti's second-floor office.

Located in a corner of the building, it was light and airy, and the many windows offered views of a small park. The high ceiling's molding looked like spiders had web-spinning contests on it, and batting was coming out of Dr. Capoletti's olive-green club chair. The covers of his sofa pillows needed ironing as badly as his shirt.

"So you found me all right," he said.

"Yes," Andie said politely. *This visit was coerced!*

She felt better about being forced to see Dr. Capoletti, however, when he got on his knees to meet Justice. He gave Justice a dog biscuit, just as Dr. Vargas always did, and patted him with more respect than Chief Malone had. Justice welcomed the attention with a friendly nuzzle to Dr. Capoletti's armpit. An Olympic champion of character assessment, Justice seemed to recognize the doctor's honest effort to be kind.

Justice accompanied Andie to the sofa and stretched out at her feet in his sphinx position so she could reach down for him, if needed. Today Andie had no intention of needing anything. She planned to get out of here as soon as possible; a quick all clear from Dr. Capoletti and she'd be back at work. Though she knew in her heart that she was still psychologically wounded, she would hide it. Whatever it took, she'd keep her feelings to herself.

"Chief Malone told me you've been exonerated. That's great news," he said.

"I was pretty relieved," Andie said. *Understatement of the year.*

"So how's it going?"

"Fine."

"Have you come to an answer about whether you did the right thing?"

"I'm still not sure. Some days I'd say yes. Others, no." *A tidy, noncommittal response.*

"Why would you think you didn't do right?" Dr. Capoletti asked.

"Oh, I don't know," Andie said, as casual as a breeze. "Maybe if I'd been less afraid, I could have handled Christopher better, and I wouldn't have shot him."

"You mean you should have been the perfect cop? Medal-of-honor brave no matter what you faced?"

"I should have kept my cool."

"I read the report. It sounded to me like you kept your cool just fine." From a table next to his chair, Dr. Capoletti picked up a tobacco tin, which he set between his knees. "Mind if I smoke?"

"No."

He pried open the tin's top and asked, "Have you always required yourself to be brave and strong?"

"No," Andie said, puzzled.

"How about when you were little? When your father died unexpectedly and your mother went to bed for weeks, and never fully recovered after that? During your hiring interviews, you told me you were only eight, but you had to take care of her and your brother. You called your best friend's mother to find out how to work a washing machine. Remember?"

"Yes. It was a difficult time."

"You said you were frightened, but you had to be strong. Do you think you should have handled Christopher the same way? Squashed down the fear? Been the superbrave cop?"

Andie could see where this was going. "I guess my reactions were the same," she admitted.

"Christopher's attack was very traumatic—perhaps as traumatizing as your father's death."

"What does my father's death have to do with what's happening now?" Andie asked.

"Because there's a link between the two events, and you're repeating a pattern," Dr. Capoletti said. "When horrible things happen to us, they can resurrect pain from earlier times. You may have tucked away your father's death so you don't think about it much these days, but it can make killing Christopher more difficult to deal with. You're handling a double whammy, past and present. Does that make sense?"

"Yes."

As Dr. Capoletti struck a match and puffed clouds of smoke that smelled like burning cherries, Andie's mind traveled back to her divorce, another time when she'd been blindsided and felt insecure and scared. She'd had to be strong then too. Her whammy wasn't double; it was triple. But she didn't feel like pointing it out and complicating the discussion.

"Being strong and brave can help you get through adversity, but it can block you from being honest with yourself and seeing that you're vulnerable," Dr. Capoletti said.

Andie insisted, "I'm really fine."

He waved his pipe through the air as if he were shooing away her denial. "When we last met, you said repeatedly that you were fine. You don't *have* to be fine. That's the point. You don't have to go through life always being strong."

"I understand," Andie said. "I really do. I get what you're saying." *Now can I go back to work?*

"I'm amazed how many police officers I meet like you who got pushed into adulthood too soon. They pick their career for the emotional security they missed out on as kids, or they want to control their environment since it was out of control when they grew up. Sound familiar?"

"Maybe," Andie hedged. "But why I joined the force doesn't matter."

"It might." Another cloud of burning-cherry smoke. "Christopher showed you that someone could kill you at any time, and you're not secure or in control. Lots of officers in your position would acknowledge they're vulnerable."

"I can live with it. I know how to protect myself if I'm attacked."

"I'm talking about more than physical safety here. I'm referring to emotional vulnerability." Dr. Capoletti puffed again. The room got quiet except for Justice's breathing. Andie didn't know what she should say, so she said nothing.

Finally, Dr. Capoletti asked, "Have you had any nightmares?"

"A couple." *Like all the time.*

"Want to tell me about them?"

"Oh, just that I was in a scary situation."

"Were you brave and strong?"

"In one I tried to shoot a gun that wouldn't go off."

"That's a typical anxiety dream. It could mirror your real-life anxiety," Dr. Capoletti said. "What would you say might be behind that dream?"

"Nothing that I know of. It didn't upset me." *That's a lie.*

Dr. Capoletti's face told Andie that he also suspected it was a lie—and silence settled between them again like a field of snow. Just like in the nightmares, Andie began to feel anxious. She feared that she was failing this interview and Dr. Capoletti would keep her on leave forever. Justice seemed to sense Andie's squirms, because he leaned against her ankle. "Please, can I go back to work?" she asked. "I really want to be there."

Dr. Capoletti closed his eyes like he was pondering. When he opened them, he said, "I was hoping you'd see that vulnerability is behind your anxious dreams. It's important to acknowledge it."

"I do. Really," Andie said. *Not true.*

Dr. Capoletti gripped a kneecap. "Okay." He paused. "I'll agree that you can go back to work on one condition. Last time we met, I warned you about nightmares, panic attacks, and flashbacks. If your nightmares continue or the other two get to be a problem, you come back and talk with me. As I said, they could be signs of something serious, like post-traumatic stress disorder."

"All right."

"And watch out for other emotional problems like anxiety and depression. I told you about them too. If bad feelings come up too often or linger too long, they can be pointing to bigger issues."

"Okay."

"Going back to work when you're still processing a trauma can help you get on track, but it might also distress you. You have to be honest with me about that."

"I will." Andie had always been proud of being an honest person. But she knew she couldn't pass a lie-detector test if challenged about a few of her comments today. She told herself to think of them as tiny fibs that she'd sprinkled into the conversation here and there. She may have glossed over the truth, but only a little, and she hadn't committed perjury under oath. Gently misleading someone didn't make her a criminal. Still, Dr. Capoletti was as perceptive as a mood ring. If she'd worn one here today, her anxiety would have turned it mustard yellow.

As Andie and Justice were leaving, she glanced at a poster behind Dr. Capoletti's desk. Written in loopy white script on a black background was: *A storm is as good a friend as sunshine.*

No, it's not, she thought. *I've had my share of storms, and they're no friends.* She led Justice down the hall to the elevator.

CHAPTER 28

The worst part about being in law enforcement was worrying about your family. For years Tom had imagined scenarios that put his teeth on edge: A driver resentful of Tom's speeding ticket could drag Lisa behind a Food Mart Dumpster and do unspeakable things to her. Or a hostile perp could get out of prison, kidnap her, and lock her in his basement for ten years. There were nutcases everywhere, and in Tom's line of work he'd met plenty. Including Franz Vanderwaal.

After a Nisqually County Board of Supervisors meeting last week, Chief Malone had taken Tom aside, put an arm around his shoulders, and informed him, "Vanderwaal is outraged at you." He had stormed into the station and snarled at the Chief, "How could any competent person conclude that Officer Brady should get off scot-free? Ever heard of miscarriages of justice? Somebody is going to pay!"

Tom was certain that he was Franz's "somebody," and, therefore, Lisa might be in his crosshairs too. Because she was small and innocent, she'd be an easy target. Franz, like Christopher, could come after Lisa with a knife on her school playground or in Mia's backyard. You could never tell what an intensely wound-up man like him might do. At times like these Tom could have used a protective dog like Justice.

On his and Lisa's last Skype call, he'd held up his gentle Sammy for her nightly wave and listened to Lisa's weather and cloud report. She told him that her mood ring was blue—so her emotional outlook was peaceful. *A good time for what I have to say.*

"Lisa, honey, I went to a wonderful private elementary school in San Julian today. You want to visit there with me on Friday afternoon?"

"Why?" She was so damned cute when she screwed up her little face. She'd pulled her hair back with bow-shaped barrettes, but rebellious tendrils wisped over her ears.

"I've been thinking you might like to go to school there starting next term. It's got a great academic reputation." *And a ten-foot spiked iron fence around the playground to keep out perverts and crazies.* "Besides the usual subjects, you can learn photography and Spanish. Even martial arts!" *One well-aimed kick to Franz's cojones, and you could have him writhing on the ground.* "The classes are small. Your fourth grade would only have twenty-one students, counting you." *The easier for your teacher to watch out for revengeful screwballs.*

"I don't want to change schools."

"You'd have field trips to the Seattle Aquarium and the Nisqually County Fair."

"I like my school now."

"Maybe you'd like this one even better."

"I'd miss my friends."

"They could visit you here on weekends. And you'd make new friends in no time."

"Da–ad. I don't want to go there."

"After I pick you up on Friday, let's just stop and look around for a minute. If you don't like it, we can leave."

"Yuck."

It was time for his ace in the hole. "The fourth-grade teacher said we could set up a small weather station for you in a corner of the classroom. I just found a perfect one online. I'll send you the link."

The kid's smile could light up a cave at midnight. "What's the station like?"

"It's got a sensor outside and a monitor you read indoors to find out about the temperature, humidity, rain, and wind speed and direction. It also tells you the moon phase, rainfall rate per hour, and other wonderful things I've never heard you talk about."

Lisa's eyes were as wide as silver dollars. "My *own* station? Not the school's?"

"All yours, and you can bring it home on holidays. The teacher was excited about it."

"Would I meet her on Friday too?"

"Yep."

Tom hung up and checked his bankbook balance. The tuition meant a sacrifice, and he might have to bribe Mia to drag herself out of bed half an hour early to get Lisa to San Julian. But anything to keep her safe.

CHAPTER 29

ANDREA

On her first day back at work, the dispatcher sent Andie to subdue two peace-disturbing neighbors, screaming at each other over their shared property line. One of the combatants, Dr. Jeremy Rosoff, was a short and squat cigar chomper, whose favorite gesture was shaking his fist. The other, Marigold Adams, looked refined in her suit and pearls, but she yelled like a drunken stevedore.

Justice flattened back his sensitive ears as he and Andie approached the mayhem. "I understand there's a problem here," she said.

Jeremy glowered at her and shook his fist at Marigold. "She started it."

"Look what that jackass did!" Marigold pointed at the fence between them.

It was eight feet tall, made of sturdy metal mesh. Newly planted along it on Jeremy's side was a line of Leland cypresses that would eventually grow to fifty feet and block the sun on Marigold's house. Every couple of yards just out of her reach if she wriggled her hand through the wire, he'd posted signs demanding: NO TRESPASSING! STAY OUT! In case Marigold didn't grasp the idea, there were other signs, of crossbones and skulls with hollow eyes and clacking teeth.

On one skull a pirate's scarf was tied at a jaunty angle above a black eye patch, hinting of plunder.

"For twenty-five years the former owners of his house let me have barbecues over there beyond those cypresses. Then he came along and decided to build his #@%★$ gazebo on our picnic spot," Marigold said.

"It's *my* property," Jeremy seethed.

"You've got five acres, and our tiny little spot meant nothing to you. You just wanted to be mean. You're a power-hungry SOB."

"That bitch was trying to take over my land!" Jeremy shouted.

"How about if we show some respect here. Calling each other names isn't going to solve anything," Andie said.

Justice, who was never keen on people he considered barbaric, bristled his eyebrows as if to do his own name-calling: *Those odious philistines. Those rancid savages.*

"I cleared a place for my gazebo. She set her wicker lawn chairs there and taped Do Not Remove signs to the seats. Can you believe that?!" Jeremy enlisted his fist into service again. "Every day I moved the chairs to her yard, and every night she snuck them back over here."

"Have you two tried sitting down and talking politely with each other?" Andie asked.

"I put up the fence to keep her out," Jeremy yelled. "The very next day I was here sawing wood for my gazebo and something whizzed by my head. She was hiding behind a bush and slinging dog shit onto my property!"

"You're not telling her what *you* did, you #!@★%^ pervert!" Marigold snapped. "I came out here the other day to water my camellias, and I looked over at the fence. He was *mooning* me! You have to arrest him for indecent exposure."

"Any video or photo of him, um, mooning?" Andie asked. "Without proof, it's he said, she said."

"I would never photograph *that*. He's the deviant, not me." Marigold looked at Andie like she had the intelligence of mold.

Andie squeezed her fingers tighter around Justice's leash and thought, *I want out of here*. In her weeks off work, she had gotten out of practice for handling wackos, and Justice looked like he had too. He turned his back to Jeremy and Marigold and let them know he had better ways to occupy his time, such as watching the neighborhood fir trees grow.

Before Christopher, Andie would have been glad to intervene in this fight. After Christopher, she knew how hard a cop's life could be, and all she wanted was to document this conflict and leave. She wanted to tell Jeremy and Marigold, *Grow up. You don't have time for stupidity like this. You could die tomorrow.*

She scribbled the San Julian court's phone number in her notebook, ripped out the page, and handed it to Marigold. "The city offers mediation. You two, give it a try."

CHAPTER 30

TOM

"Christopher Vanderwaal's homeroom teacher told me your English class was his favorite." Tom showed his badge to Miss Mildred Ware.

"His death was a terrible shock. You'd never expect a San Julian kid to come to a violent end like that." Miss Ware's delicate hand reached for the cameo pinned at her throat. Her black-framed reading glasses magnified her eyes.

Since she occupied the classroom's only chair, Tom dragged a student's desk up to hers so they could have a private conversation. Her planning period was about to start, and the room was quiet except for students talking and slamming locker doors in the hall. Glancing at a photo of Hemingway pinned to the bulletin board, Tom squeezed between the desk's seat and writing surface. High-school desks were not made for men his size.

"Was Christopher a good student?" he asked.

"He was intelligent, but he didn't live up to his potential. I'd say he was a solid C-plus," Miss Ware said. "Lots of days he'd sit at the back of the room and read novels while I taught. I'd leave him be. I figured he was doing something positive."

"Did he write very well?"

"Pretty well. He'd have been better if he'd applied himself," Miss Ware said. "He told me he kept a journal."

Bingo! A potential gold mine! "Where is it?"

"I don't know. I'm sorry." Miss Ware must have seen the disappointment around Tom's eyes, because she added, "Maybe it's in his house."

"We searched his room and school locker."

"He could have written on his laptop. Kids these days prefer to type rather than write by hand."

"Nobody knows where his laptop is."

"That's a shame." Miss Ware absently lined up three pencils on her desk.

"Do you still have any of his essays?" Tom asked.

"No. Once I grade them I hand them back," she said. "I can tell you that his best ones were personal experience, which is a lot like journal writing. Teens usually find it easier to tackle narratives about themselves than arguments about assigned topics."

"Do you remember any personal experience Christopher wrote about?"

Miss Ware ran her finger across the pedestal of a Shakespeare bust on her desk. "I guess I wouldn't be breaking confidentiality if I told you about his arrest."

Tom blinked. "Arrest" rippled through his brain. "I've never heard about it."

"Last year he and Kevin Engelbrit got caught stealing shirts from Northwest Threads. No reason for them to do such a thing. Their parents bought them perfectly good clothes. They were just acting out."

"You're *sure* they got arrested? I didn't come across any record of it."

"They spent the night in Nisqually County Juvenile Hall," Miss Ware said. "Christopher's description of it impressed me.

The specificity and vivid details. A believable tone of confusion and fear. It all rang true."

Hearing now about it fed the frustration that made Tom sometimes want to hang it up with law enforcement. He'd bet his last penny that the police and court records had been sealed. According to state law, no one could have access to them even after Christopher was dead.

The damned Vandervaals. Sure, Christopher had been as pure as the driven snow—no problems, no recent crises, nothing to upset him. Franz and Jane must have enjoyed holding back this information and thinking they'd duped Tom. He felt like wringing Franz's skinny neck.

Miss Ware's magnified eyes brightened. "I know how I can help you," she said. "Kevin Engelbrit is in my next class. He'll be here in a few minutes. You can ask him about the arrest."

Outside San Julian High School's entrance, Kevin Engelbrit aimed his shifty eyes at his grass-stained running shoes and worked his toe against a sidewalk crack. He was tall and gangly, no babe magnet, and he was clearly embarrassed to be seen talking with a sheriff's deputy as if he'd been robbing banks. As American and Washington State flags whipped in the wind above him, he fidgeted and shifted from foot to foot.

"So tell me about Christopher," Tom said. *With this kid, giving an order might work better than asking a question.* "I want to know if anything was going on with him before he attacked the officer."

Kevin shrugged. "I hadn't talked to him in a while."

"Then tell me about the two of you getting arrested."

"Nothing to tell," Kevin mumbled without looking up.

"I believe there is. Miss Ware said you and Christopher stole shirts."

"They weren't expensive. We gave them back."

"So how did you get caught?"

"The saleslady saw us stuff them into our backpacks. She called the police."

"Did a female officer come?" If Brady had answered that call, Christopher would have hated her and Tom would have his motive. He'd also know she'd withheld information far more important than Franz's DUI.

"I don't remember who came, but it wasn't a woman," Kevin said. He kept his eyes on the concrete as if it were studded with naked girls.

"Tell me about juvy," Tom said.

Kevin shrugged.

"How long were you and Christopher there?"

"One night."

"Then what?"

Kevin glanced at Tom as if he were a mentally deficient guppy. "We went home."

Contempt from a juvenile twerp is hard to bear. Tom restated the question: "The judge sentenced you to what?"

"We had to apologize to Northwest Threads' owner."

"That's all?"

"We had to pick up trash in Waterfront Park every other Saturday for four months."

"You must have been embarrassed when your friends saw you there." *Let the little bugger squirm.* "What about mandatory counseling?"

"Yeah. We did that."

Kevin couldn't seem to scrape out of his memory the name of his counselor, who might have led Tom to valuable information. "How did Christopher feel about counseling?"

"I don't know." Kevin shook his head. "He probably didn't hate it as much as the camp his parents sent him to."

"When?"

"Last summer."

"It wasn't part of the sentence? They sent him on their own?"

"I guess."

"What camp?" Tom asked.

"I don't remember."

Oh, right. Sometimes Tom's job took all his patience. "I think you do remember and you're choosing not to say."

Kevin shrugged his bony shoulders. "Just some camp in Oregon."

"Tell me the name," Tom demanded in his most authoritative voice.

Kevin shrugged again.

"If you don't tell me, I'll keep you out here all afternoon. At every class break, your classmates are going to see you talking to a deputy sheriff. They're going to wonder why."

"Sand Cliff. The name is Sand Cliff."

CHAPTER 31

ANDREA

The silver Audi was going sixty-two in a forty zone. "Got him with the speed gun," Andie told Justice. She turned on her flashing lights, pulled onto the road, and started following. Not surprisingly, when the driver saw her in his rearview mirror, he slowed to a crawl and sneaked his seat belt across his chest. Andie had seen this act of stealth more times than she could count.

When she got close enough to read the license plate, she typed it into her computer and saw that the car's owner had no criminal history. That was no guarantee she'd be safe approaching him. He could be a milquetoast in a clerical collar or a raging nutcase with guns piled in the backseat and plans to shoot up a shopping mall. On traffic stops, as with most official tasks, police never knew what they were going to meet.

When the Audi driver pulled over to the side of Koura Road, Andie let the dispatcher know her location and the speeder's license plate number. She told Justice, "Back in a minute."

His whimpers told her unambiguously that he did not like being left behind when these stops could be dangerous—and when the toll they now took on her was greater than it had been before Christopher's attack. She used to feel more confident approaching traffic violators, but now from the rise in her stress hormones and heart rate he could tell she was uneasy. Justice strained to watch her through the bars confining him to the backseat.

As Andie walked toward the Audi, she hoped the driver wouldn't be a Stop and Go, who dutifully pulled over but zoomed away as she approached his car. Maybe he'd be the kind who'd apologize profusely and claim he was rushing to the hospital to meet his wife in labor—and wouldn't you know that their last baby popped out in five minutes! Or he'd claim, *No speak English,* and Andie would have the pleasure of mentioning the twenty-dollar bill on his passenger seat, and catching him when he turned his head to look.

The Audi driver unrolled his window and gave her a megawatt smile. His eyeteeth were unusually pointed; if he'd auditioned to be a movie's werewolf, he'd have gotten the job. "Well, hi there," he said as if Andie had pulled him over to offer him a box of chocolates.

"Good afternoon, sir," Andie said.

"Why are you stopping me?"

If lambs could be so innocent. "You were going sixty-two in a forty-mile-an-hour zone."

Gasp. "Sixty-two?! Surely not."

"I'm afraid so, sir. May I have your driver's license, car registration, and proof of insurance?"

Andie did not take her eyes off his hands as he shuffled through the glove compartment, because drivers had been known to pull out guns and aim them at police. When he leaned forward to work the wallet from his back pocket, she also watched him carefully—who knew what he might reach for?

He opened his wallet and dawdled around, flipping through credit cards and photos. He whipped out a picture of his twin daughters with their beagle. "Aren't my girls cute? They're only six."

I'm not here to make friends.

He handed Andie the requested documents in one fistful and claimed, "I've got a great driving record."

That's what they all say. On his license she noted that he was James Galloway, five foot ten, 180 pounds, black hair, brown eyes. He lived on San Julian's upscale Shoreline Road.

"Are you going to give me a speeding ticket?" Another megawatt smile, more pointed teeth.

"Yes, Mr. Galloway." *I'll forget the seat belt. One violation is enough for now.*

Learning that his charm had not dissuaded her seemed to flip a switch inside him. The curve of his smile flattened to a hostile line. "Do you go after innocent people to meet a quota? Does your station need new computers or something?"

"No quota." She knew better than to argue. "I'm going back—"

"My tax dollars pay your wages," he said. "Don't you have anything better to do than harass me?"

"I'm going to my car for a minute, sir. Wait here." Andie walked away backward in order to keep her eyes on him.

Justice welcomed her to the car with small disapproving huffs of breath that let her know he did not appreciate being locked up when she needed his protection. "Just a few more minutes, and we'll be done," Andie told him.

She radioed the dispatcher her badge number, then James Galloway's name, date of birth, and license plate and driver's license numbers. She waited. In less than a minute the dispatcher said, "The driver has numerous previous incidents and parking violations. In the last twelve months a car with that license plate was stopped on January seventeenth, August third, and October twenty-eighth." *No news there. Everybody lies to cops.*

As Andie wrote up Mr. Galloway's ticket, he glared at her in his rearview mirror. If eyes could talk, his would have shouted obscenities worse than any from Marigold Adams. At least his $247 fine might teach him a lesson. There had been too many accidents on Koura Road, especially when rain slicked the asphalt.

Andie handed Mr. Galloway his driver's license, documents, and ticket. He knew he'd been defeated, but he was not the type to slink away, chastised. He flashed his yellowish eyes. "I know who you are. I remember now."

Andie replied, crisp as celery, "I'm a San Julian police officer."

"Just barely you are. You're the cop who shot the kid. I saw your picture on TV."

Andie's stomach tied itself into a full hitch. Her breath caught in her throat.

"You lucked out. You should have been fired," Galloway said.

"The investigation proved my action was justified." *Don't argue!*

"That's ridiculous. I'm a lawyer. I can tell you, what you did was criminal. You should have lost your job, and I could make sure you do." Galloway closed his window and let Andie know that he'd spoken his last word on the matter. He had the good sense not to stomp on his accelerator and speed away. But before Andie could get back to her patrol car, he was pushing forty down Koura.

She was sweating and shaking. Dr. Capoletti would warn her again that post-traumatic stress could intensify emotions. She climbed into her car, rested her forehead on the steering wheel, and closed her eyes. On the backs of her lids, Christopher ran at her waving his knife.

"I can't get away from that terrible night. Either I think of Christopher on my own, or somebody reminds me," she told Justice. Galloway's threat that he could get her fired had not distressed her as much as his attack catching her off guard. *Just as Christopher's had.*

Justice's reassuring breaths warmed the back of her head. He pressed his face against the bars to nuzzle her, but she was out of reach. His soft whines informed her, *I am here. Do not worry. If you'd let me, I'd have sunk my teeth into that man's gizzard.* When Andie put her hand against the bars, he licked her fingers.

"I feel like it's never going to end," she told him as a black cloud of despair settled over her.

CHAPTER 32

TOM

It was Shop with a Cop day, when San Julian and Nisqually County law enforcement officers took thirty disadvantaged first graders to Christmas shop at Target. As their delighted shrieks drowned out Muzak carols, the kids dragged their assigned officers along the aisles and piled gifts for their families into red carts. After the children had spent their allotted hundred dollars, they stampeded Stephanie and other department staff at a gift-wrapping station by the entrance.

There, in an alcove next to it, Tom, Andie, and Justice were waiting.

For the past few years Alan Pedersen had been Santa, but this year he was having an emergency root canal, and at the last minute he'd roped Tom into the job. He'd warned Tom that frightened or excited children might have accidents or throw up on him, so all morning Tom had been perfecting his ho-ho-hos to boom without being scary or manic. In a rented red velvet Santa outfit and a prosthetic belly, he sat on a folding chair, surrounded by artificial snow and Christmas trees, whose lights radiated heat. Tom began to sweat. After just eight on-the-knee chats, his damp moustache began slipping over his mouth, perilously close to blowing his cover—and he still had twenty-two children to go.

He gestured to Andie to send over the next kid. Andie was dressed in a green elf suit with red trim, a red conical hat, green tights, and red shoes whose toes curled up to points. Her job was to keep the children in an orderly line, and Justice was supposed to amuse them while they waited their turn on Santa's lap. Justice had not been keen on his fuzzy red reindeer antlers, but once the kids arrived he got into his role.

This was his second year as Rudolph, and he loved children. Like a therapy dog, he let them fuss over him. He listened to their secrets and nuzzled them. He washed their faces with his tongue.

A girl with fleece mittens hanging by a string around her neck finished petting him and bounded over to Tom. She straddled his knees and placed her hands on his shoulders as if she were claiming him as a personal possession. "I want a unicorn," she said.

"Er . . . that's a pretty tall order," Tom said. "Usually, I bring kids toys."

Her disillusioned eyes slanted down at the edges. "But that's not what I want."

We don't always get what we want in life, kid; I'm sorry to tell you. "I'll have to think about a unicorn," Tom said to stall. The cardinal rule for Santas was never to promise anything, because they did not know what a kid's parents could find or afford. But even the most indulgent parent wasn't going to find a unicorn to leave under the Christmas tree. "Unicorns are rare," Tom said. "Don't you want a doll or something?"

"No." She pushed out her lower lip.

"Okay, I'll see what I can do. No promises, and don't get your hopes up too high." Tom dreaded her disappointment on Christmas morning when no unicorn would be ransacking her house for breakfast.

As Tom gestured to Andie to send the next kid in line, he

pretended to scratch his nose so he could sneak his moustache back into place. But it slid off-center and lower than before. He'd be caught if he adjusted it again. "Hi there, kiddo! Nice blue hat."

The boy studied the linoleum floor but finally worked his gaze up to Tom's right shoulder. He didn't climb onto Tom's knee.

"What do you want for Christmas?"

"I don't want toys," the boy said.

Oh, brother. Don't tell me you want a unicorn. "So what should Santa bring you?"

"My dad. He's in Afghanistan. I want him to come home."

Gulp. You poor kid. Today Tom had signed up to talk about toys. He never expected a wrenched gut. "Santa can't make decisions about the military," he said. "Tell you what. When I'm flying around the world on Christmas Eve, I'll stop and check on your dad. Would that help?"

The boy nodded.

Tom wanted to hug him, buy him a plane ticket to Kabul, do anything to wipe the sadness off that face. "What branch of the military is your dad in?"

"Marines."

Tom almost said, *I used to be a Marine,* but he caught himself just in time—Santa wouldn't dream of signing up for war. "I'll bet your dad would love to be with you this Christmas. I'll tell him you miss him, okay?"

The boy nodded again. Tom wished he could spend the afternoon bolstering the kid's morale, but a line of children was waiting. It hurt Tom to tell Andie, "Next."

For the rest of his Santa stint, he tried—and failed—to keep his moustache in place, but the kids seemed willing to suspend disbelief. He got requests for an octopus and walrus— *How do kids come up with these things?* They asked for a smartwatch, quadcopter drone, Tag Solar System Adventure Pack, lizard robot, telescope, soccer ball, butterfly garden, and American Girl doll.

A boy announced that he didn't believe in Santa Claus, and Tom urged him not to tell the other kids. Another boy opened his grubby little hand, and onto Tom's palm he dropped a piece of bubblegum for a Christmas gift. "Oh, wow! This is great! I usually get the same old cookies and milk," Tom said.

Finally, at the end of the line, a girl with a patch on her tights' knee asked if Santa was fat because he ate children who got up early on Christmas morning. "That's what my mother said."

Tom ho-ho-hoed. "I've never eaten a child," he told her. "Tell you what. Why don't you let your mother sleep in sometimes? I'll bet she'd be happy about it."

Tom collected his and Andie's coats from behind a Christmas tree and finally got his moustache in place. As he helped her into her coat, he noted how pretty she looked in her elf outfit—great legs in those tights, her red hair puffed out around the pointed hat. His palm barely touching her back, he guided her and Justice through the crowd toward the entrance. After the gifts were stored on the bus, the officers were supposed to wave the kids good-bye.

Outside in the dusk, wind blew in Tom's face; Lisa's new weather station might measure the velocity at twenty-five miles an hour. Rain was falling, bad news when Santa and his elf had no umbrellas. Tom was about to suggest they make a run for their cars when lights shone in their faces.

Unsure of the source, Tom squinted against the brightness, then realized a TV camera crew surrounded them. *Wonderful! Publicity for a good cause.* He told Andie, "A local station must be covering Shop with a Cop for the ten o'clock news."

Wrong.

Sid King rushed up to Andie and thrust a microphone in her face. Looking like she'd had the props knocked out from under her, she shrank back. Justice pushed between them and growled.

Tom grabbed Andie's hand and felt her melt against him. "Come on. Let's get out of here. I'll take you to your car."

In the mob of kids, he had to strain to hear her ask, "How did he know I was here?"

"I have no idea."

Sid shouted, "Officer Brady, how do you feel about being an elf when Christopher Vanderwaal will never have another Christmas?"

"I feel . . . um . . ."

"Don't answer that jerk." Tom wouldn't mind punching Sid King.

Justice barked.

As Tom pulled Andie toward the car, the cameraman and crew walked backward just ahead of them, their lens and lights aimed at her flushed face, the red recording light bright.

"Officer Brady, are you aware that the investigation into your use of force is going to continue?" Sid's eyes glittered schadenfreude.

Tom extended his fingers so his hand looked like a giant asterisk, and he covered the camera lens. "Have some decency. We've been making these kids happy today. This isn't the time or place for your questions."

Sid tried to brush Tom's hand off the lens, but Tom held on like a bolt screwed into iron. Sid sputtered, "You can't shut us off like this. Ever hear of freedom of speech?"

"Get out of here," Tom said.

"It's a public place."

"And you're disturbing the peace. I'll be glad to arrest you." As Tom hustled Andie away, it crossed his mind that he liked protecting her.

CHAPTER 33

ANDREA

"All clear, Brady. Bring Justice to search," Tom's voice crackled on the radio. "Raid complete. Target missed."

Oh, no. Not again. "I'm on my way."

Justice, officially back to his drug-sniffing duties, jumped out of the patrol car, where they'd waited down the street from the ramshackle Victorian farmhouse of Ramon Garcia, otherwise known as the Beast. Tipped off about a heroin delivery, Tom and three deputies had turned off the Beast's water to keep him from flushing drugs down the toilet and his gas to prevent a fire. They'd knocked, cool and calm, like they were his best buddies, and lured his girlfriend, Belle, to the door. Then, guns drawn, they'd burst inside to grab him, but once again he'd outfoxed the law.

As the screen door slammed behind them, Andie and Justice stepped into the house. Belle flicked an unfiltered cigarette's ashes onto the floor and informed Tom that Ramon was visiting his mother, but she didn't know her name or address. Belle had the gaunt, inch-from-death appearance of a long-time addict. Her eyes looked as empty as those in the skulls on Jeremy Rosoff's NO TRESPASSING! signs.

One glance at the living room and Andie wanted to run outside and disinfect her shoes and Justice's paws. The house smelled decidedly of cat and rotting food, but that was the least of it. The sky might have opened up and dropped the entire state of Washington's litter onto the floor. To move around, she had to wade through debris of glass, paper, tin, plastic, rubber, and Styrofoam. An appalling sofa no sane person would sit on faced an old-model large-screen TV, the type that dealers were known to hollow out for hiding drugs.

"It's all yours, Brady. We'll stay out of the way." As Tom escorted Belle outside, he greeted Justice, who nosed his hand to ask for pets. Clearly, Justice remembered that Tom had rescued Andie from Sid King, and he'd decided Tom was honorable and worthy. Andie, who'd mentioned him in her gratitude list that night, had said he'd been "exactly what I needed."

Today she wanted to find the stash especially for Tom but also for every Nisqually County law enforcement officer who'd been trying for years to put the Beast behind bars. Though Justice might not have understood the urgency, he knew important business lay ahead. His ears alert, his face intent, he assumed his ready-willing-and-able posture.

Andie walked him into the kitchen. To show him where to sniff, she tapped gloved knuckles on the cabinets, whose doors were smeared with peanut butter and whose interiors were cluttered with trash. On the counter, Justice checked around half-drunk cups of coffee containing floating cigarettes. He and Andie searched the garbage can, refrigerator, oven, and sink, piled with dirty dishes covered with grease that cockroaches might have body-sledded down.

Justice's sniffer was in high gear, but he did not sit to signal that he'd detected drugs. If he'd spoken Spanish like the Beast, he'd have said about the kitchen, *Nada*. So Andie led him into the bedroom to another ocean of rubbish, sticking out of which like an island was a stained and verminous mattress.

On the dresser top's peeling veneer, Andie found syringes, lighters, and spoons for heating tar. She sealed the syringes in biohazard bags and the rest in plastic evidence bags, then rummaged through the drawers—and found nothing but more grunge.

"The stash has got to be somewhere," she told Justice as they went to the shriek-worthy bathroom. Surely in the last century no one had cleaned the toilet, and the mother of all molds fuzzed the shower walls. Just inside the doorway, Justice, who was a fastidious dog, froze with disgust and dug his nails into the grimy linoleum. He could not have said more emphatically, *I do not want to enter this foul and loathsome place.*

Nevertheless, he dutifully sniffed. In the medicine chest above the sink, Andie found and tossed into evidence bags four empty plastic vials that had once held OxyContin and Percocet, prescribed to Belle and picked up at a Nevada pharmacy. Andie lifted the lid off the toilet's tank, as dealers were known to hide drugs in waterproof containers there. Nada again. And worry.

As Andie and Justice continued searching the house, each stash-free room concerned her more. How reliable was Tom's nark anyway? Surely the whole afternoon hadn't been a waste of time. But maybe it had. Andie could tell that Justice was becoming as discouraged as she was.

To give his premium sniffer a rest, she decided to take him outside. As they passed through the living room, she noticed a paisley shawl covering a narrow table and hanging nearly to the floor. When she pushed the shawl aside, she found a heater vent she'd missed the first time through. She tapped. Justice sniffed and sat, unwavering and resolute. He locked eyes with Andie. *Here! Now!*

Please, let there be a needle in our haystack, Andie thought as she knelt down and unscrewed the vent. She shone her flashlight into the furnace duct and stuck in her arm.

Eureka! Got him! The Beast had underestimated Justice's nose. Tucked almost out of reach in a plastic bag were one-ounce balls of tar, packaged in newspaper squares, which the Beast had folded into envelopes. There were dozens of them, ready to sell on the street—enough to lock him away for a good long time.

Justice knew he'd accomplished something important. In his glory, he swaggered out the front door and unmistakably announced to the world, *We did it!* He acted like he expected a band to play "Hail to the Chief."

To reward him for his hard work, Andie offered his tug toy and dragged him by his teeth along the street. He tugged. She tugged. Back and forth they went till she finally let him win and he pranced, victorious, to Tom, who was standing in the side yard, his feet apart and his hands clasped behind him.

The other deputies had taken Belle to the Sheriff's Department for questioning, but Tom was waiting for Justice and Andie. "We'll get the Beast. He can't hide from us forever. Just a matter of time."

Tom got on his knees and showered Justice with congratulatory pets, which he received in his most confident maharaja position. As Andie watched, she was drawn to Tom's hands smoothing Justice's fur. They were strong, honest hands that she could imagine wielding a hammer and wrestling a bad guy. Though trained to punch and whack, his hands were now delivering gentle touches. Andie noted the contradiction and Justice's pleasure.

To stop herself from staring at Tom's hands, she knelt beside him and kissed Justice's forehead star. "He deserves every hug and pet we can give him," she said.

"I knew he could do it. He's a great dog," Tom said.

When their shoulders brushed, Andie felt his warmth radiate toward her. Their elbows bumped, but neither she nor Tom moved away.

"I have news for you. Sid King ruined my chance to tell

you after Shop with a Cop." Tom got up and grabbed Andie's hand to help her up, though she was perfectly capable of standing on her own. "I talked with Christopher's English teacher and his best friend."

"He has a best *friend?*"

"Kevin Engelbrit," Tom said. "Jane and Franz were lying about Christopher staying to himself. Turns out there's lots they *forgot* to mention."

As Justice snapped up his tug toy and continued to prance, Tom described the interviews and explained Christopher's arrest and the sealed records. "Franz and Jane sent him to an Oregon camp for troubled kids. I'm going there tomorrow."

Eyes wide, Andie shook her head. "I figured something bad was going on with Christopher, but I thought it was only family problems."

"I'm sure they were part of it. Looks like something had been building up in him for a while."

"Why would he steal shirts?" Andie asked.

"Probably just rebelling. Or doing a trial run before stealing something more valuable," Tom said. "He might have wanted money. Just because drugs weren't in his system when he died, it doesn't mean he never did business with the Beast."

"Could he have been wrongly arrested?"

"He admitted stealing shirts in an essay for his English class."

Distracted, Andie rubbed her forehead. "I don't know who the real Christopher was anymore. This makes me sad."

"I thought you'd be happy. We're finally getting an honest picture of that kid."

"How can I be happy? I killed him. I still feel terrible about it. He was a human being."

"And he stabbed Justice and wanted to stab you," Tom reminded her. "From the get-go he was a delinquent. We can feel sorry about whatever got him moving in that direction, but he's still earned some disapproval."

"I don't know. My feelings are more complicated than that." Andie's exhale seemed weighted with sand.

"Brady, you've got to make peace with this."

"Easy for you to say."

Tom narrowed his eyes. "You can't let Christopher ruin your life."

"Have you ever killed somebody?"

"No, but I came close in Seattle once," Tom said. "Look, I know how hard it is to shoot someone, and killing him would be even worse. For sure you can't forget it. But Christopher attacked you. You need to look at it right."

"How else can I look at being responsible for somebody's death? You're not seeing how painful that is."

"You're not helping yourself."

Andie bit her lip as her barometer cheeks reddened. He didn't get it. *Go ahead. Tell me how I'm wrong, and tell me what to do. Act like my lord and master.* "You can't expect me to shrug off killing a troubled kid," Andie said.

"I didn't mean it that way. Nobody can shrug off a death. I understand that."

No, he didn't understand. Andie had let down her guard and told him too much. Once again he'd managed to weasel behind her wall, and she resented it. She turned away and said, "Justice needs to go home."

CHAPTER 34

TOM

Tom had planned to ask Andie to come with him to Oregon, but he'd changed his mind after she'd left the Beast's house in such a rush. Her moods seemed to jump all over the map. She'd be approachable one minute, then turn on him the next. Maybe he'd gone a little heavy on advice, but he'd been trying to help.

Forget it. So much for her. Tom had more important things to think about right now.

Swallowing against the bad taste she'd left in his mouth, Tom turned off the highway at the Sand Cliff Camp sign he'd been told to look for and traveled down a dirt road. The camp, he soon saw, had no sand and no cliff. It was in the middle of woods so thick that the sun had to fight its way through the fir trees just to dapple the ferns and sorrel. It would be dismal here on a stormy day; no wonder campers came only in summer.

He parked beside the central log cabin. It was about the size of San Julian High School's gym. Around it were shabby Quonset huts for dorms, connected by a maze of paths. Along one of them, Tom found Christopher's counselor, Matt Stone, digging a trench for electrical wiring.

He was dour and bristly. A machete might have been the best shaving tool for his stubble, and his buzz cut was as stiff as a vegetable brush. When Tom introduced himself, he wondered how kids would like a counselor who looked like he smiled maybe once a month.

"Working hard?" Tom asked.

"We upgrade when the camp's closed," Matt grumbled. "The director decreed electricity had to go to the dorms to charge electronics. There's a pandemic of affluenza here."

"Lots of entitled brats in the world," Tom said.

"Tell me about it," Matt said.

"I'd think your boot camp would bring them down a peg."

"We're not a boot camp. Those programs scare the bejesus out of kids so they never misbehave again, but we offer wilderness therapy that lets nature heal them. We support the campers so they figure out their lives themselves."

Except the campers might not figure out much around someone so stern, Tom thought. "Did wilderness therapy help Christopher Vanderwaal?"

Matt looked like he'd just found a slug curled up in the bottom of his beer. "That kid was one of our failures. A closet sociopath."

That sounded harsh for a teen who'd only stolen shirts. "Most people I interviewed said he was neat and polite," Tom said.

"Neat, polite kids can be the ones you have to watch the most. They look like they've just left Sunday school, but under that wholesome exterior can beat the heart of a psycho."

"So Christopher was that bad?"

"Not for the first few days, but he showed his true colors on a camping trip with five other boys." Matt rammed his shovel into the loose dirt he'd piled up, and leaned his elbow on the handle. "I'd pegged that kid as shy and weak. A follower, you know? Turns out he got the other boys to follow *him.* They threw this camp into an uproar."

"How?"

"I'd been showing the campers how to get a fire going without matches. I was rolling the spindle between my hands and waiting for an ember. All of a sudden the six little bastards jumped me. Never happened at this camp before or since."

"You couldn't fight them off?"

Matt scoffed. "Ever had a pack of teenage boys drag you to the ground? Six of them, one of me. I fought and kicked. Then I thought, how am I going to explain their bruises on Parents' Day?"

Matt wiped sweat off his forehead with the back of his arm. Digging had warmed him, but recalling that camping trip also seemed to resurrect the heat of anger. The kids had beaten him up, Matt admitted, and Christopher had kept yelling, "Break his leg!" They'd tied Matt to a tree with the rope for setting up tents and taken off into the woods.

Tom made sure his jaw didn't drop; he couldn't appear so professionally unseasoned that any delinquent's story could take him by surprise. Still, he could hardly believe that Christopher had led a revolt. It sounded like a missing link between his arrest for theft and his attack on Justice and Andie; step by step, Christopher had progressed from mere acting out to increasingly violent behavior.

"I assume you rounded up the kids," Tom said.

"We had search parties, and helicopters flew around here for a few days," Matt said. "We tried to keep it quiet. Parents don't want to send their kids to a place like *Lord of the Flies*."

"But you pressed charges," Tom said, as if only a fool would refrain from going after those kids. He pictured more sealed police and court records, more frustration.

"Nope. No charges," Matt said. "The director nixed arrests, but he did expel the boys. A lot of hard feelings all the way around, I can tell you."

"Any idea why Christopher turned out to be sadistic?" *Toward Matt, then Justice and Brady*. If Andie hadn't killed him, he might have moved on to shooting up his high school.

"Ninety-nine percent of our campers come from dysfunctional families, or bad genes get thrown into the mix. If Christopher had stayed here longer, our one-on-one mentoring sessions might have gotten through to him, but I wouldn't bet on it."

"He was sure screwed up." Tom had seen too many teens like that—and always a waste of potential. It was hard to intercept the self-destructive downward spiral and turn those lives around.

"I never got a very clear sense of him because he didn't mix much. That's why I was shocked the other boys went along with him."

"Was he withdrawn?"

"Yeah. He hung around waiting for the mail every day. The only thing he seemed to care about was letters from his girlfriend."

Girlfriend?!

CHAPTER 35

ANDREA

Andie lost half an hour waiting for the cooling of her COP cakes—so named for their coconut, oats, and pears. They'd made her late for Chief Malone's department Christmas party, to which Justice, as a valued member of the force, had also been invited. To dress him up for the occasion, Andie had tied a red satin bow around his neck. She'd fed him dinner with hopes it might keep him from cornering colleagues and persuading them to share their Buffalo chicken wings.

She hurried Justice to her Honda, where he settled on the passenger seat and quickly marked the window with his damp, coal-lump nose. Though late, at the end of her driveway she stopped, hunkered under her coat's hood, and jumped out of the car. She intended to tie a red bow like Justice's around her mailbox post—her only Christmas gesture, since she'd not mustered the holiday spirit for her usual tree, wreath, and lights. *Better a little something than nothing,* she thought.

Her skirt flapping in the wind, Andie snipped the ribbon from a spool and looped the piece around the post. As she started to tie the bow in place, a black SUV approached. Its wipers squawked across the windshield as it drove by Andie, then stopped. The brake lights turned the forest red. The car backed up and parked next to the mailbox. Jane Vanderwaal stepped down onto the road.

"You're decorating for Christmas," she said.

Andie was used to Jane sounding tired and remote, but now her voice had an accusatory edge. "It's just a bow," Andie said.

"*You're* going to have a happy Christmas. What do you think it's going to be like for *us?*"

Andie froze, unsure how to answer. She could point out that her Christmas wasn't going to be a cup of egg nog, either, and she'd had to scrape together fortitude to leave her house tonight. She could take this opportunity at last to tell Jane that she was sorry. But Jane seemed too angry for an honest conversation.

"I'm not sure how happy my Christmas is going to be," Andie admitted. "You can bet I'll be thinking of Christopher." *I think of him dozens of times every day.*

Jane wound an end of her paisley scarf around her hand as a nurse might wind tape around injured fingers. Her glower pressed down her eyebrows. "I've been saving up things I want to say to you," she began. "For one, you're a liar. Christopher would never have hurt you or anyone. For another, Tom Wolski covered for you. From the start, he and his team were biased against my son. It wasn't fair you got off so easily."

Jane's heated words scorched Andie's cheeks. Feeling ambushed, she backed up to put more space between herself and Jane and left the partly tied red ribbon hanging in the wind. She started to speak, then strained to corral the right words to defend herself. Finally, she said, "Maybe you don't realize there's factual evidence. Christopher's fingerprints and DNA were on the knife he had in his hand when he stabbed my dog and intended to stab me."

"I don't know how you got his DNA and prints on that knife, but you planted it." Jane's lips were taut.

"I didn't. Honestly." *Don't get defensive. Don't argue with her.* Andie marshaled her training for dealing with explosive people and offered empathy. "You have every reason to grieve. I'm sure you're upset."

"I'm outraged." Emotion twisted Jane's face. "You never should have been found innocent. What you did was a crime. Even if half of what you claimed was true—and I don't believe any of it—you should have handled my son better. You didn't have to shoot him."

Andie felt the wind knocked out of her. Christopher's mother had just put into words the very thing that had threatened to overtake her since that night—her own personal black hole. "Doubt" had become too weak a word for such a devouring thing. Its gravity pulled her closer to certainty that she'd been wrong to shoot. She said, "I had to protect myself." But the words sounded flimsy.

"If you were protecting yourself from anything, it was from being found out. You didn't tell Tom Wolski your whole sordid story." In the rain Jane's mascara ran down her cheeks.

"There was nothing sordid!" Andie insisted.

"You should be in prison. Your crime is going to catch up with you. You'll have to live with yourself. Someday you'll be sorry for murdering an innocent boy."

"Jane—" Andie wanted to reason with her.

"You don't have kids. You could never understand." Jane stormed back to her car and climbed in. Just before she slammed the door, she shouted, "I hate you!" As she stomped on the accelerator, the squeal of her tires reverberated through the woods. She roared down Valley Road as if she wished she could run down Andie.

Andie forgot the ribbon and walked unsteadily back to her car. When she climbed into it, Justice's bow looked too merry. Tonight there were no bells to jingle. There was no joy to the world.

She could never go to the party now. She drove back down her driveway. When she and Justice got into the house, the phone was ringing.

"Where are you?" Stephanie asked.

The buzz of conversation in the background told Andie that the party was in full swing. "I'm home."

"Duh. I just called your home phone number," Stephanie said. "Why aren't you here?"

"Jane Vanderwaal just stopped me on the street."

"Bad news."

"Beyond bad," Andie said.

"Don't tell me you'll let her keep you from coming tonight."

Forget Christmas. Forget everything. "I don't feel like being with people."

"Everyone's asking about you," Stephanie said. "We're about to open the white elephant gifts. I brought a Life cereal box full of lemons. Get it? A cop's life is a lemon."

No kidding. "I'm not up for socializing."

"Can I help? Want me to stop by later?"

"Thanks, but no need. I'm okay. I just have a headache." Every throb at Andie's temples reminded her that she'd killed Christopher.

For nearly three hours, Andie sat at her kitchen table and stared out the window at the winter night's darkness and rain. Justice draped himself over her toes. By ten o'clock, her growling stomach convinced her to make popcorn, the easiest dinner. Justice would sell himself into slavery for popcorn—the more butter, the better.

She got a jar of corn from the pantry and poured kernels into heated oil. When Justice recognized their telltale clatter and sniffed ecstasy in the making, he got to his feet and waited by the stove. His pleading eyes informed her, *I am a good dog. Please, do not forget me.*

Usually, Andie shared the popcorn with Justice—a bite for him and a bite for her. It was a bonding time of simultaneous crunching, interrupted only by an occasional swallow of water for her and a lettuce-leaf palate cleanser for him. But tonight she poured half the popcorn all at once into his bowl and forgot about the lettuce. As he dove in, she returned to the table alone and resumed her brooding.

Like every kid on earth, Christopher must have loved popcorn. He probably had grabbed lusty handfuls of it and stuffed it into his mouth. Suddenly the obvious but arresting thought occurred to her that he'd never again eat it or any of a teen's other basic food groups: ice cream, candy bars, cookies, hamburgers, and pizza. Christopher would never graduate from high school or college. He'd never marry or have kids.

When Andie pictured the life he might have had, she saw him at age forty, smiling over a Thanksgiving turkey at his beautiful Norman Rockwell family, a lovely wife and three towheaded children. In his house there would be no quarrels, and everyone would be successful and fulfilled. He would look back at stabbing Justice, shake his head, and wonder how he ever could have done such a thing. And after a long and contented life, he would die peacefully in his sleep.

Andie's Norman Rockwell image of Christopher faded when she looked out her window and there he was again, a gawky teen, peering at her from the shadows. To her, *he* was a shadow who would follow her forever no matter how bright her sun. The biggest fact about Andie was always going to be that she had killed him.

CHAPTER 36

ANDREA

Andie wound her muffler tightly around her neck, zipped her down jacket to her chin, and wrapped her arms around herself. She'd forgotten how cold the beach could get on New Year's Eve when the San Julian Rotary Club set off fireworks from a barge in the harbor. Half the island's residents were gathered here to watch, but their collective body heat didn't warm the night. As hips and elbows bumped, the wind picked up and breaths emerged into a collective cloud.

"I'm worried about Justice," Andie told Meghan.

"He'll be fine," she said. "Your house is miles from here. The noise won't bother him."

"He has such sensitive ears. He hides during thunderstorms."

"Don't forget he toughed it out through the Vanderwaals' July Fourth fireworks." Meghan's hand covered her mouth. "I'm sorry. I didn't mean to mention them."

"They're a fact of my life. I can't pretend they don't exist." Especially since Jane had confronted Andie and she'd spiraled into a funk. She'd refused Christmas dinner invitations and hunkered down at home with Justice. Meghan had pestered her relentlessly until she'd agreed to come tonight.

As anticipation rippled through the crowd, murmurs swelled to excited conversations. Dads held kids on their shoulders for a better view of what was about to start. Finally at nine o'clock, when the Times Square ball was dropped at midnight Eastern Standard Time, three chrysanthemum fireworks shot into the sky and burst into red petals of fire and a communal gasp rose from the crowd. As the petals spilled into the water, a row of comets fanned out above the barge and exploded in flashes of silver. Pearls spewed fountains of red, orange, green, and gold, and peonies flared into expanding spheres of purple stars.

The harbor filled with smoke, and the smell of gunpowder wafted through the air. At each blast of fireworks, Andie flinched, then cringed. As every muscle in her body tensed, she dug her nails into her palms. The explosions kept coming one after another, too quickly for her to recover equilibrium, and she felt like she might jump out of her skin.

As her knees wobbled and she began to sweat, what looked like another chrysanthemum burst into gold sparks and boomed so loud that percussive noise struck Andie's face. The lanky college kid next to her shouted, "Wow! A Thunder Flash!" Andie scarcely heard because she was shaking and fighting to breathe.

Her face looked like she'd encountered a ghost, but what she'd encountered was Christopher. His arm raised over his head, his knife blade glinting in her flashlight beam, he ran at her. Panicked, she fired off round after round. *Bam! Bam! Bam!* The bullets' gunpowder smell made her nauseous. Her knees buckled under her, and she sagged to the ground.

"Andie, are you okay?" Meghan bent down and steadied Andie's shoulders so she wouldn't topple over. "What's wrong? Tell me what's wrong."

A girandole spun into the air, shooting off sparks, its shrill whistles assaulting her ears. A skyrocket left a trail of fire. Silver beehives flew through the sky, their sparks shooting off in all

directions like bullets that had lost their minds. Andie buried
her head in her arms as if she were warding off blows.

"Andie, can you get up? Let's go." Meghan grabbed her
elbow.

The lanky kid on the other side of Andie bent down and
took her other arm. Together, he and Meghan tugged her to
her feet, and the crowd around them pulled away to make
room for them to pass. Andie did not remember being led two
blocks to Meghan's Jeep. She only knew that she was terrified.

When Andie regained her ability of rational thought, she
realized she was huddled against the passenger door of
Meghan's Jeep. Meghan was patting her knee, squeezing her
hand.

"Don't worry. Everything will be all right," Meghan was
repeating.

"This keeps happening." Andie's mouth felt as dry as cotton.

"What keeps happening?"

"I think they're flashbacks." Andie was too scrambled to remember how Dr. Capoletti had described them, or to explain
how she'd chalked up past ones to bad memories, like anyone
could have. She could not deny that tonight's had been the real
thing. And admitting she'd *had* a real flashback was almost as
disconcerting as going through it, because she now had to acknowledge to herself that she'd crossed the line to the post-
traumatic stress that Dr. Capoletti had warned her about. The
prospect was frightening.

Meghan nodded as if she understood what flashbacks were.
She said again, "Don't worry. You'll be fine."

But the anxious worry on Meghan's face seemed to say the
opposite.

At home Andie found a shredded *Bake Away* magazine just
inside the front door and a guilty-looking Justice in the
kitchen. After her own loss of control, she could hardly be mad

at him. He may have gotten frantic at all the noise and wanted to get outside to run for his life. Or, as sensitive dogs were known to do, he could have picked up Andie's panic from a distance and been desperate to find her.

Andie thought the latter seemed more likely when she found his teddy, Bandit, on her pillow. Normally, Bandit slept on Justice's side of the bed near the foot.

When she got into bed, Justice curled up near the crook behind her knees and rested his chin on her calf. But breathing in sync with him did not calm her as it usually did. She lay there blinking in the dark till dawn.

CHAPTER 37

TOM

Kimberly Thatcher, Christopher's girlfriend, stared at her hands, balled in her lap. Once in a while, she raised her head and cast a shy glance in Tom's direction, but no one could call her an extrovert. She looked like she subsisted on celery and oxygen. In the braid down her back not a hair was out of place, and her jeans' crease was perfectly pressed. If grooming were the criterion for judging Miss Teen America, she'd win, hands down.

Tom shifted in the plaid club chair across from Kimberly's in her family's den. Through Kevin Egelbrit, he'd been able to ferret out her name. Since she'd known Christopher perhaps better than any of his peers, she could be a mother lode of insight. So much was riding on this talk. Tom couldn't fail here.

He smiled kindly. "Have you ever talked with a sheriff's deputy before?"

"No."

"We don't bite." He smiled again.

"Fine."

Obviously, he was going to have to try a little harder to connect. "I've got a daughter a few years younger than you are. She wants to play the flute. Your counselor told me you've been playing it for a long time."

"Yes."

"Are you in the band?"

"Yes."

"Do you like it?"

"Yes."

Her specialty was single syllables. *How am I going to squeeze information out of this girl?* Every teen Tom had talked with on this case had raised a drawbridge and dropped a portcullis to keep him back. Tom began to worry.

He glanced around the den, which was as immaculate as Kimberly herself—the wastebasket empty, no speck of dust on a windowsill, the hardwood floor polished to a gleam. Tidiness must run in the family. It might have attracted Kimberly to Christopher. They could have related, neatnik to neatnik.

Tom coughed though he didn't really need to. He started again. "Kimberly—or does your family call you Kim?"

"Kim." Another single syllable.

"I need your help." *Go ahead. Throw yourself at the mercy of a teenage girl. Maybe that'll do it.* "I've been working for two months on this case. I've tried to understand Christopher, but I've had trouble. I know you were close. I'd really appreciate it if you'd tell me about him."

"What do you want to know?"

Six syllables! And eye contact! Now we're getting somewhere. "What was Christopher like?"

She shrugged. "You know."

"No, I don't know. That's why I'm here," Tom pressed.

"He was okay."

"Okay" doesn't tell me much. "Did you go out on dates?"

"Not to movies and stuff. We were mostly good friends. We hung out after school." Kim picked a piece of lint off her club chair's arm and set it in an empty cloisonné bowl on a side table.

"Where did you hang out? Here? At his house?"

"At an old garage in his neighborhood."

I have to get there pronto. "Where exactly is it?"

She shrugged again. "I don't know the address."

"How would I get there?"

"Driving would be good."

Tom stopped himself from rolling his eyes. Only for the sake of information would he put up with disrespect. "Drive where?"

"To the end of a long dirt driveway off Valley Road. The garage used to be next to a house, but it's gone."

"So nobody minded you were there?"

"Nobody knew." She looked toward the kitchen doorway as if to check that her mother wasn't listening. "The garage was about to fall down. We had to be, like, careful climbing the stairs."

"Stairs to what?"

"A room. It was a mess, but Christopher cleaned it up."

Tom had to be careful to avoid alluding to any frisky business they might have gotten up to. He didn't want to put her on the defensive. "I'm assuming there was no electricity or running water."

"Probably not in, like, the last three thousand years."

Tom sat forward. He set his wrists on his knees. "Kim . . ." He used her name to sound extra-friendly and reel her in. "Why did Christopher want to be in a garage that was about to fall down?"

"To get away from his totally dorky parents. He wanted privacy to read books and write in his journal."

"Where? Where is his journal?!" *Don't get excited. Play it cool.*

"On his laptop."

Please, don't let this be a dead end. "Where's his laptop?"

"No idea."

Tom's excitement withered. "We haven't been able to find it. It's important. You're *sure* you don't know where it is."

"Of *course*, I'm sure." Her voice conveyed a twinge of the contempt that Tom had noticed too often in teenage girls and hoped he'd never detect in Lisa.

"Kim . . ." he tried again. "Did you like Christopher?"

"At first."

"Sounds like you stopped liking him."

"He started, like, smothering me. I felt kind of sorry for him," she said.

"How do you mean?"

"He tried too hard. He bought me a really fancy bracelet. My mother made me give it back."

"He obviously liked you." *A little stroke to her ego wouldn't hurt.*

"He wanted me to try dope, but it made me sick."

"What kind of dope?"

"Pot. It's legal in Washington, you know."

Yes, you little snip, as a deputy sheriff I'm aware of that. "It's legal only for people over twenty-one, but I won't tell on you." Tom chuckled like they were conspiring. "Did he want you to keep trying pot? Did you fight about that?"

She shook her head. "We fought because he got totally controlling. He acted like he owned me. He didn't like me talking to other boys at school."

"Some girls might like that. They'd feel he really cared."

"It freaked me out. I broke up with him," Kim said.

"When?"

"Three days before he got shot. That *totally* freaked me out."

CHAPTER 38

The radiator in Chief Malone's office clanged and squeaked. It sounded like a cable car was battling a deranged mouse. Months ago Andie would have hardly noticed, but since New Year's Eve her frayed nerves had made her hypersensitive, and the noise put her on edge. She petted Justice, who'd curled up at her feet, though he kept watch on the door lest the Chief come in and bonk him on the head again.

Andie checked her watch. The Chief was sixteen minutes late. She tapped an impatient finger on his desk and studied his photo of Mrs. Malone—a flinty woman, her hair pulled back severely, horizontal creases stamped into her crepey neck. Did she take umbrage at foam in the corners of her husband's mouth? Did he mind her staring from the picture with steely eyes that could pin a sumo wrestler to the ground? Mrs. Malone seemed like the kind of woman you couldn't hide your secrets from. Under her penetrating gaze, Andie felt naked.

Since New Year's Eve, she'd also felt naked on duty because she'd struggled to maintain her tough façade. She'd worried that her colleagues might share Mrs. Malone's x-ray vision and see straight through her wall to the emotionally wrecked person shivering behind it. Even if they didn't know about her flashbacks, they might sense she'd fallen apart and deem her unfit for her job. *Yep, I knew it. She's a mess,* they might whisper.

Andie reminded herself that the Chief had summoned her for only a "short chat." There was nothing to get worked up about. But she blinked extra blinks when he came into his office with Ron Hausmann. Both men looked like they might have indigestion and they'd left their smiles in the parking lot. Andie stood and shook their hands as Justice uncurled himself, got to his feet, and frisked Hausmann with his nose. He pointedly hung back from the Chief.

In one arm, Malone was carrying a stack of legal-size envelopes, which he set on his desk next to Mrs. Malone. "Brady, I'll cut to the chase," he said as Andie and Hausmann took seats across from him and Justice assumed his library lion position. "These documents were delivered this morning. Here's the one you need." He thumbed through the envelopes and handed one to Andie.

She opened the clasps and pulled out a sheaf of papers titled "Petition." Below it, she read "Vanderwaal vs. Brady," and her heart did a backflip and landed with a splat on concrete.

"You can read it if you want, but it'll put you to sleep," Hausmann told her.

Hardly. The title alone left her one rung away from a panic attack.

"Here's the deal," Malone said. "Basically, the Vanderwaals have filed civil suits against you, our department, and the city. They claim you provided insufficient first aid to save Christopher's life and you violated his Fourth Amendment protection against excessive use of force."

"I did everything I could for him!" Andie sputtered. "Everyone's agreed I was justified to shoot."

"Everyone except the Vanderwaals and their legal team. Want to explain it to her, Hausmann?"

"Sure." He smoothed his tie as if he were about to step before a jury. "The Vanderwaals claim your department didn't train you properly. They failed to teach you how to de-escalate a confrontation without killing someone and how to decide when deadly force is truly necessary," he said. "Your department's failure supposedly caused an unnecessary crisis that resulted in Christopher's death, and that's deprived the Vanderwaals of his companionship. So they're seeking damages for pain, suffering, and distress."

"What about *my* pain, suffering, and distress!? Didn't they ever stop to consider *that?*" To get control of her voice, Andie cleared her throat. "What damages are they seeking?"

The Chief's glance at Hausmann seemed to ask, *Which of us is going to tell her?*

"Six million dollars," Hausmann said.

The number punched Andie in the stomach and made it hard for her to breathe. She felt like Hausmann had thrown her into ice. Justice picked up her distress and got to his feet. He gave her the look that appeared on his face with ever more troubling frequency: *Don't be upset. I will protect you. I'm here.*

Justice seemed to feel that Hausmann and the Chief were the culprits who'd grieved Andie. Facing them, he stationed himself in front of her in his most alert Herr Commandant mode, his ears up, his front legs propping up his chest, on which, were he in the German army, would have hung medals for valor. Justice made clear that he'd be glad to take on the Chief and Hausmann were they to grieve Andie again. *You get out of line, you unconscionable churls, and it's all over. I will not let you hurt her.*

"Don't worry about the claim," Hausmann told Andie.

"How could I not worry? I could work seven days a week till I die and I'd never make that kind of money."

"Our insurance might kick in," the Chief said.

"Might" was an arrow in Andie's heart.

"You know as well as we do it's a free country. Anybody

can file a suit about anything and ask for any damages they please. That doesn't mean they can win," Hausmann said.

"What if the Vanderwaals do?" Andie asked.

"We don't think they will," the Chief said.

"Can you be sure?" Andie asked.

"Nobody can be sure of anything," the Chief said.

Hausmann jingled the coins in his pockets, another noise that sharpened Andie's edge. He said, "It's all a bunch of legal posturing and bluster. We've been expecting it."

"I haven't," Andie said.

"Don't look at it as a threat. It's just one of those irritating things we have to deal with." The Chief sounded casual, but his scowl couldn't hide the worry in his eyes, and his foam had reappeared. "We're here to stand by you."

"We'll take it as it comes," Hausmann said. "Their lawyers will want you for a deposition, but not for a while."

Andie reached for Justice's reassuring fur, but it didn't help. She tried to hide behind her wall, but a six-million-dollar civil suit was like an earthquake that cracked it irreparably—and caused a sudden shift in Andie. At that moment, something inside her forced a decision she never thought she'd make: She could not go on like this, chronically distressed, never knowing what horror might come next. She couldn't keep coming to a job that was destroying her.

For years, like her father, she'd worked for justice. Every day she'd put her life on the line and done her best to serve. But no good deeds went unpunished. For all the demanding, dangerous work, her reward had been a divorce, a criminal investigation, and now a lawsuit that could lead to garnished wages for the rest of her life. Though she'd given her heart and soul for others' justice, there was none for her. *I have to escape.*

As the radiator rattled like it was coughing up something unsavory, Andie said, "I quit."

"That's ridiculous," the Chief said.

"I can't be a cop anymore."

"Isn't that a rash decision?" Hausmann asked.

"I can't worry that something else I do might make my life even worse." Andie got up and set her gun and holster on the Chief's desk.

"You're a fine officer. I don't want to lose you," he said.

"It's too late. I'm already lost." *If you only knew how lost.*

The Chief closed his eyes as if he were taking time out from a disagreeable task, like washing out a garbage can. He formed a steeple with his fingertips, then set its peak against his lips. When he opened his eyes, he said, "Look, Brady. You've had a hard time. It's understandable. Any of us would be upset at all you've gone through, but quitting just because you're in a rough patch isn't the answer."

"It's way more than a rough patch, and it's the answer for me," Andie said.

"I'll tell you what. I'll take you off patrol. You can work here at the station and get away from the stress for a while," the Chief said. "You'll come to your senses. Give it a little time."

"I've worked here for seven years. I'm done."

"Done" seemed like the last nail hammered into her professional coffin. The Chief's face got as flinty as Mrs. Malone's. "Okay, quit if you want, but I'm not accepting your resignation. I'm putting you on unpaid leave, and I'll hold off hiring anybody else for a while."

"Take a few weeks. Think about your life. You were made to be a cop," Hausmann said.

"I'm not coming back." Andie picked up her purse. She left her patrol car's keys next to her gun but kept her father's shield.

Andie saw the Chief glance at Hausmann as if to say, *I don't have any more rabbits to pull out of my hat.* Hausmann shook his head and shrugged, like he didn't have any rabbits, either.

"Well, good luck." The Chief's swivel chair squawked as

he got up. He shook Andie's hand. "One last thing." He paused as he stepped back toward his desk. "I don't think you got over killing that kid. I'm afraid you're in trouble."

You don't have to tell me. I'm well aware. "I know what I'm doing."

"I don't think you do," the Chief said. "You need to work this out. Go see Capoletti."

I can take care of myself. When Andie started toward the door, Justice followed.

The Chief intercepted and bonked his head right on the star. Justice's glower informed him, *You are a deplorable pissant.*

"You watch after her, Justice," the Chief said.

Andie did not ask Stephanie for a ride because she didn't want to explain why she'd resigned. Rain or no rain, she would walk the two miles home. From her locker, she got Justice's yellow slicker, fitted it over his back, and fastened it under his belly. Leaving the rest of her belongings behind—who cared about her utility belt and bicycle helmet?—she buttoned up her jacket and, without a backward glance, walked out of the station.

Chapter 39

Tom

Tom was climbing out of his patrol car when Andie and Justice walked through the station's back door. He'd driven here to tell her in person about Matt Stone and Kimberly Thatcher. Surely the breakup had blindsided Christopher, and it could at least partly explain his attack. Tom might not be Andie's favorite person right now, but this important news was bound to pique her interest.

He turned up his jacket collar against the rain and hurried across the parking lot toward Andie, who, oddly, had no umbrella. As he got closer, he saw that her face looked gray and hard.

"Brady?" he called out.

When she didn't stop or turn around, he picked up his pace and caught up with her. "Brady." He put his hand on her shoulder with gentleness few would expect from an ex-Marine. "Wait a minute. I want to talk with you."

"I've got to get home." She wriggled out of his grasp and kept going, but Justice stopped and greeted him with an earnest sniff.

"Your car's over there." Tom pointed back to her patrol car. "What's going on?"

"Nothing."

"If you've got to get home, why aren't you driving?"

"Because we're walking."

"Brady, that's two miles. In case you haven't noticed, it's raining." No way could Tom let her go off down the street till he was sure she was all right. "Won't your car start? I can drive you home."

A bus chugging along the street did not drown out Andie's put-upon sigh. "I need to be alone."

"And I need to make sure nothing's wrong."

"Everything's fine."

"You want to swear that on a Bible?" Behind Andie's concrete face, Tom detected misery. He wouldn't have minded wrapping his arms around her and holding her till she calmed down, but they weren't on that kind of terms.

"I don't mean to pressure you, but I'd really like to know what's the matter." He *was* pressuring her, but so what? "Maybe I can help."

Tom couldn't tell if the noise that came out of Andie was a whimper or a scoff. She said, "That's the problem with law enforcement. We risk our lives helping other people, but nobody helps us. It's a one-way street."

What's brought all this on? "I don't do my job to get anything from anybody. That's not the point."

"What *is* the point? You tell me. Why bother?"

"We bother because our job is to keep the bad guys from taking over and to make sure people are safe. We're supposed to stop chaos. We help people."

"I'm helped *out*. This job's used me up. I don't have any more to give." Andie twisted the end of Justice's leash in her hands. At least there was animation in her face again.

"I don't get it, Brady. You want to tell me why you're thinking that?"

Her gaze aimed at Justice's ears, Andie hesitated. She had to know he'd persist till she threw him an explanatory scrap. Finally, she said, "The Vanderwaals have filed a civil suit against me for six million dollars. Christopher may as well take up permanent residence inside my skin. I'll never be free. Even if the City's insurance helps pay for damages, I could end up owing millions just because I thought I needed to protect myself."

"You did need to protect yourself. The evidence proved it. It will stand up in court."

"They claim the department didn't train me right. How do you defend yourself from that?" Andie looked exhausted. The rain had flattened her hair so it had lost its puff.

"You can go ahead and doubt yourself, but you've been trained just fine," Tom said. "None of us wants a civil suit, but you'll be all right. Hausmann will watch after you."

"I'm not counting on it."

"You may think that today, but you'll see. They won't hang you out to dry." Tom pulled a handkerchief from his back pocket and handed it to her to mop rain off her face. When she didn't take the handkerchief, he mopped his own. "So why are you walking home?"

"Because I just quit. I gave the Chief my car keys. I'm not a cop anymore."

Had Tom heard right? "Are you nuts? You're not thinking straight." When Andie's beautiful cheeks turned red, he knew he'd crossed a line and stirred her up again.

"Do you judge everybody or is it always just me?" she asked.

"Look." Tom tamped down his frustration so as not to raise her hackles more. "In the investigation I had to judge. It was my job. But I'm not judging you now. You can be sure of that."

"I have a right to quit if I want to."

"Of course you do, but that doesn't mean it's a smart decision."

Andie set her jaw and turned away. As she started down the street, she made clear that the encounter was over—and she and Justice wanted to be alone. *Let her stew in her own juice,* Tom thought as he walked back to the parking lot.

By the time he got into his car, however, he realized that shooting Christopher had been harder on Andie than anyone had understood. Including him. Nobody would guess that someone with her strength could be so vulnerable, but he supposed there was a limit to how much even a tough cop could take. A lawsuit and a potential six-million-dollar judgment would take the starch out of any officer. He should cut her some slack.

Tom drove back to Andie as she stormed down the street with Justice, who looked like he didn't understand her storm any better than Tom had. He rolled down his window and inched along beside them as they sloshed through puddles along the sidewalk. The rain was coming down harder, and Tom's windshield wipers were slinging it onto the hood. "I'm in a helping profession, lady, and I don't want you and that wet dog walking two miles in this weather. You'll catch colds."

"A little rain never hurt anybody," Andie said.

"Come on. Get in the car," Tom ordered.

"No."

"I don't want to arrest you for being stubborn, but I will."

Andie stopped. He pulled his car over in front of her, helped Justice into the backseat, and opened the front passenger door. "Get in, lady."

Andie did.

CHAPTER 40

TOM

Searching for the dirt driveway that Kimberly had mentioned was starting to feel like a game of Dupe the Cop. On Tom's third pass down Valley Road, he wondered if she'd lied about hanging out in a garage with Christopher, but he didn't relish going back to her house to confront her.

As usual for January, the afternoon was overcast. The rural neighborhood looked dreary. Though Andie and Mildred Hawthorne kept up their properties, few others did, and plenty of greenery along the road had grown out of control. Blackberry thickets were rampant, and ivy vines were choking trees into untimely deaths. The vegetation seemed aggressive; if you stopped too long, it might wrap itself around you and swallow you, boa-constrictor style. Tom passed the Vanderwaals' house and was glad his days of questioning them were over.

When he approached Andie's, he slowed and craned his neck to look down her driveway, but for the third time today its curve through the woods blocked any glimpse of her. He wasn't sure what he hoped to see unless maybe she was outside raking debris blown from the trees in last night's storm. He could get out of the car and offer to help. *Any other bright ideas, Wolski?* As he'd told her when he'd dropped her off at home last week, if she needed anything she knew where to find him.

He was worried about her—not so much because of the emotional wear and tear of Christopher's attack and the Vanderwaals' lawsuit, which he believed they would lose. His main concern was Andie's decision to resign from the force. That reaction, it seemed to him, showed how badly Christopher and his parents had messed with her mind. It would take more than a civil suit to make him leave his job. Brady's choice made little sense when she had the department behind her.

Better to leave her alone, give her space to process the whole damned ball of wax, he thought. But then he asked himself, *Why should you care about Brady?* And he answered, *Well, because.* Sorry not to see her, Tom took off down the road again.

Thinking he might have better luck searching for the garage on foot, he pulled over and parked at the intersection of Valley and Birch. As he walked along Valley feeling thwarted all over again, he saw what might once have been a dirt driveway's entrance—but it was hard to say because blackberries, alders, and madronas grew in the middle of it now. He stopped and pushed back branches for a better look. There *had* been some kind of road here. And through the underbrush, someone had worn a path, carefully hidden. Unless Tom had been looking for it, he'd have walked right by and never known it was there.

He stepped onto the path and let go of the branches behind him. In some places he had to stoop or turn sideways to get through the brush and branches, which scratched his hands. When it started to drizzle, he wished he'd not left his hat in the car.

Just as he was imagining how fools felt about their errands, up ahead he saw a brick fireplace and chimney, all that remained of a house that must have burned to the ground. Just beyond it was a structure that looked as if one strong gust of wind could provide it with a merciful death. Weather had stripped off the paint, if there had ever been any, and the roof's splintered cedar shingles were a breeding ground for moss. Boards were missing from the walls, and in the two upstairs windows cardboard covered broken panes. Someone had nailed signs to what might once have been a garage door: NO TRESPASSING! DANGER! BEWARE OF DOG!

Tom walked around to the back and found a door hanging on hinges that squawked when he forced it open. Beyond it was a flight of stairs daring anyone over sixty pounds to climb. But footsteps in the dust told Tom that not long ago someone *had* climbed them. The steps could lead to something promising. *What to do?*

This could be the break Tom had been hoping for. He'd come too far to turn around just because the steps were rickety and he was a large man. Unwilling to wait for the fire department to bring ladders to reach a window, Tom took the flashlight off his utility belt and shone it ahead of him.

He thumped his knuckles on treads he could reach from where he stood. A few looked more rotten than others, but the stringer seemed sturdy enough. He could pick and choose what treads might hold his weight; to get around those that he might fall through, he could step over to the stringer. Though the disintegrating banister would never support him if he fell, it might help him keep his balance—slow going, but doable. And dangerous.

Tom stepped on the first tread. *Wobbly, but no problem.* He tried the next—a creak. Another and another. *Not bad.* To bypass the next two disintegrating steps, he put his weight on the stringer. Now he'd come high enough that falling through a stair could land him in the hospital.

Anxious step by anxious step, Tom made it to the top. He met another door, whose hinges squawked worse than the one below had. He stepped into a room and shone his flashlight on the opposite wall. *Wonder of wonders.* The oddly colored eyes of David Bowie, who'd loomed over Christopher's bed at home, looked straight at Tom from a poster nailed to the wood.

A watery light fought its way through the windows' few remaining panes. In a quest for tidiness, Christopher had swept the room and hauled away whatever had been stored here. All that was left were wooden apple crates turned upside down for tables, a transistor radio that had seen better days, candles crammed down bottles' necks, a Mason jar of pencils, and two faded lawn-chair pillows that someone must have put out on Valley for garbage pickup.

Tom squatted down and rummaged through a plastic trash bag. He found empty Coke cans and apple juice cartons, potato chip bags, Snickers and Butterfinger wrappers, and ancient copies of *Outside* and *Popular Science.* No cell or laptop anywhere. *One more dead end. Damn.*

Tom was about to leave, disappointed and no more enlightened than before he'd come, when his flashlight beam skimmed a warped floorboard that rose half an inch higher than the others. Something about the board compelled him to figure out why. To lift it, he worked his nails along the edges, but a splinter pierced under his thumbnail and nearly sent him through the roof. He shook his hand, but that didn't shake away the pain. Still, pain or not, he could never leave without being sure that Christopher hadn't hidden anything here.

Tom jiggled the board loose and pried it up with his pocketknife. There, wedged between two floor joists, were the very laptop and mobile phone he'd been searching for all this time. *Hallelujah! Gotcha!* Despite his throbbing thumb, he smiled.

Since he'd already tracked down Christopher's friends, the cell's contact list might not help much, but photos could shed light. And if Kimberly had been correct, the laptop contained

Christopher's journal, into which he might have poured his heart and soul. It would be as close as Tom could get to interviewing him. It might be the key to unlock his motive.

An apple was emblazoned on the green plastic case, which was smudged with fingerprints. Tom raised the lid and pressed the power button. *Damn. But no surprise.* The laptop's battery was as dead as the phone's.

Tom put it in his pocket, gripped the laptop like a lifeline, and carefully navigated the stairs again. He rushed to his patrol car to get back to his office.

CHAPTER 41

ANDREA

The Barkery was a doggy bakery, where customers could buy Red Velvet Pupcakes, Carob Delights, or Cinnamon Honey Heart biscuits for their dogs, then enjoy tea and scones at French café tables themselves. An ever-changing exhibit of local artists' work brightened the room. The morning sun streamed through the plate-glass windows, along the bottom of which were posted flyers for such events as San Julian Playhouse productions or the Nisqually County Fair. Delicious smells drifted from the kitchen, which was located toward the back behind a half wall.

For Andie, working at the Barkery meant a fresh professional start. Her new job allowed her to use her baking skills, and, psychologically, it was as far as she could get from the San Julian Police Department. Instead of patrolling streets and issuing traffic tickets, she could sift flour and cut out cookies. She could replace a hard-edged masculine world with a softer, feminine one and, most important, avoid anything that would remind her of Christopher. But of course, he and his parents were never far from her thoughts. On her new annual salary of twenty-five thousand dollars, she figured she'd have to work 240 years to pay the damages that Jane and Franz were after.

No longer cooped up in the back of a patrol car, Justice

could wander around the Barkery and greet dogs who came by with their people, or he could lounge on his round blue bed, which looked like a giant morning glory blossom. Perhaps his greatest bonus was sampling the merchandise. The kitchen became his personal smorgasbord, and the sound of Andie's spatula lifting something off a cookie sheet brought him running to vacuum up whatever might fall to the floor.

This Friday morning he was playing possum on his bed, and Andie was kneading dough for Woof Supremes, which were dog-bone-shaped cookies iced with peanut butter. His premier sniffer informed him that ecstasy was in the making. He raised his head to check on Andie's progress and to remind her of his debilitating hunger: *Please remember I am here. I am fond of Woof Supremes, and I am ravenous. I have not eaten in two hours!*

Onto a marble pastry slab, Andie sprinkled flour and spread it around with her palm. As she set down her lump of dough and reached for her rolling pin, the cowbell hanging from the front door's knob clanged and the Laser Lady came in. Wearing purple slacks, a fake leopard fur jacket, and sunglasses with rhinestones, she walked over to the glass case of baked goods next to the cash register and stooped down for a closer look at the dog and human treats. Andie pushed errant curls off her forehead with the back of her floury hand and waved from the kitchen. She left her dough and stepped behind the counter.

"Why, my goodness. What are *you* doing here?" the Laser Lady asked.

"I'm working."

"I hardly recognized you out of uniform." The Laser Lady removed her sunglasses for a better look at Andie. "You don't look the same."

"It's still me." To dodge the Laser Lady's inevitable question—why Andie had changed jobs—she asked, "How's Alistair?"

"Oh, he's fine."

"Any more breaking and entering?"

"No. He seems happy living in the shed with the other feral cats."

"Good." Andie wiped her hands on her white apron as outside the Barkery window a commuter in a suit and wingtip shoes made a dash for the ferry. "What can I do for you this morning?"

"I need some people crackers for a dog's third birthday party," the Laser Lady said.

"Good choice. What size? Small? Medium? Large?"

"Medium. The dog's a beagle. I'll take a pound."

Andie dug a red plastic scooper into a cracker vat and poured a crowd of firemen, mailmen, and policemen into a brown paper bag. She weighed them and added a few more. "There you go. A pound." She handed the bag to the Laser Lady. "Whose dog has the birthday?"

"The man north of me at the end of the block. He's the only neighbor I trust."

Andie remembered him, a kindly senior citizen who'd called her when a skunk had sprayed the birthday beagle. "Um–hum," she said.

"He's not like that communist across the street," the Laser Lady said. "That man is planning to kill me. He put a for-sale sign in his yard and aimed it straight at my house. A hostile act if I've ever seen one."

"I doubt he means any harm," Andie said.

"My front window is directly across from that sign. He could attack me when I'm watching TV." The Laser Lady dug into her purse and handed Andie a ten-dollar bill.

As she dropped change into the Laser Lady's hand, a middle-aged man, his hair swept up into a pompadour, walked in.

"I was going to call you this afternoon about getting a re-straining order," the Laser Lady told Andie.

"Sorry, I can't help you," Andie told her, and smiled at the man. He stepped back, looking startled.

"I'm sorry, sir. I meant I can't help *her*, not you," Andie told him. To the Laser Lady, she said, "In the old days I'd have been glad to talk with your neighbor, but I'm not a cop anymore."

"You were a cop!" Clearly recognizing Andie, he pointed at her.

Her pulse racing with the urge to run, Andie hesitated. "Yes."

"I've heard all about you."

"Okay." *Don't let him be an Islander for Collaborative Policing.*

"I work with Jane Vanderwaal. She's a close friend."

"Oh."

"She said you'd left the police department. I guess you had to when people were blaming you for murdering an innocent kid."

The Laser Lady blanched. "Where's a murderer?!" Her eyes wild, she looked around the Barkery for enemies who might have sneaked in.

"A lot of people at the hospital are worried Jane's never going to be all right." The man looked worried too. "She's broken. The poor woman. But it's no surprise after what you did."

Andie raised her fist to her mouth to stifle a cry. She tried to speak to defend herself, but her vocal cords wouldn't work.

Her legs stretched out across cold ceramic tile, Andie leaned against the Barkery's locked bathroom door. She felt like a catapult had flung her heart into the street and a Sherman tank had run over it. At the sink, Christopher, in his black hoodie, pressed the soap dispenser and lathered, then rinsed his hands. He shook off excess water and turned on the automatic dryer. It roared in Andie's ears.

More than ever, she now knew that wherever she went or how hard she tried to escape, Christopher would come along. He was as much a part of her as the breath she was trying to catch. And accompanying him would be his parents, who would persecute her, and the judges and haters, who viewed her as a murderer with blood dripping from her fangs. Changing jobs had done nothing to stop the anguish. It would always be the same.

Andie heard sobs that sounded like the wrenching sounds of a tortured animal, then realized they were coming from her. In the months through Tom's investigation, her return to the force, and the Vanderwaals' filing their suit, Justice had not seen her cry a single tear, and now she was wailing into her hands. He sat in his ready-willing-and-able position as close to her as he could get, his presence there to comfort her. But even he didn't help. As the cowbell clanged and puzzled customers entered and left the empty Barkery, Andie cried uncontrollably behind the locked door.

Her emotions gravely distressed Justice.

But they gravely frightened her.

The wall she'd carefully constructed of stone and reinforced with her own steel had cracked on the day she quit the force. Now the wall crumbled around her, its rubble pulverized to dust, impossible to rebuild. As hard as she'd tried to keep going, she knew that she had no more fight left. Chief Malone had been right; she was in trouble. She closed her eyes and thought, *I need help.*

CHAPTER 42

ANDREA

Justice tugged Andie from Dr. Capoletti's waiting room into his inner sanctum and personally delivered her into the doctor's kind hands. He stooped down and gave Justice a dog biscuit as Andie sank into the sofa; she looked like a monsoon had taken up residence inside her. Sensitive to her turmoil, Justice lay on guard at her feet, but he seemed relieved to let Dr. Capoletti take charge. The room filled with Justice's biscuit crunches.

Outside the windows was the chilly darkness of a late January afternoon, but Dr. Capoletti's brass bowls and table lamps made the room feel warm and bright. A Buddha looked down serenely from the bookcase. The spiders who'd spun webs along the crown molding last fall had closed up shop and headed for the hills.

Andie glanced at the poster above Dr. Capoletti's desk and read again: "A storm is as good a friend as sunshine." *Pure sap and drivel,* she thought. The storm she was weathering now was no good friend. It was a cannibal.

"I'm glad you called." When Dr. Capoletti settled into his chair, the arm's loose batting bulged from the rip. "So how are you doing?"

"Not very well." With his encouragement, Andie poured

out her run-in with Jane, her New Year's flashback, the Vanderwaals' lawsuit, her resignation from the force, and her emotional
crash in the Barkery's bathroom. "I manage to get to work every
day, but I keep crying. I can't sleep or think straight. I'm falling
apart." With her fingertips she swiped at tears.

"You mean you're vulnerable?"

"Yes. In every way. I admit it. You were right."

"I knew this was coming, Andrea." Dr. Capoletti nodded
toward the tissue box near her elbow. "You can't sweep a
strong feeling like that under a rug. It'll chase you till you look
it squarely in the eye and deal with it. It's been waiting for you
to acknowledge it for a long time."

"I feel so sad and scared."

"Nothing wrong with that. It's good for you to feel those
things. It's the first step back to health." As Dr. Capoletti tapped
his pipe's ashes into a bowl beside his chair, the brass rang like
a meditation bell. "Did you ever decide if you were right to
shoot Christopher?"

"No. I still ask myself that question dozens of times every day."

"Then let's keep talking about it. It's important," Dr. Capoletti said. "What if you *hadn't* shot him? What would have happened?"

"He'd probably have stabbed me."

"Could you have stopped him without shooting him?"

"I don't know."

"What if you'd gotten into a fight over the knife?"

"I'd have grabbed it or knocked it out of his hand and
kicked it away."

"So that would have been the ideal outcome. Maybe it
would have worked out, maybe not." With a small steel tool,
Dr. Capoletti scraped out his pipe's remaining ashes. "What if
you couldn't get the knife away from him? What if he had a
black belt in karate, flipped you to the ground, and stabbed you
in the heart?"

"Most likely it would have been the end of me."

"Yes. Hardly ideal. You could have died."

A sobering shiver zigzagged through Andie as she considered that her obituary could have been in the paper. She wrapped her arms around herself. For months she'd focused on Christopher's death, not on her own.

"You look distressed," Dr. Capoletti said.

"I am."

"What are you thinking that's upsetting you?"

"About my death. It scares me."

Dr. Capoletti put a pinch of tobacco into his pipe and tamped it down with his index finger, then added another pinch and tamped. "Do you realize that all we've just been talking about are things that *might* have happened? You might have fought over the knife. Christopher might have killed you. Those were only possibilities. It's important to recognize that they were *not* facts. You sitting here alive is a fact. See the difference?"

"Yes."

"The possibilities of what could have happened are not real, but they can affect you as if they are. They can depress you or make you anxious," Dr. Capoletti said. "Have these unknowns—these possibilities—been on your mind lately?"

"They've been on my mind for the last few months," Andie admitted. "All the 'what-ifs' and 'maybes' and 'mights' about Christopher and the Vanderwaals. They plague me. I see what you mean."

Dr. Capoletti nodded, struck a match, and lit his pipe. "You know, you have every right to be angry about that attack and lawsuit."

Andie shrugged.

"Why aren't you mad, Andrea? You could hate Christopher and his parents if you wanted to."

"I don't. Mostly I just feel bad."

Dr. Capoletti puffed his burning-cherry smoke. "I know from your file that you've been known to have a temper. Where is it now?"

Andie shook her head. "I don't know."

"Do you feel that anger isn't justified in your case?"

"I can't *tell* myself to be angry. It doesn't work like that. I have to feel it."

"Fair enough," Dr. Capoletti said. "But some cops might sit where you are and fume. They'd tell me that they responded in the only way they could, and they'd be gearing up to give Christopher's parents hell in court."

"It wouldn't do any good."

"Why do you say that?"

"I'd still feel bad."

"Depression can be anger turned inward," Dr. Capoletti said.

"Maybe I'm angry, but I don't know it. Is that possible?"

"Possible, and probable. Denial is a good defense till you're ready to see what's going on." When Dr. Capoletti puffed his pipe again, the tobacco glowed. "You know, we psychologists have a saying. 'What you resist will persist. What you feel you can heal.'"

Andie didn't know what to say. She listened to Justice breathe and Dr. Capoletti's desk clock tick. Finally, feeling obliged to add something to the conversation, Andie admitted, "I guess I've had a wall around me."

"To hold in your feelings?"

"Yes, and to keep people from seeing them. I thought it would help me get through the ordeal."

"Has it?"

"At first, I guess. Lately it's been crumbling around me."

"It sounds like the wall got lodged between you and your deeper self. That can happen when people cut themselves off. They lose touch with what's going on inside them."

Andie nodded. He was right. More clock ticks punctuated the silence. She grabbed another tissue and swiped at the tears that continued leaking from the corners of her eyes. "I still worry about Christopher. It wasn't fair for him to die."

"Would it have been more fair for *you* to die?"

Andie paused. "No. It was an impossible situation. It's still impossible. I don't know how I'm ever going to get out of this mess."

"You can get out of it. It won't be a quick process, but we can work on it. Do you want to come back here and try?"

Andie would swim across Puget Sound to talk with Dr. Capoletti again. "Yes."

"Same time on Friday? How about we meet twice a week for a while?"

"Okay." Andie wasn't sure why she felt lighter, but she did. When she got up to leave, Justice roused himself and stood with her. She picked up her purse and umbrella and said, "It was good to talk about what might have happened if I hadn't shot Christopher. I see it's just a possibility. But I still don't know if I did the right thing."

Dr. Capoletti set his pipe into the brass bowl. "Sometimes an answer to a question like that can take a while. One day when you're least expecting it, it may leap out at you."

That night Andie wrote her list and dropped it into her basket:

1. Christopher didn't kill me. I'm alive!
2. Dr. Capoletti understands.
3. Even if I end up an indentured servant for the next 240 years, there's hope.

CHAPTER 43

TOM

Brady should be on patrol instead of here, but at least it's a decent place. Tom shoved his hands into his jeans pockets and looked around at the Barkery's tables, chairs, and seascapes. Though geared to dogs, it was a typical small-time eatery. But if Tom did say so himself, nothing in it could compete with police cars, handcuffs, and badges. In the glass case below the counter, he studied the treats made by Andie's own hands—a mashed-potato frosted hamburger cake, doggy banana bread, and pumpkin pupcakes iced with cream cheese. *She may be a star baker, but she should still be a cop.*

Sammy and Justice had greeted each other with ardent sniffs. She was lapping water from his blue ceramic bowl when Andie hurried around the half wall separating the storefront from the kitchen. She wiped her hands on her apron and left flour streaks. "Long time, no see," she said.

"Two and a half weeks." *But who's counting?*

Her hair was pulled back in a ponytail, and Tom liked its energetic bounce. But she looked shopworn; she may have started a new job, but her face still showed the wear and tear of recent months. "So it's true? You really are working in this place?" Tom asked.

"I am. I like it," Andie said, a touch defensively. "Who told you I was here?"

"Stephanie. She and the rest of your department are scheming to get you back."

"They can scheme all they want. I'm not leaving. I miss them, though."

"They miss you. You belong there, Brady. You can't let a bogus lawsuit drive you away."

With a damp cloth, Andie wiped imaginary crumbs off the brushed chrome countertop. "Isn't Lisa with you this weekend?"

The change of subject let Tom know that he may have pushed his opinions too far . . . again. "Lisa's at her ballet class till noon. I stopped by because I've got big news."

"Oh?"

"I guarantee it'll interest you."

"Why?"

"Just because," Tom said. "What do you want first? The big news of the county or the smaller news of a case I'm working on?" *Which also happens to be about you.*

"Okay, tell me the county's."

"First we need a trumpet fanfare," Tom teased.

"It's that important?"

"You bet. And you'll never guess." *It's fun to make you curious.* "Yesterday an amazing thing happened in Bremerton. Are you ready?"

Andie's attention seemed to rise a notch. "Yes."

"A couple of our guys were having lunch at the Harrison Diner on Front Street. Eating their burgers and passing the time. Not expecting anything unusual. Guess who walked in."

"I have no idea."

"Take a guess. The guys were ecstatic about it."

"Angelina Jolie?"

"No, you're nowhere close."

"Come on, please tell me," Andie said.

"I love to see you beg," Tom joked. "The Beast walked in! He's cooling his heels in the Nisqually County jail as we speak."

"Wow!" When Andie clapped her hands, Tom noted her grin was genuine. "Justice! Did you hear that?" Andie left the counter and hugged her dog. While she was at it, she hugged Sammy too. "They got the Beast!" Justice may not have recognized the name, but he wagged his tail.

"It would have been nice to see his face when they cuffed him," Andie said on her way back behind the counter.

Just what I wanted to hear. "You might have seen it if you hadn't left the force. You're missing a lot."

"All I'm missing is knife attacks and lawsuits."

Tom could argue with that, but he let the remark go by unchallenged. "You want to hear the other news?" he asked.

"Yes."

"Christopher had a girlfriend. I interviewed her." Tom described the garage, the perilous stairs, and the Bowie poster. He mentioned his splinter, which had been a bear to remove, and finally worked his way to prying up the floorboards. "That's where Christopher hid his laptop and cell."

Andie's eyes were wide. "You mean you've *found* them?!"

"They're at the lab. It's going to take a while to break the passwords, but we should know more in a month or so."

"I can't believe it." Andie sounded breathless. "It's a miracle."

"According to Kimberly, Christopher's journal is on the laptop. That could tell us a lot about what was on his mind."

The prospect of a journal seemed to surprise Andie even more. As they discussed what might be in it, she shook her head with what Tom hoped was wonder, not worry. "His journal may be better than interrogating him. He'd be more open and honest," Tom said.

"Possibly," Andie said with a nod as a timer buzzed in the

kitchen. "Excuse me a minute. I've got cookies in the oven. I forgot to ask what I could get for you and Sammy today."

"We can wait." But Tom decided not to wait. As Justice and Sammy chased each other around the storefront, Tom followed Andie behind the half wall into the kitchen.

Since the Barkery had no dishwasher, dirty pots, pans, and mixing bowls littered the counters and cups and dessert plates were piled in the sink's soapy water. Next to it, the few plates Andie had managed to wash this morning were lined up in a dish drainer. Without asking if she needed help, Tom picked up a sponge and went to work.

"You don't need to do that." Andie pulled two sheets of cookies shaped like fire hydrants from the oven.

"I'm glad to help. Nothing else to do this morning." Tom had groceries to pick up before Lisa, but for now he'd rather be here.

As Andie scooped up the fire hydrants with a spatula and placed them on a wire rack, Justice was so busy cavorting with Sammy that he did not charge to the kitchen and remind her that he was a professional taster. She added the cookie sheets to the pile of unwashed pots and pans and started drying cups and plates as Tom set them in the drainer. In a companionable silence, they worked as if they'd been washing and drying dishes together for years.

Andie stacked a plate on others in a cabinet. "May I ask you something?"

"Fire away." Tom sloshed the sponge inside a cup.

"Before I went back to work, Dr. Capoletti told me that many law enforcement officers dealt with hardship as kids. They had to grow up too soon," Andie said. "Did you?"

What a question. "Why do you ask?"

"I've just been thinking about it."

As Tom rinsed off the cup and handed it to Andie, he

thought about how to answer, then decided, *I have nothing to be ashamed of.* "I had a brutal father. Cops should have picked him up for child abuse, but nobody ever did."

"I'm sorry."

"Don't be. I'm fine."

"Couldn't your mother stop him?"

"She was afraid of him. We all were."

"Who's we?"

"My mother and my little sister. I had to take care of them," Tom said. "By ninth grade I got big enough to stand up to my father, and that helped."

"Are you still in touch with him?"

"Not since I left for college. My family's pretty much fallen apart. We avoid one another now. Too many bad memories."

"That's sad."

"I know, but I'm not sure I want to do anything about it."

Andie added a dry plate to her stack. "Dr. Capoletti said that after a difficult childhood, some people look for law enforcement jobs because they offer security and control."

"That could be true," Tom said. "I grew up in a house where you never knew what was going to happen from one minute to the next, so I like law and order."

Andie picked up a washed cup and handed it back to Tom. "Lipstick on the rim," she said.

"You can't get decent help these days." Tom rubbed the sponge over it. "What about you, Brady? You grow up too soon?"

"Age eight. My father died, and my mother had a breakdown. I had to hold our family together."

"I heard your father was a cop. Did he get killed on duty?"

"No. A heart attack out of the blue. I've been wondering lately how that's influenced me. I've been trying to figure it out."

"And?"

"Christopher's attack was a shock like my father's death. Zero security and control," Andie admitted. "Both traumatized me."

"Understandable." Tom handed back the cup, minus the lipstick.

"Good job," Andie said.

"We aim to please," Tom said.

"It pains me to see you wash dishes on your day off."

"I'm actually enjoying it." Tom had never told anyone, even Mia, about his father. He was surprised that he'd been so open with Andie. But he couldn't say he hadn't liked today's conversation. "What else have you been thinking about besides growing up too soon?" he asked.

"Oh, a lot of things." Andie dried the cup and added it to her stack. "After living with your father, you can probably relate to the main one that keeps coming up."

"And what's that?"

"That life is unfair."

"That's true. But it can still be good," Tom said.

When Andie didn't respond, he looked over at her. She was drying a mixing bowl and staring at the wall. "Did I say something wrong?" he asked.

"No." Her eyes went back to him. "I was just wondering if life could be unfair and good at the same time."

"Unfairness is an equal-opportunity condition. It's something everyone on earth needs to learn. Nobody's immune."

"I guess you're right."

"I know I'm right," Tom said. "Aren't you divorced?"

"Yes."

"We both learned all about unfairness by the time our spouses' lawyers chewed us up and spit us out."

"I don't even want to think about it." Andie smiled.

"You're pretty when you smile. You ought to do it more often." Tom liked that he'd coaxed another one out of her. "See?"

"See what?"

"Right now your life is unfair because of the lawsuit, but it's also good when you smile. They're not mutually exclusive."

"I never expected you to be so wise," Andie said.

"Try me."

CHAPTER 44

ANDREA

After work, Andie turned into Mel's Groceries' parking lot to pick up supper items. As usual, she scoured the lot for Jane's SUV to make sure there was no chance of running into her. One advantage of the Barkery was that the Vanderwaals didn't have a dog and Jane was unlikely to show up there. Dr. Capoletti said that the day would come when Andie wouldn't feel so defensive about her.

Andie pulled into a parking space and told Justice, "I'm going to get you a *chicken* breast!" She boomed "chicken" so he couldn't miss that he was about to get a treat. It was her best way to thank him for loyally hanging out at work with her. It was starting to become clear that he was not pleased with the arrangement.

When she reached over to the passenger seat to ruffle his forehead star, she wondered if he'd not heard her mention chicken. With a laser beam's intensity, he was staring out the window at two men standing between cars. One, in his forties, looked like the disheveled sort who might camp under freeways. The other, wearing an expensive suit and Hermès tie, was reaching for his wallet.

Andie knew the signs of a drug deal. Justice did too. He sniffed at the window's open crack and whimpered staccato sounds of urgency. He marched his front legs on the seat and panted and whined, desperate to spring out the door. *Foul miscreants! Let's get 'em! Come on!*

"Justice, I'm not a cop anymore."

Last week Andie had said that very thing to him when he'd tried to tell her in every way he could that he missed his K-9 job. All morning he'd followed her around the Barkery and plopped down on her toes to make her stop what she was doing and pay attention to him. He pined, sighed, paced, and stared out the windows, on the lookout for druggies.

When a teenage boy about Christopher's age came in to buy Peanut Butter Wonders for his sheltie, Justice jumped up from his morning glory bed and gave him a fervent sniff. Then he sat like a soldier at attention, his sign that somewhere on the kid were drugs.

Andie ignored the alert, but Justice was determined. He hurried behind the counter, clamped his teeth gently around her wrist, and tugged her toward the boy. In no uncertain terms, Justice announced, *Cocaine! A user in our midst! Don't let him get away!* When the teen sauntered out without being arrested, Justice, despondent, flopped on his bed and resumed his morning mope.

That was when Andie had reminded him that she was no longer on the force. The disappointment on his face had replied emphatically, *The Barkery is a colossal drag. I am shriveling from boredom. I want to go back to work.* He stared at the ceiling as if he were counting the ways he was bored: no dope, no peddlers, no searches, not even a trip to the Laser Lady's house. Lying around, purposeless, all day was a monumental bummer, unbefitting a German shepherd, who had so much to give.

Andie climbed out of the car and locked the doors—not that any thief would dare break in and wrangle with Justice's teeth. She called to him, "I'll be back in a minute."

On her way into the store, she glanced at the men, and a pang for the old days sneaked up and pinched her. As much as she didn't want to admit she missed being a cop, she wouldn't have minded rounding up the men and reminding them of the error of their ways. But she shoved that thought out of her mind. *You are a doggy baker, a perfectly respectable job. You are safe from teenage stabbers and money-hungry plaintiffs.*

Inside the store, Andie pushed her basket along the aisles and dodged other after-work shoppers who wanted to get home as badly as she did. She picked up lettuce, tomatoes, a package of chicken breasts, and Sweet Potato Maple Walnut ice cream, for which Justice would gladly join the French Foreign Legion and march across the Sahara. She headed to the checkout stand.

In Mel's and just about everywhere else on the island, Andie used to worry about running into hostile people she'd arrested or given traffic tickets to, but now, out of uniform, she blended in with everybody else. Anonymity was a relief. Or was it? She used to be proud to wear her uniform. She hadn't minded standing out.

As the checker itemized Andie's purchases, her glitter-tipped nails clicked against the cash register keys. Andie paid with a credit card and stuffed her groceries into a canvas tote. When she reached the car, she expected Justice to stand and swish his tail, excited to see her, as usual. But he remained seated. Though the two men who'd captured his attention were gone, he turned his face resolutely toward the window.

Undaunted, Andie addressed the back of his head. "Ready for your *chicken!?*" She lilted her voice at "chicken" to underscore the ecstasy.

Justice's silence boomed his disapproval of being a kept and unemployed dog.

"Come on, Big Guy. I know you love chicken."

Not a whimper or whine. Not even a disinterested pant.

Okay, so she'd launch a full-court press: "I got Sweet Potato Maple Walnut ice cream too! You can have some after your chicken."

Nothing. She felt censured, dismissed. Justice was telling her that she ranked lower than a rattlesnake scale. As she drove through the parking lot, he stared out the window as if his life depended on memorizing the license plates of cars they passed.

However, in his silence, an entire waterfall of words splashed onto the Honda's dashboard: *I am bored. I have no purpose. I want my job back. And if you want to get down to brass tacks here, I want you back. You're not yourself. I want us to feel alive again.*

CHAPTER 45

TOM

At first Miss Evelyn Granger, Lisa's fourth-grade teacher, looked like her forty-one years in the classroom had carved a permanent scowl on her forehead. She looked like she delighted in whacking rulers on knuckles; and if she were reincarnated, she'd come back as something hard and prickly, like a thistle.

But then Miss Granger smiled, and her wrinkles became a road map to Pleasantville. Tom felt comfortable in her presence. He'd been right to send Lisa to this school and this warm teacher, who'd taped Valentine hearts of red construction paper to all the classroom's windows.

Still in his khaki uniform, Tom hoisted himself onto the art table for his Back-to-School-Night conference with Miss Granger, her back ramrod straight, at her desk. The one-on-one portion of the evening had been set up like speed dating; a student's parents got five minutes with her before a bell rang and the next student's parents moved in. Mia had not been inclined to attend, so Tom had come alone. With so little time, he had to talk quickly, so he got right to the point.

"I'm worried about Lisa. Last week her mother announced she's getting married again." It was hard for the bitter admis-

sion to pass through his lips. He hated his daughter having a
stepfather.

"Does Lisa like the fiancé?" Miss Granger asked.

"I don't know. She never says much. Has she mentioned
him to you?"

Miss Granger glanced down at a science textbook on her
desk. A panda was on the cover. "Once in a while she says her
mother's boyfriend took her to a car wash or the grocery store—
never anywhere exciting. I'd say she doesn't have strong feelings
one way or the other."

"That's pretty much what I've concluded."

"Do you like him?" Miss Granger asked.

"I've only met him a few times. I feel sorry for him ending
up with my ex, I can tell you."

"I hear that from a lot of divorced parents," Miss Granger
said. "Why exactly are you worried about Lisa?"

"Maybe 'worried' is too strong. I'm uneasy. Fathers aren't
universally kind." As Tom knew all too well from his own. "I've
been working on a case about a teen who tried to hurt a cop.
As far as I can tell, his stepfather was a . . ." Tom searched for a
polite word to describe Franz. "His stepfather was mean to
him. I'd hate for Lisa to get into a situation like that. I don't
want her to be a troubled kid."

"Lisa's nowhere near troubled. She's got a good head on
her shoulders. Most days her mood ring ranges from a happy
dark blue to an upbeat blue-green." Miss Granger's eyes twinkled. "She's taught me how to read the colors. It's amazing
what I learn from kids."

"She's taught me names of clouds." Tom swung his dangling
size-twelve feet. "So you don't think some soon-to-be stepfather
is abusing her? I see way too much of that on my job."

Miss Granger shook her head. "I think I'd sense abuse," she
said. "The main thing you need to do right now is keep com-
munication lines open."

"We talk by Skype every night."

"Good," Miss Granger said. "I wish all my students were as loving and sweet as Lisa is. She's our weatherwoman. She's adjusted quickly here."

"I'm always trying to compensate for not being a full-time dad. I wish I saw her more than on holidays and weekends, but I have crazy, ever-changing hours." Tom could have talked with Miss Granger all night, but the bell rang, shrill and cold-hearted, and bumped him out of this reassuring conversation into the night.

As he got up to give his place to the smiling couple at the classroom door, Miss Granger said, "I've heard about the terrible schedules you officers have. If you decide to marry again, find someone who's also in law enforcement."

All the way home, Tom pondered that.

CHAPTER 46

ANDREA

In the weeks that Andie had been seeing Dr. Capoletti, Justice had begun to consider his office a second home. He bounded in like he owned the place and waited for his biscuit by Dr. Capoletti's white ceramic jar. Then as peaceful as the bookcase's Buddha, Justice sprawled out on the Oriental rug. Confident that no threats lurked here, he conked out for each fifty-minute hour.

For Andie too, the office had become a haven. Dr. Capoletti's burning-cherry smoke that lingered in the air was familiar to her now, and the batting escaping from his chair's arm seemed charming. This was the one place besides her home where she could leave behind all pretense of being tough, strong, or in command. She could just be.

What she was being today was gloomy. She sank into the sofa as if buzzards were roosting in her heart, and explained that she'd slid back into a psychological morass. "My anger is tearing up my insides. One minute I hate Christopher for ruining my life, but the next I blame myself for shooting him. Then I hate his parents for their lawsuit, but I know I killed their son," she said. "I can't decide who are the offenders and who are the victims in this mess."

Dr. Capoletti pulled a handkerchief from his back pocket

and honked a loud and boisterous honk that rallied Justice enough to open an eye before he went back to his nap. "Tell me, how are you the offender?"

"Simple. I killed Christopher. He's my victim."

"What if you reverse that? How are you the victim?"

"Christopher hurt Justice and attacked me."

Dr. Capoletti picked up his pipe and clamped it, unlit, between his teeth. "You didn't ask for the attack."

"Of course not."

"He came at you and surprised you, didn't he? You didn't have time to ponder your response."

"No, I didn't. It was pure survival instinct."

"Exactly! Survival!" Dr. Capoletti toasted the air with his pipe. "That night when you shot him, you survived physically. Now we've been working on how you survive emotionally."

For Andie, who felt like sharks had been circling her leaky boat for four months, survival sounded like a good idea.

"Do you know the difference between a victim and survivor?" Dr. Capoletti asked.

"No."

"After a trauma, a victim gets depressed or discouraged or, at worst, immobilized. She often feels responsible for what happened even if that makes no rational sense."

"You said 'she.' You're talking about me, right? Because I'm depressed and blaming myself, you're saying I'm a victim?"

"Do you think you are?"

"Yes, because I *was* victimized. You can't ignore it. It's a fact."

"It was a fact when it happened. But you don't have to stay a victim forever. You can grow out of it and become a survivor."

"What's the difference?" Andie asked.

"If you're a survivor, a trauma makes you stronger, and you take responsibility for *recovering* from it. You stop being passive and depressed, and you become a fighter. You rise like a phoenix from your ash heap of anger and guilt."

"You can't just will away those bad feelings," Andie said.

"But you *can* cut off the bad feelings' power over you," Dr. Capoletti said.

"That sounds impossible."

"Not if you work at it."

"How?"

Dr. Capoletti struck a match and lit his pipe. *Puff, puff.* "You work at it by giving up trying to forget what happened, because you never will. And you stop beating yourself up because that accomplishes nothing. Instead of feeling victimized, you celebrate your resilience and strength."

"What if you have no resilience and strength?" Andie asked.

"You think you don't?"

"Do you always answer a question with a question?"

"Most of the time." Dr. Capoletti's lips parted in a smile. "I'd say you've shown plenty of resilience and strength all your life. Think back on the hard things you've overcome. You've been a survivor."

"I never looked at myself that way."

"Maybe it's time."

When Andie stood up to leave half an hour later, she felt like in her chest doves were spreading their wings, about to take flight.

On the ferry ride back to San Julian, Andie thought so hard about being a "survivor" that the idea sprang to life in her mind, like an imaginary friend. She named her the Stalwart Cookie and because Andie had watched a safari video the night before, she pictured the Stalwart Cookie researching wildlife in Uganda. Her hair damp under a pith helmet, she always pushed forward, and she ignored Uzi-bearing poachers peering at her through binoculars. As silverback gorillas climbed trees above her head, she batted tsetse flies and hacked her machete through tangled underbrush.

The Stalwart Cookie forged her own path and met life on her own terms. No one would guess that two years before, a protective mother elephant had charged her open-sided Land Rover, flipped it over, and jabbed a tusk into her thigh. It had taken her months to regather courage to go back to the wild. But there she was, a survivor, moving on.

Ahem. The Stalwart Cookie elbowed Andie's ribs. *In case you're not seeing what's in front of you, you were a survivor supreme when your father died and that unworthy twit of a husband abandoned you.*

Andie supposed that was true.

If you can do it twice, a third time won't kill you. Get some spunk. Go live your life.

Andie stroked Justice's shoulder as the ferry approached San Julian. In the darkness, the town's lights twinkled, full of hope.

When the ferry pulled into the dock, for the first time in months Andie didn't feel like going home. Though it was dinnertime, she drove down Main Street to Stephanie's condo, which was two blocks from the police station. Andie had not seen her in weeks.

"Wonders never cease! The hermit emerges! Welcome back." In a ruby fleece top and jeans, Stephanie was brandishing two knitting needles and holding a ball of crimson yarn. "I'd drop a stitch if I put these down," she said. "Come on in. Want some tea?"

"I can only stay a minute. Justice needs his supper." They followed Stephanie into her kitchen, where red enamel pots and pans hung from a ceiling rack and every hour a clock tweeted the song of a different bird—such as a cardinal at one and a blue jay at two.

At the smell of stew in Stephanie's Crock-Pot, Justice's nostrils emphatically announced, *I want. I want. I am famished. Starve me at your peril.* But when Andie sat at the table, he politely wriggled underneath and curled around her feet.

"I wanted to see how you are," Andie said.

"No complaints." As Stephanie resumed knitting, her needles clicked.

Andie picked a red-and-white-striped watch cap from a pile on the table. "Did you make these hats?"

"To sell at the Crafts Fair in two weeks. Thirty-five dollars a pop, and I can make the hats fast with these fat needles. Plus I've been knitting on the sly at work. Great Barrier Reef, here I come."

"Good for you," Andie said. It felt like she'd visited here just yesterday and she and Stephanie were picking up where they'd left off. "Promise you haven't been an artist's model."

"At this time of year it's too cold to parade around and show much flesh."

"I'd have worried about you." Andie wound, then rewound a red yarn scrap around her index finger. "Everything okay at the station?"

"Fine except everybody misses you."

"I miss all of you," Andie said.

"We think you're nuts for leaving. Old crusty Malone is waiting for you to see the light."

"Well . . . um . . ."

"Why don't you come back? What's the problem?"

"I haven't wanted to be a cop again."

Exasperation flickered across Stephanie's face. She poked one needle under the other and looped yarn around it.

Andie was about to say that she was never coming back, but the Stalwart Cookie wielded her machete at another vine and growled, *Never say "never."*

"I'm taking it one day at a time," Andie said.

"Sounds reasonable," Stephanie said. "Meanwhile, how are things with you and Wolski?"

"What do you mean?"

"Every time I see him, he asks how you are. I was embarrassed to admit I hadn't talked with you in weeks."

"I'm sorry. Really. I've needed time to get myself together."

"Are you together now?"

"More than the last time I saw you." It seemed like she'd resigned from the force in the Jurassic Period.

"Good. Welcome back to the land of the living," Stephanie said.

CHAPTER 47

ANDREA

Dr. Capoletti seemed to reside in Andie's head. Whenever unsettling possibilities invaded her thoughts, he appeared in her mind and shooed them away, insisting, *They're not facts!* Or when she pondered snippets of his other observations, such as "what you feel you can heal," anger at Christopher seeped out of her. Or when a nightmare left her sweating in the dark, she told herself, as Dr. Capoletti would have done, "You are a survivor." She understood that since age eight she'd forced herself to *act* strong; now she knew that her strength was real and it had always been inside her.

At a session in early March, Andie told Dr. Capoletti of this progress, and they began discussing the concept of justice, whose basic purpose, they agreed, was to set things right.

"You think you've gotten justice with Christopher?" Dr. Capoletti asked.

"I was exonerated for shooting him," Andie said.

"That's law-and-order justice. It set things right for you legally. How would you go about setting them right emotionally?"

"I don't know."

"It would probably involve an apology and forgiveness, wouldn't it?" Dr. Capoletti asked.

"I guess."

"They're part of what's called restorative justice. To repair the psychological harm of an offense, some judges actually help criminals say they're sorry and their victims to forgive them. It's a deeper kind of justice than a punishment or an eye for an eye. Everybody can heal."

Pie in the sky, Andie thought. "Forget apologies. Christopher's dead, and I can't wait a hundred years for the Vanderwaals to get around to it. And anyway I can't forgive. I've tried." Whatever forgiveness she'd mustered had had the consistency of straw that would require years of chewing to digest. A grudge against Christopher and the Vanderwaals had lodged itself inside her.

Dr. Capoletti puffed his pipe. "Maybe you're thinking about forgiveness as kissing and making up, but I'm talking about a different kind. It's the forgiving Justice has done." At hearing his name bandied about, Justice interrupted his possum playing and shifted positions.

"Justice isn't brooding about being stabbed. He's managed to let it all go and move on with his life," Dr. Capoletti said. "Do you think you can do that? Forgive, let go, and move on?"

"I don't know."

"Here's a good way to start," he said. "Write Christopher and his parents a letter and pour out all your thoughts and feelings. Then destroy the damned thing. Bury it or drown it or send it up in smoke."

Three days later, Andie sat on a driftwood log and watched Justice sniff tide pools down the beach. He seemed rapt by the starfish and crabs' smells. Not enthusiastic about wet paws, however, he sniffed only till a wave had the impertinence to come too close, and he jumped back. Justice may have been courageous, but he ran from foamy water.

The wind picked up, and the afternoon sun hid behind

rolling hills of clouds. As they floated across the sky, Andie wrapped an arm around her knees and dug her heels into the pebbly beach. She rubbed her eyes, scratchy from lack of sleep. Until late into the night, she'd written the letter that she and Dr. Capoletti had discussed, and she'd wrung out her negativity and ambivalence.

Free at last to feel anger, Andie lashed Christopher with fury. "You practically ruined my life, but I'm sure you could care less. You're a screwed-up brat, and you deserve a major thrashing. You put me in an impossible situation. What was I supposed to do? I didn't want to kill you, but I didn't want to die."

She described her nightmares and flashbacks. "Do you have any idea how terrifying they are? All because of you, I wake up screaming in the middle of the night. Or I'm out somewhere, and I remember you, and I break out in a sweat and feel like I'm going to faint. You still haunt me sometimes, and I don't understand why you attacked Justice and me. You had no reason to be so cruel. We'd done nothing to you."

As Andie's tears fell on the letter, she told Christopher, "You'll never know how much guilt you've caused me. I hate you for it." But then she begged him, "Please forgive me. I'd give anything if you were alive. I'm so sorry. Wherever you are, I wish you well."

Next, Andie railed at the Vanderwaals. "You were lousy, irresponsible parents. How dare you appear on TV with Sid King and blame me for what happened? *I'm* not guilty of criminal behavior. *You're* the ones who should rot in hell. You may have filed a lawsuit against me, but you can only get my money. You'll never have my soul."

Singling out Jane, Andie said, "Before Christmas, you verbally assaulted me. You refuse to see the truth about what Christopher did. You're mean and blind, and you owe me an apology, big-time." But by the end of the letter, Andie herself apologized to

Jane and Franz and begged their forgiveness as fervently as she'd begged Christopher's. "I can never express how sorry I am. There's nothing in the world I wouldn't do to bring back your son."

Now as Andie watched Justice exploring the beach, she felt emotionally spent but also purged. And she felt lighter and freer because the heft of her complicated feelings weighed down the letter instead of her heart. It was as if psychological Merry Maids had shown up and dusted, mopped, and scoured her heart till no dirt or cobweb of hate could be found. Internally, Andie was cleaner. It was time to scrub away the letter too.

She began ripping up her five single-spaced pages and dropping the pieces onto a slowly growing mound between her rubber boots. On the ragged paper scraps, she could still make out a few words—"unfair," "hell," "pain"—but they no longer belonged in sentences, and every yank of her fingers eviscerated the damage behind them. As she worked, she thought that she was also eviscerating her own misery of the last four months— and she snatched and attacked the paper till nothing was left but a pile of bits. She wadded it in her fists, got up, and started toward the water.

Justice, who always seemed to grasp when something significant was happening, bounded over to her. As she sloshed into the shallow water, he sloshed, *semper fi,* beside her. Unlike before, he did not back up when waves threatened his paws. He stuck to her like a faithful barnacle.

In an act of celebration, Andie raised her fists into the air and hurled the paper toward the sky. The pieces flew away like confetti thrown from windows onto a victory parade, and the wind swept them over the waves. Finally, they landed in Puget Sound, which would take them to the ocean. There they would dissolve in the great pool of life.

But suddenly in horror Andie shouted, "Yikes!" The waves

were returning the scraps to shore. Barking, Justice ran with her as she scrambled around, frantic, catching as many as she could and tossing them back into the water.

No matter how far she threw the pieces, they kept bobbing back. She realized that the waves were an incoming tide. She and Justice could chase and rail at the paper for the rest of the afternoon, but that would do no good. They were up against a natural force; the tide would not go out until the moon said so. Dismayed, Andie called Justice, and they made their way back to the log.

As wind blew tiny paths through Justice's fur, he sat in his maharaja position, his bottom on the pebbles, his regal face toward the water. Andie put her arm around his back and, together, they watched the soggy paper pieces litter the beach. Something she'd wanted so badly to let go of refused to do her bidding. Like most everything else in life (*except your attitude,* she heard Dr. Capoletti say in her head), she had no control over the tide. It was almost comical, how insistent the little scraps of paper were.

Andie was not sure how long she and Justice sat there, but just as surely as the waves rolled in, so did her thoughts. What slowly came to her was that maybe expecting to be done forever with shooting Christopher was too much to ask. Maybe she wasn't supposed to close a door on his death and walk away. Maybe she needed to learn that he was a fact of her life—perhaps *the* fact of her life—and she must accept and work around it, and bravely play whatever cards the Vanderwaals dealt.

Surrounded by pieces of a letter she'd hoped would rid her of Christopher and his parents forever, Andie admitted that nothing ever would. They'd always be a part of her. She said, "Justice, I'm not going to fight anymore."

When he panted, he exposed the heart-shaped spot on his tongue. It reminded Andie that all the thinking in the world wasn't going to solve her problem; it was her heart she needed to worry about. In other words, as Dr. Capoletti had said, she needed to forgive—just as she'd begged Christopher and the Vanderwaals to forgive *her* in the letter.

Andie could never hug and kiss the Vanderwaals, but in her heart she could cordially shake their hands and wish them well. As for Christopher, she'd take a lesson from Justice; she'd let go of that horrible night and move on. When Christopher inevitably turned up in her thoughts, she would picture him, his knobby knees at odd angles, riding a celestial bike along a celestial tree-lined street—heading toward a loving home. That would be the best way for her as the victim to bestow forgiveness.

But what about her as the offender? How was she supposed to *receive* forgiveness when it could never come from Christopher and would likely not come from his parents in her lifetime? Andie decided that it was up to her to go whole hog and set right everyone's offenses, including hers, in her own heart.

I may never know if I did the right thing, she thought. She might die still wondering if shooting Christopher had been a mistake and wishing she'd handled him better. Still, on the night she'd killed him, she knew with rock-solid certainty that she'd done the very best she could. She'd never ever wanted to hurt anyone.

She would forgive herself.

CHAPTER 48

TOM

Tom parked on Main Street a block from the Barkery. He intended to walk to the library, because the librarian wanted to talk with him about participating in an identity theft workshop. He locked his car, stepped onto the sidewalk, and started down the block past Woof Gang Pet Store and the Chat 'n' Chew Café.

He stopped. The librarian said she could meet anytime from ten till noon, and it was only ten fifteen. No rush. What if he went to visit Brady for a minute first? He hadn't seen her since they'd washed dishes together last month, and she'd been on his mind. More than he liked to admit.

Would it be right to show up for no reason? asked a cautious streak in himself.

Hell, yes, answered his red-blooded all-American male.

What if she's baking something and doesn't have time to visit?

It wouldn't hurt her to take a break.

Tom couldn't remember a time when he'd been so circumspect about a woman. Sure, Andie had broken their date years ago and wounded his pride. But today it seemed to him like more than that. Maybe he'd invested feelings in her. No maybes about it—he had—and now he had something to lose.

Tom's red-blooded male grabbed his arm and walked him back toward the Barkery. At this hour of the morning, commuters had left on the ferry, mothers had dropped off their children at school—and shoppers, coffee klatchers, and delivery people had taken over downtown. A man in a fedora was studying a map in front of Rainier Bank, and a mailman was stuffing envelopes into the Family Smile Dentist's box. Tom's red-blooded male escorted him past DIY Hardware and Village Vittles Kitchen Store and stopped him in front of the Dippity Creamery.

Bring her an ice cream, the red-blooded male ordered.

Nobody eats ice cream for breakfast, argued Tom's cautious streak.

So you think ice cream hours are from exactly two to ten p.m.? You get fined if you eat Rocky Road in the morning? Loosen up. Brady will like a surprise.

A pervasive but pleasant smell of milk hung in the air. Written on a chalkboard were the day's flavors, and Tom pondered Going Nuts and Peppermint Kiss but finally settled on Industrial Chocolate because every woman in her right mind liked chocolate. From a girl with a gold stud in her tongue, he ordered two cones, two scoops each. Since chocolate was bad for dogs, he also asked for a small cup of Vanilla Bean for Justice.

How am I going to open the Barkery's door if I'm carrying all that? wondered Tom's cautious streak.

Cool it. You'll figure it out.

A woman in an iridescent orange coat was leaving the Barkery with her Pomeranian as Tom arrived, and she held the door open for him. When Andie heard the cowbell's clang, she stopped wiping off a table, looked up, and smiled a warm, welcoming smile.

"Hello there," she said.

Tom didn't need Lisa's mood ring to conclude that Andie was glad to see him, and his cautious streak took a hike. He held out the cones, still pressed against the cup for transport. "You'd better get going on one of these before it melts. They're Industrial Chocolate."

"What a treat!" Andie smiled again and worked a cone out of his full hands.

Justice's champion sniffer informed him that ice cream had entered his domain, and he got up from his morning glory bed and moved in for the kill. He planted himself in front of Tom and gazed in a way designed to force him to submissive knees. *Surely you intend to share that,* said the bead of drool about to drip from Justice's tongue. *You would not be cruel and heartless and ignore me.*

"I'm sorry. He's a beggar," Andie said.

"That's why I brought him some Vanilla Bean." When Tom set the cup in front of Justice, he shoved his muzzle into it, and with ebullient licks he scooted the cup across the floor.

"You look different," Tom told Andie.

"It's the same me."

"No, you seem taller and straighter. It's hard to explain."

"It could be the Industrial Chocolate. It does that to people," Andie said.

That was an actual joke. A first. Something's changed. Tom started on his own cone with a smile.

"Any word about the laptop and cell?" Andie asked.

"Not yet, but the lab's working on them. I'll let you know when there's news," Tom said. "So how's it going?"

"Better since you came."

The red-blooded all-American male high-fived Tom. *What did I tell you?! Chortle, chortle.*

"Customers hassling you this morning?" Tom asked.

"No." Andie licked a drip that was about to slide onto her thumb. "I'm glad you stopped by because I needed a boost."

"For what?"

"A deposition. At one thirty the Vanderwaals' lawyer officially starts coming after me."

"Wow. Nobody's wasting any time." From a Barkery dispenser, Tom pulled out two napkins, handed one to Andie, and wiped his mouth with the other. "I didn't expect any discovery for another few months at the least."

"The sooner the lawyer piles up billable hours, the better for his bank account," Andie said.

"You scared?"

"Yes. It's taking all my courage, but I'm not as afraid as I'd have been a month or two ago."

"What's the difference now?"

Andie licked another drip. "I guess I know whatever happens, I'll survive somehow."

"You'll be fine," Tom said. "The last I heard, thumbscrews were outlawed. Nobody can demand strips of flesh to pay for damages."

Andie laughed.

"And you're laughing on a day like this," Tom said. "A few months ago you didn't have a laugh in you."

"I've been working on my attitude."

"Good for you." Tom had to hand it to her. She'd always been tough, but now she seemed easier in her skin. He liked the change. "You go tell that lawyer you did what you had to do. You've got truth on your side."

"I hope you're right."

Justice, who'd given up trying to lick a hole through his cardboard cup, looked like he would now angle for Industrial Chocolate. He abandoned the cup under a table, cocked his head, and fixed Tom with keen eyes. *You still have ice cream. I want ice cream. Can you spare a lick for a hungry dog?*

Tom tried to ignore him, but he felt his eyes bore into him. "Is Justice going to the deposition with you?"

"Ron Hausmann said I could bring him for moral support."

"Good. Follow his example."

"You mean by being brave?"

"Definitely that. But look at him."

Justice's gaze threw spears at Tom and pinned him to the wall. The intensity in his eyes was meant to make Tom fall down and crumble before him.

"See? Justice will never give up," Tom said. "After Christopher stabbed him, he could have moped around, scared, for the rest of his life, but he's probably stronger than ever. And he knows it. Ain't nobody gonna mess with him."

"You think I should be like that too?"

"You already are," Tom said. "This afternoon let it show."

CHAPTER 49

ANDREA

Ron Hausmann was waiting for Andie outside the entrance to Twombly and Fixx's law firm, which was located on Main Street in a white Victorian house. He leaned against the porch railing and waved to her and Justice, climbing the steps toward him. "Are you ready?"

"As ready as I'll ever be, I guess," she said.

Hausmann reached for the front doorknob, embossed with a lion's face. "Remember what we talked about. This is a deposition. You're not here for a chat."

"I know."

"Norm Fixx is going to dig for things to use against you in court. Stay focused on the questions, and say the minimum. Don't give him rope to hang you."

"I'll try."

Andie remembered Tom's suggestion that she follow Justice's example. He not only tried; he never gave up, and he was confident and strong. That would be her goal today. The Dr. Capoletti in Andie's mind reminded her, *You can't control what happens, but you can choose your attitude toward it.*

The fluorescent lighting in the reconfigured breakfast nook bleached out the face of Norm Fixx. He pumped Andie's hand like he was after well water. His self-satisfied smile hinted of the Laser Lady's Alistair, surrounded by canary feathers.

"Mr. Hausmann said it would be okay to bring Justice," Andie said.

"Why, sure! Justice looks like a fine dog!" Fixx said. "I love German shepherds. They're remarkable animals. You know, I had one as a kid."

In that case, he should have known to hold out his hand for Justice's get-acquainted sniff, but he bonked Justice on the head as insensitively as Chief Malone had, right on the star, exactly where Justice did *not* like to be bonked, and especially not by a clearly unpalatable stranger like Fixx. Justice's glower told him that he was as worthy as smog. *I'd like to introduce you to my teeth, you reprehensible slug.*

Indeed, a slug might have occupied a prominent place in Fixx's gene pool; one glance at him and you'd expect spiked antennae and a trail of slime. His hair, combed back in a European style, was on the oily side, as was his skin. The crest on his pinky ring might have represented the barony of Sing Sing.

A court reporter in wire-frame glasses swore in Andie, and everyone took a place around a former built-in breakfast table. Fixx began, "As you know, the Vanderwaals are litigating against you and asking for six million dollars to compensate for their son's death."

Before, whenever Andie had heard that sum, her heart would buckle over in a swoon. But lately her heart had been stouter. Today she quickly gathered her grit and told herself to stay focused. The Stalwart Cookie cheered her on.

Fixx flipped open a folder of notes and fired preliminary questions: What was Andie's name, age, and address? What was her employment history? How long had she been on the force? That groundwork laid, he turned the page and said, "Let's move on to that night." He grilled her about exactly what had happened.

"How long did it take the deceased to run from Justice to you?" he asked.

"I'm not sure," Andie said.

"One second? Two? Three?"

Andie shrugged. *Don't let him stress you.* "He walked a step or two toward me, and then he started to run. I didn't have a stopwatch. Maybe five seconds, but I don't know."

"As he came toward you, what expression did he have on his face?"

"I couldn't see. I don't know."

"Was he laughing? Crying? Any signal of his feelings?"

"She told you she couldn't see his face," Hausmann said.

"What about his posture? Any sign there?" Fixx asked.

"I'm not sure. I didn't have time to evaluate it."

"Did he say anything?"

"Not that I heard."

"Could he have whispered?"

"I don't know if he whispered or not."

"Tell us what you *do* know about Christopher approaching you, Ms. Brady." Fixx's arched eyebrow was doubtless intended to intimidate her as readily as his barrage of unanswerable questions.

Andie sat up straighter and reminded herself that she did not need a carapace of toughness to protect herself from a slug. All she needed was a strong heart. "I do know I came home from work and Christopher . . . the deceased . . . was waiting there," she said calmly.

"Of all the things the deceased might have done that night, why do you think he chose to come to your yard?" Fixx asked.

"Objection. Speculation," Hausmann said.

"All right, then I'll ask this way." Fixx turned the page. "Tell me, are you divorced?"

"Yes."

"Why did you divorce?"

"Incompatibility," Andie said to keep the answer short.

"I don't understand." Fixx acted like "incompatibility" was too complex a term for a simple man like him. "Explain. What do you mean by that?"

"What other people mean by it. Our marriage didn't work out."

"Were you faithful to your husband?"

"Objection. Irrelevant," Hausmann said.

Andie pierced Fixx with her eyes and said anyway, "I was faithful."

"Have you ever had a relationship with a much younger man?" Fixx asked. *Heh-heh.* His smile exposed yellow teeth.

"Objection! Ambiguous. What do you mean by 'younger'? Younger relative to what?" Hausmann said.

"I'll rephrase," Fixx said. "How friendly were you with the deceased?"

"I hardly knew him."

"How *did* you know him?"

"I saw him around the neighborhood. He knocked on my door one day and sold me a raffle ticket."

"Oh, *really?!*" Fixx's well-practiced eyebrow arched again, this time suggesting that buying a raffle ticket was a danger-ously salacious act.

"Yes, really." *You're trying to fluster me, but I won't let you.*

Fixx coughed and fumbled with his notes so he appeared to be looking for something, but the awkward silence was obvi-ously intended to pressure her into saying more. Perhaps he wanted her to admit that the raffle ticket was a prelude to a de-licious affair, that she and Christopher had groped and thrashed during after-school trysts and their hot breath had fogged her patrol car's windows.

When Andie did not volunteer rope to hang herself, Fixx coughed again. "What if the deceased had come back to sell you a magazine subscription? What would you have done?"

"Objection. Irrelevant." Hausmann pounded his fist on the table.

"All right. We'll get back to that." Another of Fixx's smiles told Andie, *Sweat it out while you wait.* "Let's return to the deceased running toward you. Why did you think you were in danger?"

"He stabbed my dog. I saw his knife."

"Have you had training in de-escalation tactics?"

"Yes."

"What was it?"

"A workshop given by our department psychologist, Dr. Capoletti."

"So what did he teach you about calming down somebody?"

"Basically, you ask open-ended questions and get him talking. You paraphrase what he says and repeat it back to him so he knows you're listening and you understand. You build rapport."

"Did you ask questions and build rapport with the deceased?" Fixx asked.

"I had no time to talk with him. He was running at me. De-escalation tactics wouldn't have worked."

Fixx continued to badger her. He tried to get her to admit she'd cut corners and not bothered to try an alternative to force. When she didn't buckle under his questions, he finally moved on to her knowledge of first aid and asked, "Did you have any training to take care of wounds?"

"Yes, at the Academy. Since then, I've had to be recertified every two years."

"So you'd say you're an expert?"

"No, but I know what to do," Andie said.

"When did you notice the deceased was bleeding?"

"Soon after he fell."

"And you started first aid immediately," Fixx said, as if any competent officer would have jumped right in to save a life.

"I had to call for help first and make sure I was safe."

"How did you do that?"

"I kicked away his knife, checked him for other weapons, and cuffed him."

"When did you *finally* get around to helping him, Ms. Brady?" Fixx asked with sarcasm.

"Objection. Mischaracterizes her testimony. She administered first aid after following necessary protocol," Hausmann said.

"I saw he was bleeding badly, so I wound a tourniquet around his leg," Andie said.

"Where?" Fixx asked.

"Above the wound. In the middle of the bend between the front of his leg and his hip, as high up as I could."

And so it went. Fixx circled around and around, stopping one topic and picking up another and returning to the topic before. Why did Andie apply the tourniquet and then leave the deceased? When the police arrived, why was she bent over her dog?

Andie stayed cool as lettuce even when he brought up her "relationship" to Christopher again. And again. Fixx weaseled around and tucked that topic into most lines of his questions. He seemed obsessed with it. When he pursued her history on the force, he asked if Andie had a boyfriend. Did she ever fantasize about teenage boys? Would she say that she was sexually fulfilled?

After four hours of Fixx's grilling and his threat to require her to return for more, Andie got up and walked outside into the gathering darkness with Justice and Hausmann. She didn't need her lawyer to say she'd done a good job today because she knew she had. She wished Tom were here so she could tell him that she'd done what he'd suggested. Ain't nobody messed with her.

CHAPTER 50

TOM

Andrea was raking leaves in front of her house when Tom drove up in his patrol car. She was wearing jeans and a sweatshirt, and her cheeks were flushed from exercise. As Tom tucked a manila envelope under his arm and started across the grass, Justice galloped over to him. Tom held out his hand for the requisite sniff.

"Hey, Brady! It's almost April. Don't you know you're supposed to rake leaves in the fall?"

When Andie smiled, her green eyes could conquer nations, including the Nation of Tom. On her small hands, her leather garden gloves looked like mitts. "I didn't feel like cleaning up out here before," she said.

"Need some help?"

"I'm done." Andie tied her last bag of leaves closed and set it with others lined up on her flagstone path.

"Aren't you going to rake that side of your yard?" Tom pointed to what once had been the crime scene.

"I can't get myself to go over there. I don't park in front of my house anymore, either."

"Why?"

"It gives me the creeps."

"Park wherever you want, but if you let that part of your

yard go to hell, by summer the grass will be up to your windows."

Andie shrugged. "It doesn't matter."

"Tell that to the fire department. Tall grass is a hazard. If you find me over there raking and mowing someday, you'll know why," Tom said as Justice nudged his hand to ask for pets. Tom stooped down and scratched Justice's chest, which was one of his favorite spots.

As Andie took off her gloves and stuffed them into her jacket pocket, Tom noticed that she looked puzzled, and he realized she might be wondering why he was there. Dropping into the Barkery with an ice-cream cone was different from showing up at her house. Crossing a boundary called for an explanation.

"I wanted to talk with you about something," Tom said.

"Good or bad?" Andie asked.

"Depends on how you look at it."

"Now you have me worried."

"It's just some news."

"Um . . . do you want to talk out here or come in for a cup of tea?" Andie asked.

"Let's go in." Tom was a put-hair-on-your-chest espresso man, but for her he'd stoop to chamomile.

Tom had not stepped through Andie's front door since the shooting. After such a violent incident, even the house had seemed shocked, like it had been shaken to its foundation. Tom had turned on all the lights to chase away the gloom pervading the place. Wishing he didn't have to be there, he'd zipped up his jacket against the chill.

But today sun shone through the windows, and the rooms felt light and airy and warm. Tom was aware of bright, friendly colors coming at him from all directions—the stained-glass lamp hanging in the entry, the rug and sofa pillows in the living room, the red geraniums blooming in the windowsills. It felt like the house had come to life again.

He followed Andie into the kitchen, and just as he'd helped her wash the Barkery dishes, he set the breakfast table with the place mats, spoons, and cups she handed him. They discussed Andie's deposition and Ron Hausmann's belief that she'd stopped Norm Fixx in his tracks. Tom did not mention that he'd almost waited for her outside the law firm that day. But then he'd decided that if she'd walked outside defeated, however unlikely, she might have wanted to be alone.

Justice Hoovered down a people cracker, and on his golden kitchen throne he lay on his side and thrust out his legs so his body formed a sideways U. His sagging eyelids announced that Tom could take over as guard and protector until Justice finished his nap.

At the table across from Tom, Andie poured tea into his cup, and steam billowed up between them. He took a gulp and winced—it *was* chamomile. *How could anybody drink this stuff?* Still, it was pleasant to be here. He'd have welcomed sitting around for a friendly chat, but the manila envelope next to his elbow reminded him that he'd come here on business.

"I've got some things to tell you," he said. "The lab's still working on Christopher's cell, but they got into his laptop. I printed up part of his journal."

All the way across the table, Tom heard Andie's sharp intake of breath. "Did he write terrible things?"

"He's left us a lot to think about."

"Like what?" Andie asked.

"For starters, we were right that Christopher didn't have good parents." Tom unclasped the envelope and slid out pages, which he'd marked with yellow Post-it notes. "Christopher always refers to Franz as 'the Jackass' and Jane as 'the Slave.' There's no dad or mom mentioned anywhere."

"That's sad," Andie said.

"It gets worse." Tom set the first marked page on top of the others. "You want to read this yourself, or should I summarize?"

"Summarize."

"Okay. Here's an example of something that happens pretty regularly, because it's clear that Franz is emotionally abusive. He tells Christopher to make him a chicken sandwich for lunch. So Christopher picks some meat off a carcass in the refrigerator, puts everything together, and brings it to Franz, who's glued to a Mariners game." Tom read: "'The Jackass took a couple of bites and started yelling about chicken fat and why hadn't I cut it off. I didn't know chickens *had* fat. I mean, BIG DEAL. Who cares? But apparently I'm a LOSER who'll never amount to anything because I don't know about chicken fat? And no wonder nobody likes me, because I'm too stupid to make a sandwich.'"

Tom continued, summarizing, "Franz threatens to ground him for disrespect—apparently Christopher is punished for no good reason all the time—but after Franz's flash of anger, he loses interest and goes back to the Mariners. Then Jane comes home that night."

Tom read again: "'I didn't bother telling the Slave what the Jackass said because, as usual, she'd act like it wasn't important. She'd say what she always does: "Oh, that's just Franz's way of talking. He doesn't mean any harm. YOU need to try and get along with him better." Like it's MY fault he's an asshole. She doesn't get it. I don't matter to her.'"

"That's horrible," Andie said. "But Christopher was wrong. He did matter to Jane. When she stopped here before Christmas, she was really upset."

"Maybe he didn't matter enough. Or Jane could have been trying not to rock the boat with Franz. Maybe she's scared of him—he could mistreat her too," Tom said. "You can see why Christopher stole shirts and attacked the camp counselor. In a house like that, he had to put his anger somewhere." Tom hid his grimace as he swallowed more chamomile. "It's a shame Christopher couldn't have hung on till he grew up a little. Once he got bigger, he could have stood up to his dad." *Like I did.* Tom knew what Christopher had felt.

"Jane should have left Franz." Andie's face looked as dark as it had during Tom's investigation. "Abuse like that can be so damaging to a kid. It's awful nobody intervened."

"I know you think you should have, Brady, but forget that. There was no way," Tom said. "And Christopher's girlfriend didn't help. You want to hear about her?"

"I'm not sure I can stand it. But go ahead."

Tom flipped to another page and read: " 'I called Kim five thousand times yesterday, but she wouldn't talk to me. She got her parents to say she wasn't home. Like I really believed them. I called this morning at seven and she was still "gone." RIGHT. I can't believe I was ever dumb enough to think she cared.' "

When Tom looked up, Andie had dropped her head to her hands. She looked like she couldn't bear to hear another word. "I didn't mean to upset you, but I thought you needed to know," Tom said.

"I do. It's just hard. He must have felt so alone," she mumbled against her palms.

Tom appreciated that Brady, the tough cop, was more sensitive than she probably liked people to believe. And the truth was that he himself didn't exactly enjoy thinking about that sad kid. In Tom's work, he came across troubled teens like Christopher every day, but the numbers of them out there didn't make knowing about him easier. "I can stop if you want me to."

"No." Andie raised her head again. "Keep going."

"Christopher rants all through his journal about the Jackass and the Slave. But two days before he attacks you and Justice, he keys a teacher's car, and he gets into a brawl with Joey.

Christopher calls Kim a 'coldhearted bitch' and says he wants
to kill her."

"You think he meant it?"

"We'll never know." Tom set another page on top of the
others. "He admits he's been doing things he knows are wrong
and he doesn't even want to do them."

"Like what?"

"Besides the shirts and camp counselor, he probably means
the keying and the fight. I'm not sure. He says he doesn't want
to be like that anymore. He wants to move on to a better place
and start over," Tom said. "I imagine he was pretty lost."

"That makes what I did worse." Andie scrunched up her
face like she might cry.

"No, Brady. Christopher brought it on himself. I'm sure he
was upset about more than he writes in this journal. It all adds
up. Near the end, he says he doesn't want to live anymore."

"I made sure of that."

"That's why I came to talk with you." Tom wanted to
reach across the table and take her hand, but for now he was a
messenger, not a comforter. "The most important thing you
need to know is that Christopher wanted to kill himself, but
he couldn't work up the courage. He decided to buy the knife
and run at you and force you to shoot him. Look at his final
journal entry. . . ." Tom set a page between them and pointed
to the last two lines. "He says: 'I'm going to commit suicide by
cop. Tonight I'm going to die.'"

"Die" echoed around the kitchen. Andie looked like she'd
been slapped, and her cheeks looked feverish. She pressed her
lips together like she was stifling a wail.

"It's hard to hear. You're shocked." Tom got up, found a
glass in Andie's cupboard, and filled it with water. He set the
glass in front of her. "Here, drink this. It'll help." In the quiet
kitchen, Tom listened to Andie's swallows. Down the road,

someone was using a leaf blower. Crows were cawing in Andie's trees.

"If I'd only known what Christopher was thinking that night," she finally said.

"It wouldn't have made any difference. He didn't give you time to talk him down. He wanted you to shoot, and he chose to die. He basically asked for your help," Tom said. "Christopher put you in a terrible position. He used you. He was too young to see how he'd affect your life."

"All this time, I've felt responsible. . . ." Andie's voice drifted off.

"You may have pulled the trigger, but you're not to blame for Christopher's death. You carried out his wish."

Tom finally did what he'd wanted to do for a long time. He reached over and took Andie's hand, which felt like ice, but maybe he could warm it. "Now you can let yourself be at peace."

CHAPTER 51

ANDREA

Andie was pulling Beef Yummies from the oven when the Barkery's phone rang.

"Glad I caught you," Ron Hausmann said.

"I'm still here." *Please, don't tell me I have to face another deposition.*

"I've got news."

Andie braced herself.

"Norm Fixx just called. Christopher's journal has changed everything," Hausmann said. "The Vanderwaals realize they don't have a case. They've dropped their civil suit."

When Andie grabbed the stainless-steel counter to steady herself, she almost knocked the Beef Yummies onto the floor.

"You're free, Andrea."

"So that's it? No legal fight? No six million dollars? I don't have to do anything else?"

"Nope," Hausmann said. "How does it feel to walk away from such a mess?"

"I'll let you know after it all sinks in."

Could she ever walk away from such a mess? Not completely.

As she drove to the beach, the same worn and tattered question gnawed at her: *Did I do the right thing?* Suicide by cop had blurred the answer to her question. Tom Wolski was right that Christopher had used her—her actions had been a foregone conclusion to him. It tarnished the freedom she felt now that the Vanderwaals had dropped their suit.

Andie parked and got out of her Honda. When she opened the passenger door, Justice, who'd moped in the Barkery all afternoon, took a flying leap. The instant his paws touched the parking lot's gravel he rejoiced at being in his favorite place. In contrast to her pensive mood, he danced, ecstatic, around her feet.

Andie grabbed her army blanket and followed him as he pranced along a path through the woods. They passed blackberry thickets, ferns, and sorrel until the canopy of branches thinned and the greenery got scruffy. Finally, they stepped into the light, slanting from a slowly setting sun, and the beach lay before them. Justice's sniffing nostrils shouted, *Crabs! Sea cucumbers! All for me!* and he dashed away. Andie walked alone.

Now that April had arrived, the weather was warmer. The water's steely winter gray had changed to a silvery blue, reflecting the sky. Along the beach, willows and alders glowed with the green aura of renewal that was about to burst forth in new leaves. Geese and great blue herons had flown in from their southern winter sojourn and were sunning themselves on the pebbles.

The last time Andie had brought Justice here, the tide and wind had carried her letter's scraps back to shore. But today the tide was going out, and the wind had calmed—and there wasn't a piece of her paper left anywhere. Nature had brought her anger and guilt out to sea and drowned them so now mostly what remained was her regret, which came in occasional bouts. Like now.

Though Christopher had wanted Andie to kill him, she still felt sorry that she had. She wished he were alive today and had decades left to sort out his problems. She told herself that if she'd known he'd be waiting in the bushes she could have come home earlier or later when he wasn't there. If she'd been willing to die, she could have risked Tasing or Macing him or fighting him with her bare hands. If she'd been a mind reader, she could have befriended him and headed off his death wish.

But an "if" governed each option, and she had shot him, and her regret wouldn't change an iota of Christopher's death, which was cast in the stone of the past. The only thing that Andie could change was her attitude, her internal Dr. Capoletti reminded her. And now it struck her with a jolt that instead of feeling sorry, she needed with all her heart to accept what had happened. Really accept it. Live with it. Let it sink down to her core, work into her bone marrow, and flow into the nuclei of her cells. Let it become so deep a part of her that recriminations couldn't reach there.

She also needed to accept that sometimes in life when she tried her best it still might not be good enough. Sometimes life would pit her against forces greater than her measly self and she'd have to give up the fight and walk on. And sometimes, as Tom had said, her life wouldn't be fair, but she'd have to cling to the thought that it could still be good. When such a truly terrible thing as killing Christopher had happened, there was nothing left to do but claim her rightful place in the world and ask the sun and sky and sea to give her strength to keep going.

And that was exactly what Andie decided to do.

She spread out her blanket and sat down, cross-legged. The war of tension between her back and shoulders called a truce, and the heartburn that had been her constant companion for months packed up and went home. Accepting seemed like such a simple act, and yet it was huge.

As Andie watched Justice wander the beach, charging geese and sniffing footprints, she thought of her final visit with Dr. Capoletti. He'd reminded her that she'd always carry some sadness about Christopher. His suicide had been like a rock thrown into the still lake of her heart, and the ripples would go on and on forever.

"He forced you to shoot him. He wanted you to. In that way, he is more responsible for his death than you are. You were a pawn. He didn't leave you much choice."

"I guess so," Andie agreed.

"You can't let what happened define you. You must be more than the cop who killed a kid."

Andie had agreed to that too.

Now as she sifted pebbles through her fingers, it occurred to her that the tragedy wasn't hers—it was Christopher's. The snarl of emotions behind his death belonged to him, not her. Would he have gone through with killing her if she hadn't shot? Andie would never know. All she could know for sure was that she had a right to live and she'd done the right thing for *herself*—and as Dr. Capoletti had said, no one could take that knowledge away from her.

Andie lay back, closed her eyes, and listened to the waves as relief flowed into her. She felt as if a storm had sunk her ship, but now she'd washed ashore and was lying in the sun, slowly gathering her wits, grateful to be alive. And tucked into her gratitude was the peace that Tom had told her she could let herself feel.

She had lain there for ten minutes or two hours—she'd lost track of time—when Justice's paws shuffled over the pebbles and she heard a *plop*. She snapped open her eyes.

A nasty sand-and-drool-covered stick sat inches from her face, above which Justice's eyes were begging, *Throw! Oh, please! Throw!*

Andie got to her feet and hurled the stick as far as she could, and Justice tore after it. As he ran, the wind flattened his fur and his body exuded power and strength. His gait showed no sign that he'd been stabbed and come close to death. He wasn't stiff. He didn't limp. He was pure beauty flying toward the waves.

Justice testified to the miracle of healing and restoration. He embodied spring's rebirth. *So could I,* Andie thought. Because of the storm of Christopher's death, she'd come to the sunshine of acceptance and growth into her true, strong self. She'd needed both the storm and the sun, her good friends.

Plop. Moist eyes begging.

Andie threw the stick again. As Justice ran after it, she told him, "Last time. We've got to go home. I have something important to do."

CHAPTER 52

TOM AND ANDREA

On Sunday nights the ferry riders had been acting like thugs again, yelling at one another, making obscene hand gestures, and cutting into the line of cars waiting to board. Ferry traffic was heaviest on Sunday nights, and the drivers needed someone to make them behave. Tom had just agreed with Chief Malone to be that someone starting next week, not that he was looking forward to directing traffic in spring rain.

As he walked out of the San Julian police station, however, he was not thinking about Sunday nights. He was thinking about Andie. When she'd been back at work after his investigation, he'd liked seeing her around there. Without her, the station felt like somebody had dimmed the lights. And bummer of bummers, the Chief had just said he'd kept her on leave long enough and next week he'd advertise for her replacement.

Tom lamented that Andie would never again be the department's Christmas elf. He wouldn't be able to raid her cookies in the roll-call room or see her at Cops Night Out, an event she'd organized every summer for the police and sheriff's departments. Now that the case was closed, he had little reason to see her. Too bad life wasn't always the way he wanted it, he told himself—just as Andie materialized out of nowhere, as if she'd picked up his thoughts and come to prove them wrong.

Next to his patrol car, she climbed out of her Honda, leaving behind Justice, who looked highly displeased. His furrowed brow said to Andie and anyone else who might see his forlorn face, *I belong in that building. Why the devil do I have to be locked up? Somewhere on this island there are drugs to be sniffed!*

"Hey, Brady," Tom said.

"Hey, Wolski."

They were off to a flying start. After just hearing of the Chief's plan to replace her, Tom wasn't sure what to say, so he settled on an original and scintillating question: "What's going on?"

"Not much."

"The Chief just told me the Vanderwaals dropped their suit. That's fantastic."

"At least I won't have to pay them six million dollars."

"So life *can* be fair," Tom said.

"Even if it isn't, it can be good," Andie said with a smile. "I have a lot to thank you for. You really helped me. Without your continued investigating . . ."

"I'm glad."

Andie was holding a business envelope that looked like a white flag of surrender, and Tom itched to know what was in it. At long last her formal resignation letter? A legal form she'd signed for Hausmann? Not to be an overt snoop, he nodded toward it and asked obliquely, "Important business?"

"I don't know yet." Andie tapped a corner of the envelope against her thumb as a motorcycle passed by, its muffler loud enough to raise the dead. "Just for the record, I'm doing what you wanted."

"How so?"

"I'm asking the Chief to take me back."

Yes! If Tom's smile had extended another few inches, the

corners of his mouth might have touched his ears. "That's great news."

"You think it's great because you told me I should be a cop."

"Great minds, same channel," Tom said. "Justice sure will be happy."

Right now he was as glum as rain. He stared them down with his most crestfallen expression. *I want out of this Honda.*

"Justice won't be happy if the Chief says no," Andie said.

"I'm sure he'll be glad to have you back." Why did Brady have to look so damned good in that sweater? It fit in all the right places.

His red-blooded all-American male began to joust with his cautious streak again, and only one was going to stay on his horse.

Go ahead. Ask her out.

Remember, buddy, she broke the date before.

The red-blooded male guffawed. *That was six years ago! Are you the Guinness World Record holder for the lamest grudge?*

Andie glanced toward the station door. "Only one way to find out what the Chief will say."

"That's true." Tom had wrestled mammoth bruisers to the floor and tackled wing-footed kingpins. It was ridiculous for a strapping man like him to hesitate about much of anything. He was about to ask Andie out when she looked back at him and said, "Can I take you to dinner tonight? You know, to thank you for all the work you did to find the motive." It sounded innocent enough, but a blush had crept into her cheeks.

Tom almost laughed out loud before he caught himself. "I'd like that."

After Andie left her letter for the Chief in the mailroom, she stopped to visit Stephanie behind her glass window just inside the front door. She was weaving wands of lavender, which she'd dried in her closet all winter, to sell at a church bazaar.

"I've started a new business as a hangover helper," Stephanie said. "On mornings after, I bring Gatorade and a burrito to college students' apartments. If they've had a party there the night before, I also help clean up."

"I hate to think of the mess," Andie said.

"Cleaning up messes pays good money."

"Are you close to what you need for the Great Barrier Reef?"

"Depends on how luxurious I want the trip to be. Scuba diving isn't cheap."

"You'll get there." Andie hugged her. "I have to hurry. I have a date. Sort of, anyway."

Stephanie raised a hand to her forehead like a Victorian lady swooning on her settee. "Pardon me while I faint. Tell me! Who?"

"Wolski," Andie said, "and if you don't close your mouth a fly might buzz in."

"I *knew* he had the hots for you."

"It's not the hots. . . ." *Well, maybe it's the mutual hots.* "I gotta go."

Andie rushed to the parking lot. She had to get Justice home and feed him supper. With luck, she'd have time to change out of her jeans and sweater and get her hair to behave.

When she climbed into her car, Justice was still in major woebegone mode, his forehead grievously rumpled. Andie patted his shoulder. "I'm sorry I left you, Sweet Boy. I didn't think you'd mind if I went in for a minute."

When he fixed his eyes on her, white crescents appeared below his pupils, his darkest, most lugubrious look. *You went into the station without me. I wanted to see my friends.*

"If the Chief lets me come back to the force, you'll get daily doses of our colleagues," Andie promised.

As she drove home, Justice got back to his old self. His

damp nose streaked the windshield while he looked for bad guys and squirrels he could round up.

When Andie turned onto Valley Road, Justice whimpered with anticipation of hauling Rosemary around in his mouth and eating his dinner. Andie turned into the driveway before she realized that she'd passed the Vanderwaals' without thinking of Christopher. For the first time since his death, she'd driven by without a flinch, because she'd been thinking of Tom and her first date since Christopher had attacked her.

For months she'd been measuring her life in terms of "before Christopher" and "after Christopher" just as some people gauged events before or after they moved away from home, or started their first job, or met the person they would marry. Before and after Christopher had even applied to where Andie had parked, for heaven's sake. *Ridiculous.*

She drove down her driveway but did not head toward the side of her house. She went straight to her "before Christopher" parking spot in front of it. As she pulled her key from the ignition, she resolved that it was time to look for a better life-organizing principle than Christopher Vanderwaal.

She opened the passenger door, and Justice ran to the bushes to hunt for Rosemary. Andie walked over to the side of her yard that she'd avoided for months and Tom had threatened to mow. Evening was coming, and the forest was peaceful. A soft pink streaked the clouds. Last night's rain had washed the trees, and she breathed in the clean, fresh smell of cedar and fir.

Andie walked over the grass Christopher had run across. She ran her hand along the bushes where he'd hidden. She stood on the dirt once pooled with his blood and gazed at her house.

Though she'd lived here for years, she felt as if she'd never truly seen any of it before. It was no crime scene. It was her home. She was exactly where she belonged—in her rightful place—and it was more beautiful than she'd ever understood.

Maybe there were no befores and afters or beginnings and ends, she thought. Life just kept moving, and you muddled along the best you could. Once in a while, the worst got thrown at you like a tornado that sucked you up and spit you out and you had to find your way back home. But as long as you kept muddling along, you reached it, and, like Andie, maybe you saw it with new gratitude, as if for the first time.

EPILOGUE

Being a faithful and hardworking dog, Justice rejoiced at being reinstated as a San Julian P.D. K-9. He guarded Andie with extra vigor and, when asked, sniffed his heart out. In May, after the Beast was tried and put away, Justice nabbed the Brute, who'd moved in on the Beast's turf. In June, on a tip from a Bremerton nark, Justice charged into an upscale house, where one would have expected to find upstanding people, and he led Andie, Tom, and a tactical response team to an entire drug lab—with eighty bricks of heroin and twenty-eight thousand dollars in cash.

In August Justice had another chance to shine at the annual San Julian Cops' Night Out, which Andie had been organizing for months at Waterfront Park. The whole town—including Dr. Mark Vargas, the Laser Lady, the once-mooned Marigold Adams, and the fastidious Kimberly Thatcher—turned out. As the enticing smells of free hot dogs, popcorn, and cotton candy drifted through the air, dozens of children crawled through a demo ambulance and police car. At booths manned by police, parents picked up brochures on fire safety, emergency preparedness, and crime prevention.

Unperturbed by the crowds, Justice demonstrated his sniffing skills. With the focus of a conscientious homing pigeon, he zeroed in on stashes that Andie hid in the backpacks and pockets of colleagues planted in the audience. After their applause, he assumed his maharaja position and allowed petting hands as a pope might allow signet-ring kisses. Though modest, Justice basked in his glory.

Popular as he was, he could only lay claim to being the evening's second-greatest attraction. The first was the pie-eating contest, which began as the sun set and floodlights came on all over the park. Andie was the emcee, and the judges were Meghan (minus Rosemary) and Stephanie, who was packed and ready to leave in the morning for the Great Barrier Reef. Contestants were the bravest members of the San Julian Police Department and the Nisqually County Sheriff's Department.

Andie called them all up to the stage. Reluctant but good-natured, Tom dragged himself there first, and next came Chief Malone, Doug Baker, Ron Hausmann, Alan Pederson, Ross Jackson—and Justice, whose eyes glittered at the prospect of food. Facing the audience and lined up across the stage, all of them but him sank to their knees before one of Andie's blackberry pies, waiting on an apple crate.

Justice was in a different category. Andie had prepared him a small pie of browned hamburger, topped with mashed potatoes. Meghan stood with her hand up in front of him to keep him from lunging at it before the contest began.

As Murphy handcuffed the contestants behind their backs, Andie announced that first prize went to whoever finished the most pie, and second, to whoever's face got the purplest. She rang a bell and bedlam broke out onstage. There were chomps, gulps, chokes, coughs, and porcine grunts. Noses rooted through pies. Purple goop and clumps of crust fell all over the stage.

The Chief slobbered berries down his shirt's front as he raised his head to chew, and Alan Pederson got so worked up that his signature crescent moons of armpit perspiration appeared on his shirt. Once again Ross Jackson could have used intravenous feeding. He dipped his forehead and chin into the pie and rolled his cheeks from side to side so purple completely covered his face and managed to reach his bald head. Blackberries found their way into his ear and up his nostril.

As Lisa screamed from the audience, "Go, Dad!" Tom ratcheted up his eating speed and gulped full blast. He attacked the crust and swallowed blackberries whole. As he gluttonized at rocket speed, berry juice got slung around and stained the sergeant's stripes that Andie had recently sewn onto his sleeve. Next to him, Justice, who'd polished off his hamburger pie in twelve seconds, was licking his chops.

Finally, Andie rang the bell again and Stephanie and Meghan examined sticky faces and pies' remains. Tom, dubbed the "Eager Eater," won first prize, a gift certificate for the Dippity Creamery. Ross Jackson, the "Purple Piglet," came in second for two Sweet Time Bakery pies of his choice. As the crowd cheered, Murphy removed everybody's handcuffs and Ross Jackson strutted around the stage, his hands clasped above his head like he'd just knocked his opponent out cold in a boxing match.

Andie claimed her man. With a moist towel she tenderly wiped Tom's face. She flicked bits of blackberry off his cheeks and planted a congratulatory smackaroo on his sweet purple lips. No longer needing a wall around herself, she gladly showed anybody who cared to look what her feelings were, and no one could doubt that she loved Tom. She now thought of events as "before Tom" and "after Tom." He, not Christopher, was the organizing principle of her life.

Too regal to sink to jealousy that Tom, not he, was Andie's organizing principle, Justice approved of any smackaroo that took place in his presence. After the long, winding road the three of them had traveled since last November, they'd finally reached their destination, all of them together. They were a family in the making with long hours and crazy, ever-changing, dangerous shifts. And Lisa would live with them on weekends.

Justice pressed himself against Tom's and Andie's legs. Just as he liked to prance around proclaiming that Bandit was his personal teddy, he now proclaimed to the contest audience that Andie and Tom were his personal people. And if anybody like the Beast showed up and caused them any grief, Justice had some teeth he'd be delighted for them to meet.

ACKNOWLEDGMENTS

A Healing Justice would not exist without the kindness and support of special people. I would never even have started the book, for example, if I'd not signed up for the Citizens' Academy at the Bainbridge Island, Washington, Police Department and made good friends on the force. Sergeant Trevor Ziemba, who should write novels himself, generously steered me toward the idea for my story and helped me with the plot. Officer Carla Sias supplied me with information again and again and never complained about my constant impositions. Detective Aimee LeClaire patiently explained how crime scenes are investigated, and she drew diagrams to help me understand. And every time I saw Chief Matt Hamner, I bombarded him with questions, which he cheerfully answered. All four of these people would have been justified to run when they saw me coming, but they didn't—and I will be forever grateful.

Rachel Strohmeyer, DVM, described how Justice would be treated for his wounds. Alexandra Kovats, Ph.D., introduced me to restorative justice, which is a main theme in this book. Kirkham Johns, J.D., taught me about depositions. Todd Dowell, Senior Deputy Prosecutor in Kitsap County, Washington, explained how records are sealed in juvenile court. And Barbara Wood, my friend and fellow German shepherd lover, shared stories of her dogs, some of which have found their way into my story.

Then there are the people who were midwives at *A Healing Justice*'s birth. Cullen Stanley, my A-plus agent, shepherded me along from the book's idea to its completion, and Michaela

Hamilton, my gracious editor, inspired me and cheered me on. Others on the Kensington Publishing Corp. staff were always kind and helpful: Lynn Cully, publisher; Kristine Mills Noble, book cover designer; Paula Reedy, production editor; Karen Auerbach, publicity director; and Vida Engstrand and Alexandra Nicolajsen, two marketing geniuses.

My many friends, of course, bolstered me while I wrote *A Healing Justice*. You know who you are! And in this category I include Jordan Taylor, who took the photo of the German shepherd on the cover and of me on the last page.

As for my family, Lonnie Matheron, my niece, is my consultant in just about everything. And John, my beloved husband, is my personal Polar Star. As I have said many times, without him there would be no books. I thank him for his intelligence and understanding.

Also in my family over the years have been six German shepherds. Needless to say, I have loved every one of those dear dogs. Woofer came to me as a breeder from Guide Dogs for the Blind in San Rafael, California, and Ludwig was her son. Anna, Noble, Logan, and now Bridget were rescues. I can't imagine how sad my life might have been without them. They aren't dogs—they are saints in German shepherd outfits. Justice is a combination of them all.

A HEALING
JUSTICE

Kristin von Kreisler

ABOUT THIS GUIDE

The following discussion questions are included to
enhance your group's reading and discussion of
A Healing Justice.

DISCUSSION QUESTIONS

1. Andie's most urgent question through most of the book is: *Did I do the right thing?* How would you answer for her? What's the difference between being justified to shoot and right to shoot?

2. Andie often says that life isn't fair. Do you agree with her? Does Tom? Was it fair for Andie to be viewed as a criminal suspect? Or for the Vanderwaals to file a civil suit against her?

3. Shooting Christopher causes Andie great emotional stress. Do you think it's unusual for a police officer to feel that way? Or should she have considered the use of deadly force as just part of her job? Why is it important for her to acknowledge that she is vulnerable?

4. Who is to blame for Christopher's death? Is it his own fault? Should Andie be held responsible? His parents? His girlfriend? Fate?

5. Is building a wall around herself a good defense for Andie? Would something else have been better, or was that all she could do? How does the wall change in the story? And how does her relationship to it change?

6. In the story's first paragraph, Andie feels that the fir trees around her house are both a plus and a minus. Could the horrible night when she kills Christopher be seen as that too? What else in the story might be a plus and a minus?

7. How does Andie's attitude toward being a police officer change in the story? What's her attitude like before she kills Christopher? And after? What about at the end of the book?

8. What does Dr. Capoletti's poster mean—that a storm is as good a friend as sunshine? How does that idea apply to Andie and the story? How does her attitude toward the saying change?

9. What does Justice teach Andie? How does he influence her thinking and her life?

10. How do you feel about the media's attitude toward Andie? Do you think it's unusual? Realistic? Necessary? Unfair? Is Sid King just doing his job, or is he relishing going after her? How do you react when you read in the news about a police officer's use of deadly force?

Kristin von Kreisler will be happy to meet with your reading group by Skype, or in person if you're in the Seattle area. Contact her at www.kristinvonkreisler.com.

Connect with Us

Visit us online at
KensingtonBooks.com
to read more from your favorite authors, see books
by series, view reading group guides, and more.

Join us on social media

for sneak peeks, chances to win books and prize packs,
and to share your thoughts with other readers.

facebook.com/kensingtonpublishing
twitter.com/kensingtonbooks

Tell us what you think!
To share your thoughts, submit a review,
or sign up for our eNewsletters, please visit:
KensingtonBooks.com/TellUs.